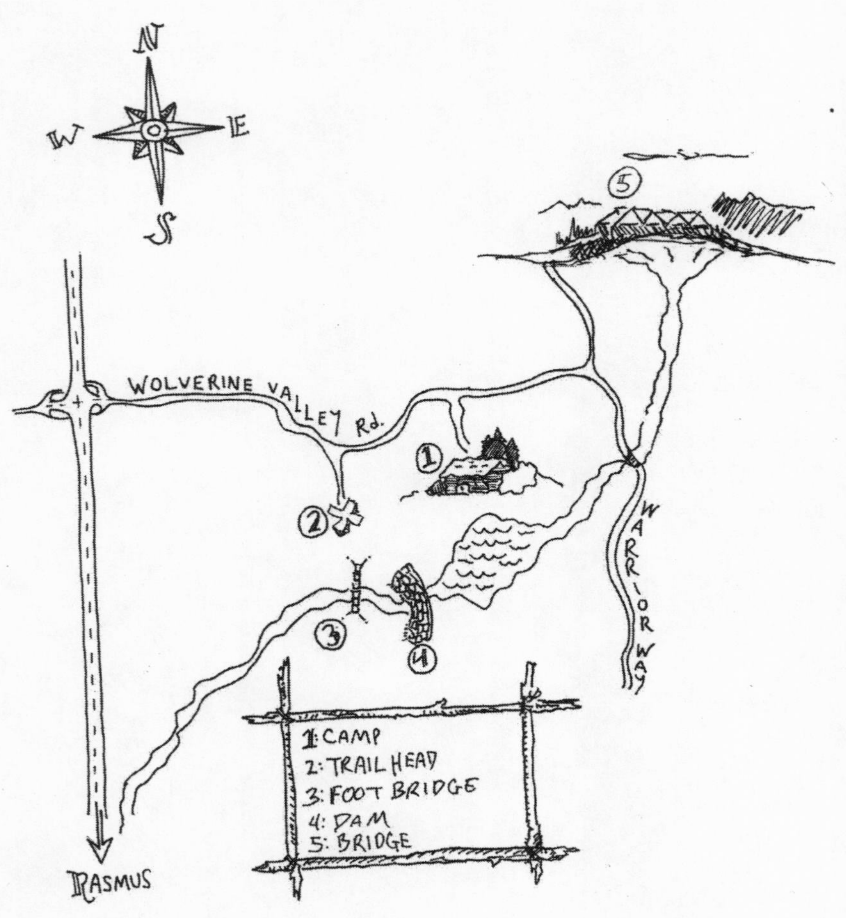
N
W
E
S
5
WOLVERINE VALLEY Rd.
1
2
3
4
WARRIOR WAY
RASMUS
1: CAMP
2: TRAIL HEAD
3: FOOT BRIDGE
4: DAM
5: BRIDGE

SPARROW RIVER

Death and Intrigue in the North Woods

By
Kevin J Garrity

SPARROW RIVER

Sparrow River is a work of fiction. Names, characters, incidents and places are either the product of the author's imagination or are used fictitiously, and any resemblance to actual persons, living or dead, businesses, companies, or events, is purely coincidental.

Cover photos by George V. McKim
Sparrow River Map by Cris Carver

Hammer Handle Press
6197 Quaker Hill Drive
West Bloomfield, MI 48322
(248) 757-2751
www.kevinjgarrity.com

Published by Hammer Handle Press

ISBN 978-0-9853310-0-9
ISBN 978-0-9853310-1-6 (eBook)

Acknowledgements

With thanks to my brother Michael, a man blessed with an abundance of faith, to George, Teemu, Charles, Cris and everyone who helped put the little pieces together, and especially to Deanna, the one who makes the world go 'round.

THE WATER
1

The icy water came thrashing over the moss and weed-covered boards, a million eels racing to see who could be the first downstream. Glossy slick and crusted with zebra mussels all at the same time, the boards seemed as if they had been there forever. A poor-man's dam that held back the river in the good times, it merely postponed the inevitable during the spring run-off. The pool behind the dam was caked with a floating slab of skim ice. It had been solid enough to walk upon not two weeks before, but now was merely a dollop of cream hovering over the turgid waters below. Driven by the river beneath, the sheet of ice thrust itself against the narrow dam, grinding itself into shards before joining the torrent pounding the topmost boards.

The dam had not really been there forever, it merely seemed as if it had. It was in the early 1920's that Hanson Jones and a few of his well-to-do buddies managed to pull a few strings and secure themselves a little over 800 acres of prime hunting and fishing land, smack-dab in the middle of the Huron National Forest. No one knows exactly who's strings were pulled, or how hard, but the end result was a private island of tranquility surrounded by a couple million acres of even more pristine public land. One of the country's premier trout streams runs right through the heart of it all. A camp was built. At first a single log structure, with a privy out back. Here and there another small outbuilding was added, as the circle of friends expanded slowly outward. Indoor plumbing came soon, as the membership of the club grew and matured. Eventually a little earth and wooden dam was erected on the site, because after all, what was the point in a hunting and fishing camp if it didn't come with its own private pond?

Earth and wood, it turned out, weren't enough to hold back the volume of water that races through the Sparrow River in the springtime. "Sparrow," a misnomer if ever there was one. In the dog days of summer it flows smooth and shallow. It meanders through her deeper stretches, hiding cool dark holes where the big trout lay until the evening hatch. It riffles and purls its way across the gravel bars that stretch like fingers into the her current. It wraps around corners and dumps sand from her load, only to pick up where it left off and continues upon its former course. In the summer months hikers are easily enticed to take a dip, washing off days of sweat accumulated during their hike across the lower peninsula's shore-to-shore trail. Horses have watered there since before time was measured. The Sparrow can seem gentle enough, but most of the locals called it the "Bitch River" for a reason.

Winters in the northern lower peninsula are harsh, with often more than one hundred inches of snow that eventually freezes into walls of crusted ice. The Wolverine Valley experiences overnight lows dropping to thirty-five degrees below zero in January and February.

Come spring, the thaw arrives with little warning. A brief warming spell usually shows itself by late March, when the mercury finally creeps above the freezing mark. The Sparrow gorges herself on the thousands of feeder streams and creeks that work their way down from higher ground. Mounds of what appear to be white granite dissolve until the river literally bursts at her banks in pursuit of relief. It doesn't last. The thaw will last for a few days, a week at the most. Most of the snow will hang on well into May. But for a few short days when that temperature spikes, all hell will break loose.

In April of 1957 one of those temperature surges caused the dam to give way, sending a twelve-foot wall of water racing downstream. It destroyed everything in its sight. Not to be defeated, the Hunt and Fish Club put up another dam, only this time using concrete instead of mud as its base. Removable wooden boards were stacked end to end at the top of the dam, allowing the club to control the depth of the pond, and to regulate the downward flow of the Sparrow. Hanson Jones and his friends were certain that they had tamed the beast for good.

Once the water makes it past this speed bump, it is clear sailing for about a mile, before the river takes a sharp left, and then a sharp right to straighten herself back out. The banks are undercut by a good two to three feet at both of these turns, and any log or limb that finds its way into the river above will wedge under the overhangs with its brethren. These logs extend along the bank a good twenty yards before the current rights herself. In summer the holes in front of these undercuts might be at most three to five feet deep. Deep enough to hide the big, marauding brown trout from the summer heat, deep enough to take a quick dip and cool off if you happened to be backpacking through this stretch of the forest.

THE WATER

After the first two turns the river quickly finds its rhythm, and settles into a surge of roiling energy. Occasionally it deflects a few degrees to the north or a few degrees to the south, changing momentum and losing steam before regrouping and building its head toward Lake Huron, some eighty miles to the east. Sometimes a boulder, a little "sorry we stopped by, you weren't home" card left over from the last glacial era, will appear midstream and halve the flow, before the two currents meet up and rejoin their purpose. In a few spots the Sparrow widens into a series of riffles over gravel, before tailing out into yet another deep hole. Sometimes the river just plows ahead, regardless of what lies in its path.

It was late March, and the deep holes in front of the banks were easily 10 to 12 feet deep. The laconic stream that purred along at forty cubic feet per second in August was now pushing one-hundred and eighty cubic feet per second. The river was angry and seething, rife with the weight of the dwindling snowpack. Anything that interfered with its progress was likely to lose the battle. Deadheads and beaver-chewed logs stacked along the turns and projected a good 6 feet out from the bank, little log cabins full of froth and broken crystals. The occasional styrofoam cup bobbed along in an eddy, modern man's message in a bottle, finding safe harbor from storm.

The ice shield floating above the damn attempted to join the downward push, so that what sounded like breaking glass was the only noise in the forest.

WALT
2

Walt turned off the pavement and onto the two-track path, fishtailing left and right as he made the cut onto the untreated frozen surface. Wolverine Valley Road could be a bear unto itself in the winter, but with the warmer temperatures this week the road surface was merely wet. No fresh snow had fallen in over a week. Black ice, the silent killer that could send any vehicle spiraling out of control, wasn't a threat today. He was at least thankful for that. The two-track, on the other hand, was a completely different story. It was less a road than a suggestion. In the winter it never got plowed, and by spring was often indiscernible from the fields which surrounded it. The rare driver that was either brave or stupid enough to pull off the main road and onto this trail only managed to pack its snow down harder, and a glassy layer of water and ice accumulated atop the twin-rutted surface. "Slicker than hot cat shit on linoleum," as his Uncle Bert used to say.

"Tom Dewers is an asshole," Walt cursed under his breath. Walt was the only person in the van. "The biggest asshole to ever walk the face of the earth," he added. Walt knew for a fact that Tom Dewers was an asshole, because Dewers had gotten to work fifteen minutes before Walt, and Dewers had checked out the last of the new F250 crew cab trucks that the department had bought this year. Tom Dewers was sitting in the driver's seat, warming up the engine, when Walt came skidding into the parking lot. Walt couldn't help it if his piece of shit Suzuki Samurai didn't want to start this morning, or that he spilled coffee all over his crotch at the gas station. He couldn't help it either if he had to use the restroom at Speedway and tried to dry himself under the automated hand dryer. Some guy walked in on him as he was doing the limbo beneath the blower. He didn't want the guys at work to think he'd pissed himself. "There's another asshole," Walt thought aloud, sitting in the van and pondering that other customer in the restroom. "Backtracking out the door like he'd just walked in on Charles Manson or something. Probably some jerkwad snowmobiler from downstate," he muttered, to no one in particular. "I hope I see him on the way back to town, so I can run him over."

WALT

The upshot of Dewers claiming the last of the new trucks was that Walt was now driving the last of the '98 Astro Vans. "Government issued POS, that's what I get to drive. Piece of junk a soccer mom would be embarrassed to drive. Worthless in snow, defroster only works when it feels like working, and a crack in the damn windshield like it's a Playbill cover for a Broadway production of Charlotte's Web," he once told a guy who had made the mistake of asking. Walt could be unusually eloquent when the mood struck. He was also extremely chatty when it was just him in the van, or when he brought his dog Doofus along for the ride. The US Geological Service had just upgraded most of its automotive fleet for the first time in over a decade, yet kept a few of the old Astro's around, just in case. Being the last guy to reach the office, on a day when all hell was breaking loose, almost guaranteed you'd be in that "just in case" category. Walt had bragging rights to the Astro more often than not.

He didn't have far to drive down the two track, and truthfully it's not like you could bounce your way out of the foot-deep ruts even if you tried. You could keep moving forward, or sit and spin. Sure, you'd slosh around side-to-side and maybe loosen a few teeth along the way, but you learned to grin and bear it. This was a two-way ride, either in or out. There was no turning around once you'd started. The Astro pushed forward, scraping away the softer snow beneath its center at the expense of the vehicle's undercarriage, until it finally came to a small clearing at the trailhead to the river.

Walt packed a little snuff in his lower lip, cursed Dewers one last time for good luck, and stepped out of the van. The sun was shining. It was forty-two degrees, and it could have been a nice day if he didn't have to strap sixty pounds of gear onto his back and hike another half-mile through waist-high snow drifts. In most places the snow was merely knee deep, unbroken except by the occasional deer prints. The trail was soft and wet. Each step took effort, the drifts sucking and pulling unrelentingly at the cheap steel-toed boots Walt bought from the Goodwill Store. Where the trees were sparse the wind cut freely, glossing the surface as swiftly as could any broom. Every now and then he would come to a treacherous hollow, filled in by the white, hidden ankle-breakers that could be felt but not seen. Another guy Walt worked with had torn ligaments in his ankle just last year, making one untimely step into an invisible coyote den. Walt was cautious that he not be the next one, and he cursed the coyotes for good measure.

Walt slogged the half mile toward the river, meandering left, then right, trudging along the course of least resistance. When he eventually reached the Sparrow River, he found it flowing at what might possibly be an all-time high. In less daunting conditions he would have put on his chest waders, traversed about twenty yards into the flow, and quickly uploaded the data from the submerged equipment of his gauging station. That was one option, but not an appealing option on a day like today. On a day like this, he referred to that as "plan B."

There was, after all, a footbridge spanning the river, about two miles downstream from the dam and not far from this footpath. The bridge was built by the Civilian Conservation Corp. back in the thirties, a glorious quilt of hand-hewn logs and rough-cut boards that had somehow withstood both time and the elements. Walt loved that bridge, in all its rustic elegance. His check station was just a few yards upstream from the CCC bridge. If he lie prone on top the bridge and leaned just the right way, Walt could snag his submerged equipment with a gaffing hook, pull it up atop the decking, and avoid the chance of a springtime swim that might instantaneously turn fatal. It usually took a few tries, and in this current you couldn't see a damn thing, but it was possible. Once Walt snagged his equipment, he'd have to watch that it didn't get caught on a log or any of the other flotsam that was coming hard at him. A current like this could smash a couple of grand in equipment in a heartbeat. "Hey, everything has its risks," he'd told the other guys more than once. "So a fishin' we will go," he whispered now. He still had the hike in and the hike out to contend with, but this beat wading in and the risk of getting wet.

On his first couple of attempts Walt came up empty. He lie on his stomach, stretched out as far as he could reach, steering the eight-foot steel pole toward his invisible target. It didn't help that every few seconds a log or limb would drive into the gaff hook, throwing the pole off course and throwing Walt slightly off balance. A few times the gaff got pushed back into the pile of debris jammed amongst the bridge footings. He'd pull the hook out covered in weeds and sticks, clean if off, and try again. Upper body strength was important if you were going this route. On about the twentieth try, or maybe it was the fiftieth, because there wasn't much point in counting by now, Walt again got the pole jammed amongst the logs. When he pulled the tool out to clean it once more, he was dumbfounded. "It looks like a human hip bone," he murmured, though it well might be a bone from a deer. What would a human hip bone be doing out here? There was no cemetery upstream, no Indian burial grounds in the area that he'd ever heard mentioned. He took a closer look.

Walt had killed his first deer last November, a small buck that, while no Pope & Young prize, still put food on his table. He had been hunting state land a few hundred yards behind his office, and had stumbled across the buck on the last day of firearm deer season. This was the first time Walt had ever hunted deer. He knew a lot about guns, and was an excellent marksman, but he hadn't had much chance to hunt large game growing up in Rhode Island. He'd decided to call a friend to help him gut the deer, to show him the ropes.

Walt thought back to that cold day, freezing drizzle falling down as they field-dressed his kill. This bone, glistening in the river's spray, was definitely not from a deer. The dimensions weren't right, weren't even close. His mind quickly ran through a list of wha other game animals would have a hip this size. Nothing came to mind, and he began to feel a slight sense of dread. "It's gonna be a long ride back to town," he mused, to no one in particular. Half an hour later he was back in Sturgeon, then heading southbound on the interstate for a quick forty-mile drive back to the office.

AUTHORITY
3

"Shit, Bill, how the hell should I know how it got there? I work for the Geological Service, you're the cop." This conversation was in no way going the way Walt had hoped it would go. He thought he'd bring his discovery to the office with him, give it to one of the Conservation Officers working in the other half of the building, and get right back to work. They might say "Thanks Walt! Great work, buddy," or "Hey, this is something!" Instead it was turning into a bunch of b.s. questioning about where he'd found the bone, how he'd found it, how many swats with the gaffing hook did he take before hooking onto it. How long had he stayed at the scene? Did he disturb anything? All in all, it was rapidly turning into a miserable day for Walt. What should have been a moment of glory was instead becoming an inquisition.

"Disturb anything? Don't you think that river disturbs everything around it?" Any idiot could see that this bone had been bleached clean. It had probably been in the river forever, or at least for a few years. It might have been lodged in one of the overhanging banks for over a decade, purged and purified of any soft material a long time ago. Hell, it might have even come from above the dam, two miles upstream. He was beginning to regret this day more than he regretted most days. His head felt like it was splitting in two, and he could really use a belt of something stronger than the putrid coffee Dewers had brewed that morning. Walt had never been one to drink while on duty, but it was beginning to look like a good time to start.

"Walt, you pull in here looking and smelling like a sled dog that just won the Iditarod, drop what you claim to be a friggin' human bone on my desk like it's some sort of trophy, and you think I'm going to thank you or something?" Bill Fourshe was not a happy man. He was capable of being a happy man, once he was home with his wife and three girls, or out working in the field by his lonesome. But right now, in this time and place, he was not appreciating the company or the situation in which he found himself. God knows where this bone came from, or how it got there in the river in the first place. Now he had to deal with an irritating Walt Pitowski on top of it? Why'd this clown bring it to *him*, and not to the County Sheriff's Department? "I'm a

Conservation Officer, genius, why drop this on my desk?" he finally asked. Fourshe considered himself "law enforcement," but with Walt Pitowski involved, he was trying to put as much distance as possible between himself and what Walt would describe as a "real cop," and to do it in a language that might sink in to Pitowski's thick head. Retirement was looking better every minute, but it still hovered a few years away. Fourshe opened his right desk drawer and began rummaging around. He'd seen a roll of antacid tablets somewhere in that clutter, and they were calling his name. Maybe if he didn't look up, Pitowski would just go away.

"It was in the river, Bill, wedged up against the footbridge. National Forest land. Whose jurisdiction would that be? I think that's Natural Resources Department turf. It's not my problem, either way. I'm reporting it to the proper authorities. You're an authority. Plus, those guys at the sheriff's department don't like me. Amberson pulled me over last week and wrote me a ticket for a chipped windshield on the Suzuki. Who the hell *doesn't* have a chipped windshield in this county, with all the logging trucks going back and forth? *Seriously*, a chipped windshield? Now I've got to drop a hundred bucks that I don't have into a fifteen-year-old car that barely runs, and the car is barely worth a hundred bucks as it is. You call the County, Bill." Chipped windshields were an ongoing gripe in the county, with the state selling off logging rights to everyone and their little brother in their quest to balance a beleaguered budget. It seemed as if logging trucks were tearing up every road in northern Michigan, night or day, and it wasn't uncommon for wood chips and debris to take out the glass of vehicles that trailed behind them.

"I can't understand why the boys at the Sheriff's office don't like you, Walt," was all Fourshe could get out. He was trying to maintain a straight face. He'd dealt with Walt too many times before. Couldn't say he "liked" him, but then didn't outright "dislike" him, either. It was kind of like having a rattlesnake around the property. Sure, you weren't happy when you first discovered him, but after a while you just sort of *knew* that he was there. As long as you stayed out of his way, he wasn't likely to bite you or anyone else. Walt did have some good qualities, they were just a little hard to find. Fourshe briefly pondered the idea of writing Walt a ticket for fishing out of season, just for his own personal amusement, but then thought better of it. *Having* a rattlesnake on your hands was different from *provoking* the snake, particularly when the snake was already agitated. Fourshe mulled the thought over for a few more minutes in his head. "I'll call Matt Amberson and see what he wants to do," he finally decided.

YOGA THE BEAR
4

In March of 1976, the Hanson Jones Fishing Club voted to disband and sell its property. Its founding members were well into their seventies and eighties. The three hour drive north from Detroit (five and a half hours for those that live in Chicagoland), was becoming less and less enticing for a group of aging men with prostate issues. Their forays into the woods and streams were becoming even less manageable and less frequent.

When the club was originally founded they were all hearty, wealthy men in the prime of life. They could retreat to their northern haven for a week or two of deer camp, long days sitting in the woods chewing venison jerky, followed by long nights of drinking and carousing back at the main lodge. Summer would find them fly fishing the Sparrow, or wading one of the other three blue-ribbon streams within a fifteen minute drive, until the daylight ran out and the whiskey began to pour. In the early days parties rolled well into the night and past dawn, seeming to last for weeks on end. Occasionally the fun would lead to an excursion into the town of Cheboygan, where the Gold Front Lounge offered slightly racier entertainment.

Over the years, the energy of the club's members had waned. The Fifteenth of November (first day of firearm deer season) still took on a major significance, as did the last Saturday in April (trout season opener). But those were largely ceremonial observances. In between those two big events, visits to Hanson Jones became fewer and fewer. The club's nighttime activities began to die down even before the eleven o'clock news came on. In the last few years the club had become nothing more than a poorly-attended gentlemen's drinking social for septuagenarians. The summer of 1976 marked the end of an era.

The property fell to the auctioneer's gavel that June and the high bid, to the surprise of nearly everyone, came from a little known group operating under the ambiguous title of "Sparrow Lotus, LLC." Not one of the Hanson Jones Fishing Club members had ever heard of a Sparrow Lotus, or even knew what the hell one was, but Sparrow Lotus money was as good as any, and the check cleared. The property changed hands with minimal fanfare.

Sparrow Lotus immediately issued a press release, noted by no one, announcing their intention to manage the camp as a new age retreat and yoga instruction center. The facilities were ideal for these purposes. There was a large lodge with bar and dining room, though it was sorely in need of updating. There existed a handful of outbuildings and a few smaller cabins, and of course a private lake big enough to row across, yet not so big that one could get lost on it. The thinking was that in this vast northern tract of woods, water, and campgrounds, an endless queue of hippies and yuppies would pay handsomely for the opportunity to commune with nature. The camp was at once isolated, and yet only 14 miles from the little town of Sturgeon. From Sturgeon you could pick up the interstate south, and head for the bigger cities. Smaller roads led to the tourist towns of Gaylord or Charlevoix. The camp offered hiking and fishing in the summer, cross country skiing and snowshoeing in the winter, and meditation and spiritual healing any day of the year.

Sparrow Lotus Camp managed to go largely unnoticed until the summer of 1984. During June of that year the camp carelessly drew down the water level of their pond, releasing a flow of silt and sediment into the river which killed every fish for miles downstream. The caretakers that operated the camp claimed that they didn't realize that they needed permission from the State of Michigan Conservation Department before changing the flow of the river. They were merely lowering their pond so that they could do some repair work on the dam. No one at the camp seemed aware that tons of sludge would go with the flow. That was their story.

As a result, fishing was ruined in the lower stretches of the river for the better part of a decade. Fishermen across the country screamed in outrage, and local businesses suffered lost revenues. Environmental groups, despite their usual sympathies with the camp, jumped on the bandwagon and howled for remediation. Eventually Sparrow Lotus was fined heavily by the State, castigated in the local media, and vowed never again to be a bad neighbor.

Local resentment toward the camp festered, but local resentment is a way of life in the northern woods. It's all part of the stew that makes a small community work, and eventually someone new will tick people off even more than the last guy did. You don't always have time to revisit old wrongs. New ones keep turning up. Fish gradually returned to that stretch of the river, and things continued much as they had before the incident.

FISHING FOR ANSWERS
5

The Bell canoe drifted lazily across the lake's surface. Seventeen feet of smooth green canvas and cedar, cutting the surface of the water like a knife. It was a sturdy craft, tracking well on the flat water of Shambarger Lake. Walt paddled effortlessly from the stern, leaving a glistening swirl in his wake. In the bow sat his friend Elvin, gently flipping a floating balsa lure amongst clusters of lily pads.

To some the visitors to Sparrow Lotus were spiritualists, on a quest for higher understanding and a little less technology, if only for that weekend. To Walt they were mostly hippies, pot-heads and dykes, doing god-knows what on their privileged little piece of paradise that they didn't share with the rest of the neighborhood kids. The bastards probably didn't even pay taxes, hiding under the label of 'nonprofit organization.' Walt couldn't quite put his finger on it, drifting around the lake with Elvin in a canoe, but he was sure the yoga camp had something to do with that body in the river.

"You want me to paddle, Walt?" a half-hearted question wafted from the bow of the craft.

"You fish. I've got it," Walt replied.

The two men had met several years before, both transplants to a small town where friendships were forged in high school or sooner, and latecomers to the ball had to dance with whomever might be leaning against the gymnasium wall. It wasn't that the community was necessarily unwelcoming of new arrivals, but tight bonds reached back for decades. Guys who drifted up from the big city in their mid thirties had to forge tenuous friendships wherever they could find them. Flaws needed to be overlooked if you desired companionship. The dating scene was even worse.

Walt had been married when he and Elvin had first met three years back. It wasn't a good marriage, though it had its good moments. Walt had married young and for the wrong reasons, and things were just coming to a head about the time the two men met. Shortly thereafter Walt found himself single again, with a wife moving back to Rhode Island, and all the while bleeding him dry. Elvin said Walt was lucky that he and Dora didn't have kids, that it would be easier to move along with his life. Walt didn't see it that way. If they'd had a kid, maybe it wouldn't have been as easy for Dora to leave him. Maybe that would have been enough to make her stop and think about what she was doing. Still, Elvin and his wife were what friends Walt had, and they helped him get past those first few months of starting over. He stopped by sporadically, and Elvin and his wife lent a cup of coffee and the occasional ear to be bent.

Elvin was a stay-at-home dad who, along with his wife D.J., had decided to downshift his career and raise two kids at a slower pace of life. He was forty-five years old. Walt was forty-two. The two men were as close in age as they were different in temperament, but they had managed to develop a semi-silent camaraderie. Theirs was a friendship built on a mutual willingness to ignore the other's sins, combined with a set of two shared interests.

It was the last Saturday in May, the bass opener. A religious holiday in Walt and Elvin's eyes, and neither of these two men was going to miss it. There weren't many people with the desire to paddle around in this cool, not-quite summer weather, but Walt and Elvin were not going to let Mother Nature cheat them out of a holy day of obligation. The fishing might not be great, but it was still fishing. That was shared interest number one. In the autumn, their friendship centered almost exclusively around bird hunting.

"You sure?" Elvin asked again. He was feeling a little guilty about getting first crack at all the good spots, but then, Walt did like to paddle more than he liked to fish, and Elvin liked to fish more than just about anything else. Guilt was a relative thing, so Elvin kept casting his line into the shallows. Occasionally a little swirl would appear next to his lure, but it was the sign of curious fish, not necessarily hungry one. The lure continued to twitch along the surface, ghost swirls chasing behind. He wasn't having a lot of luck with the fish.

"No, I've got it. I need to get in shape anyway, and you're never going to be in shape," Walt jibed back. Walt prided himself on his physique, and was as toned as most men half his age. He had the muscular, compact stature of a middleweight boxer. When he wasn't working, he spent much of the winter hauling and splitting firewood by hand, stoking the firebox in the drafty cabin he called home. Once spring arrived and the ice started breaking up, it was paddling season. Walt had always aspired to compete in the Grand Limoneaux River Canoe Marathon, over 16 hours of paddling, endurance, and sheer hell. The Marathon created a brotherhood amongst paddlers that was forged in blood. Last year he entered the race, but wasn't able to finish. He still remembered the sour taste in his mouth when he'd had to withdraw from the event. This year he intended to complete the grueling competition. Anything short of that he'd consider failure.

Elvin, on the other hand, could best be described as "stringy," though he'd rather be referred to as "svelte." He had a body built for running, not the grueling abuse that the Canoe Marathon dished out. Part of this was just a lack of interest on his part. Sixteen hours of nonstop paddling, when your back was killing you, you were dehydrated, and your hands were turning to raw meat? Why do things the hard way if you didn't have to? Now if you could take a three or four day drift to the river's mouth in Hohner, in a stable boat, napping along the way, well that might be his kind of canoe trip. There would have to be snacks on board, not the Power Bars and 'Energy Goop' that the marathon racers survived upon. Maybe a few drinks, too, and a book for when the fishing was slow.

"You ever hear any more about that bone you found?" Elvin asked a few minutes later.

"Cold case, I guess," Walt shot back. "Fourshe says the State cops found most of the skeleton, probably been buried in the river forever and got kicked loose by the high run-off. It took them most of a week to put the parts together, but they know it was a man. There's been no missing persons around here in the last 20 years, at least not that anyone can recall. Police aren't sure how long it was in the Bitch or how far it drifted before I found it, let alone *who* it could have been. Their best guess is that it was buried in the mud for about ten or twelve years. Amazing the porcupines didn't find it first and eat the bones. You know why you hardly ever find bones in the woods? Porkies and mice, love the calcium and minerals in them. Fourshe doesn't want to deal with this mess, the sheriff doesn't want to touch it, and the state police have better things to do. I think they've seen the writing on the wall and given up before they ever really started."

"Fish on!" was Elvin's response. He promptly hauled up a small bluegill that was quickly released back into the lake. "Two for me, none for you.

You'd think someone would notice, somewhere, if a person disappeared forever," getting back on subject.

"You'd think. *I* sure as hell noticed, because whoever died, he was in *my* river and he screwed up two weeks of *my* time. I wish he'd have *stayed* disappeared. I had to answer the same stupid questions over and over from Bill. I burned one whole day taking Fourshe and Amberson out there, and then another day when those dip-shits from the state got involved. Then I had to answer a million questions from the county, and again the state cops asked me the same stupid questions. In the meantime I've got that jackass Dewers calling me 'The Bone Collector' all day at work, like he thinks he's the King of Comedy or something. I'm not sure you can really call what you just had in your hand a 'fish,' by the way. I think 'minnow' would be a better description."

"Gee Walt, you ought to solve this quandary," his friend shot back. He knew it would rile Walt up. Just the use of the word "quandary" would probably piss Walt off. Sometimes you had to poke the bear, just to see if he'd growl. "Stick it in Amberson's face a bit. You figure the mystery out when he can't."

"Screw you," Walt shot back. "You think I have time on my hands? And what's with 'quandary?' Did somebody give you a dictionary for your birthday? You are such a pretentious prick sometimes."

"I love you, too," he laughed. "You're right, Walt. Amberson's a professional. He's probably better at solving problems than you could ever be," he pushed back. This was getting more fun by the moment. He could see the color rising in Walt's face. If he had a blood pressure monitor he could probably keep score.

"Screw you again, Elvin. Amberson couldn't find his own pecker if you gave him a flashlight and a GPS." Walt knew when he was being provoked, but couldn't resist rising to the bait. What if Walt *could* find some answers, and dangle it in Amberson's face? If he just looked around a bit on his own, without letting on what he was doing, what could that hurt? It might even shut Dewers up for a while.

"Fish on!", yelped Elvin. "Hey Walt?" once more.

"Yeah?"

"Maybe it was Jimmy Hoffa," he kidded.

MAKING FRIENDS
6

Two hours later they were done fishing for the day. Dusk was creeping over the horizon, and with it a light fog levitated just above the water's surface. A loon, hidden in one of the back bays, mournfully called for its mate. Mosquitos and black flies took the setting sun as their cue to attack in full force. The two men silently hefted the canoe and began their mile-long walk, back to where they'd parked their vehicles. The two men were satisfied yet bloodied. With their hands full of canoe, the mosquitos had eaten Walt and Elvin alive. They were both silently assessing their damage from the little vampires.

A few minutes later the Bell canoe was strapped upside down atop Walt's Suzuki, extending a few feet past both the front and back bumpers, and looking for all the world like some cartoonist's idea of a joke. Walt tied a red kerchief to the back of the canoe. It was better to be safe than to have someone smack into the overhanging boat with their car.

"Hey Walt?"

"Yeah?"

"Thanks for fishing with me." It was a small gesture, but heartfelt just the same.

With that they parted ways. Elvin jumped in his Ford Ranger and headed back to his wife, once again boasting the honorary title of Gillmaster at Shambarger Lake. It was a long running joke between the two. They had long ago decided that the title of 'Gillmaster' was only good until the next time they fished together.

Walt started the little Samurai and turned toward home, only a few miles down the state road. After thinking about what waited for him at the house, an eight-year-old golden retriever named Doofus and an empty refrigerator, Walt decided a quick drink at the Deer Track Inn was in order. It would help fortify him for a lonesome evening later on.

'The Deer Track Inn' was a fairly grandiose name for a pole barn masquerading as a bar, thought Walt, as he pulled into the lot. What it lacked in polish it more than made up for in absence of charm. It was far enough outside of town that it didn't attract but a handful of locals. And by "locals," one meant hard-core alcoholics who had lost their drivers' licenses. It was a place for those who couldn't *get* themselves to town, along with those that were no longer permitted in the "real" bars that featured bands and dancing, and the occasional stray that wanted to drink without the scrutiny of the town's immoral majority. The Deer Track wasn't really on the way *to* or *from* anything, other than Walt's house and Shambarger Lake, and neither of those was going to rival Yellowstone as a tourist destination. There wasn't a lot to recommend the Deer Track, when you got right down to it. But then here it was, and the lights were on. That in itself Walt considered a minor miracle.

The Deer Track parking lot bespoke of compacted sand and potholes, with a smattering of desolation for good measure. There was an older Pontiac with a mismatched right front fender and a cancerous Chevy pickup truck in the lot when Walt arrived. A Rascal scooter was parked at the front entrance, one man's detour around drunk-driving laws. A basket was attached to the Rascal's handlebars, some relic from a little girl's bicycle, woven plastic plastered with faded synthetic daisies. A ten-foot orange flag, the kind you'd find on a dune buggy, was zip-tied to the rear corner of the frame, and a reflective orange triangle, the universal sign for 'slow moving vehicle' was duct taped to the back of the seat. The owner must have assumed that these modifications made it road ready. "Too bad it doesn't have turn signals, a license plate or an air bag," Walt thought to himself.

The wooden screen door yelped as Walt opened it, then slammed shut loudly enough that everyone turned to see who had entered. "Everyone" included a pair of twenty-something women at one table, one grizzled northerner quietly in his cups at the far end of the plywood bar, and the bartender. Walt didn't recognize the two women at the table or the mountain man sitting at the bar. The guy might be Rip Van Winkle, from the looks of him. He could be fifty or he could be a hundred, sometimes it was hard to tell around here. He hadn't wasted much time shaving or bathing in the last year, and he hadn't bothered to put his teeth in for the night, if he even owned a set. Walt was pretty sure that old Rip was the owner of the Rascal tied to the hitching post out front.

MAKING FRIENDS

Walt checked out the two women seated at the table. The dark-haired one looked physically fit. He might even describe her as "muscular." She was dressed like she could have stopped in from a long day of hiking, only it didn't make sense that anyone would be hiking down the state highway. Not unless she was very, very, lost. Her red-haired friend was dressed similarly, wearing jeans, a red plaid shirt, and a black fleece vest. She was good looking, thought Walt, but a little on the chunky side. If he were a betting man, and he was, the truck out front would be theirs. If he were a betting man, they probably weren't here to find themselves a betting man. They were here to find a betting woman or two, seemed more likely.

The bartender, or was it "bartendress" nowadays? He could never really recall what was politically correct, and usually didn't give a shit either way. The Person of the Bartenderly Persuasion he had seen once before, a full-figured bottle blond in her early fifties. Pam or Patty or something like that, he couldn't remember her name. He hadn't had a chance to talk to her that first time, as the bar had been hopping with six or eight customers. Six or eight customers constituted a big night at the Deer Track. Pam or Patty had a few miles on her, but that's the way Walt liked them. Maybe tonight he'd get his chance to know her better.

"What'll it be?" she asked Walt.

"Beer and a bump. Patty is it?" He took a shot in the dark.

"It's Pam. Here's your beer. Stroh's o.k.?"

"Sure. I've been fishing with a buddy over on the lake," he started hesitantly. Small talk didn't come easily in a place like this. "We did alright. I caught about a dozen."

"Yeah? You must be doing awfully well by yourself, that you can spend your weekends fishing," she replied. Something between a smile and a smirk crossed her lips. Her expression suggested that maybe she remembered him from his previous visit, after all.

Walt couldn't explain exactly why, but he found this woman difficult to resist. She was a hard read. Was her remark sincere or sarcastic? He had a hard time telling the difference since his divorce. Women in particular, who really knew what was going on inside their heads? She sure wasn't your classic beauty. Doughy features, far too many wrinkles and crows' feet for her age, and probably carrying an extra thirty to forty pounds. Maybe it was her gruff demeanor that he took for a challenge. It could be he liked to be mothered. Walt had always had peculiar tastes in women, tastes even Walt didn't understand. "A handsome woman," is how Elvin described Walt's last girlfriend. That relationship had lasted all of two weeks. "Handsome women are grateful," was Walt's reply. Maybe in a drink or two, pondered Walt, this Pam might be worth pursuing. "Hit me again, please." Maybe he could make her grateful. He'd have to be on his best behavior.

The old guy at the end of the bar was nursing a shot of something, mumbling under his breath. Maybe he was still fighting a war somewhere in his head. Probably the civil war, from the looks of him. He didn't seem like he needed much maintenance from Pam beyond a continuously full glass.

The two women at the table were talking quietly to one another, occasionally glancing up at the television that hung mute from the ceiling. The local weather was on, and it didn't manage to hold their attention. They each had a beer in front of them. Maybe he could get one of them to dance with him. A little jealousy often helped light a fire, and he hoped to light a fire under Pam.

Walt wandered over to the jukebox, plugged in a dollar, and punched some buttons, but no sound came out. He punched the buttons again, and still no sound came out.

"That hasn't worked in over a year, honey" Pam noted, as if the thought had not occurred to her until this very moment. "Sorry." It was hard to tell if there was a true "sorry" in that voice, or just a heaping helping of "snide-a-la-mode."

"It just ate my buck," seethed Walt, "can I get that back?"

"How about a shot on the house, and we'll call it even."

"I guess that will have to do," he conceded, and settled back to his bar stool. Now that they were friends, he'd get back to working on Pam. "You know those bones they found up in the Bitch River? That was me," he boasted. Walt firmly believed that no woman could resist a hero.

"Really," she raised one eyebrow. Was she truly interested, or was feigned interest merely part of her job description? "No one put a name to that corpse yet?"

"Not yet, but I'm working on it."

"Ah, you must be FBI or something. Who do you think it was? Colonel Mustard in the study with the candlestick?" she asked. Now she had him on the spot. He wanted to look like a man in the know. How was he going to impress Pam if she thought he was a clueless rube?

"Not FBI, USGS."

"What in God's name is an UsGus?"

"It stands for United States Geological Service. We study water quality, stuff like that. Stream flow, velocity, you know. My theory is that the body was someone from the yoga ranch, you know? Who would notice if some freak from the big city disappeared? You'd never put it together, a missing person from a big town and pile of old bones up here. I'd bet hundreds of people go missing from Detroit or Flint or Saginaw every year, and no one even notices. Maybe it was some gay lovers' quarrel that ended in murder or something."

"Excuse me, could we get another round?" interrupted one of the women from the table. It was the redhead, he thought, not her friend with the black hair. He tried not to turn around and stare. She sounded impatient, like they were both on the verge of imminent dehydration.

"Cows," whispered Walt, more out of habit than true malice. He was finally making progress with Pam and those two were throwing sand in his wheels. Why couldn't they wait a few more minutes before interrupting?

"Coming right up," shot back Pam, as she stepped into the storage room to grab another case of beer.

"Now I'm getting somewhere," thought Walt, and that was the last thing to drift through his mind before the lights went out.

A HAIR OF THE DOG
7

"What the hell happened?" asked Walt as he grudgingly opened his eyes. He wasn't entirely sure where he was, or if anyone was around to answer his question. His head felt like someone had removed the top of his skull with a can opener, and he was lying on a pine floor that wasn't nearly as clean as the pit toilets in a state forest campground. Everything around him smelled faintly of urine and stale beer. He hoped the odor was not emanating from him. How long had he been unconscious? Finally a face hovered above him, with the halo effect of a second, identical face directly behind it. He couldn't quite place her, but the sturdy women who spoke from above seemed familiar.

"Hey, lover boy. You're alive! You're on the floor of the Deer Track. I closed shop over an hour ago. You've been napping."

The two faces were starting to become one. It reminded him of his last trip to the optometrist. "Now tell me when the two images are directly aligned," the doctor implored. They weren't quite there this time, but they were getting closer. The effect somehow made Pam/Patty seem more attractive. Two Pams or Pattys, it was like a gum commercial he'd once seen. Twice the flavor, twice the fun, something along those lines.

"What the hell happened?" Walt asked again. "Is it Pam?"

"My, you are a quick one. What did you say to those women that they had to knock you out? One minute I'm in the back room getting another case of beer, the next minute you're lying on the floor and I'm missing two customers. You must have used one of your smoother lines on them."

"Who?" Walt was a little slow returning to his senses. He was almost able to sit upright. He wasn't bleeding, and he was fairly certain he didn't have a concussion. At least not a *real* concussion. His head hurt, but his tolerance for pain was higher than most men. At least that's what Walt told himself. He knew he wasn't thinking as clearly as he could, but things were starting to come back bit by bit. "Who hit me and why? I think someone got me with a bar stool." If he was lucky, Pam had a thing for innocent victims.

"Do you know them?" questioned Pam.

"Who?" Walt still wasn't sure how he'd ended up on the floor. He was slowly rising to his feet now, then gingerly sitting on a chair, just until the vertigo abated. He was starting to suspect the two women at the table had suckered him, if only because the old drunk had looked barely able to lift his drink, let alone a stool or a chair. He hadn't known Pam long enough yet for her to wish him bodily harm, and he didn't remember seeing any of his exes lurking around outside the place. "The two cows at that table? Is that who hit me?" he tried.

"Ah, I think we have an answer to one question, lover boy. You called them 'cows,' did you? Either those two ladies didn't appreciate your particular kind of flattery, or they killed some guy and threw him in the Sparrow River when they were about ten years old, and they know that you're on to them. Unless you have a third, still unmentioned theory, I think your two lady friends took exception to your tone. Try honey instead of vinegar next time, genius."

"Ever seen them before?" Walt tried, with false hope. His head was still buzzing, though not quite as loudly. He was increasingly certain it was because of those two women that he hurt, and increasingly doubtful that Pam was the pitying kind.

"No, but I did hear them talking earlier about a retreat. Unless they're reenacting the civil war, I'd think they might have been up at that yoga camp on the Sparrow River. And it wasn't a bar stool, sweetheart. One of them must have hit you with a fist. My bar stools are right where I left them. Your head might not be as tough as you think it is."

"Did you call someone?"

"You weren't bleeding and I didn't think you were going anywhere," Pam grinned. There was a little gap between her front teeth, something he hadn't noticed until now. It made her seem even more attractive in Walt's eyes. Maybe they were going to be friends after all. "Can I get you something?"

Walt thought she was looking better already.

A HAIR OF THE OTHER DOG
8

The sun was nearly up when he slid into his clothes and slipped out the front door of Pam's house. It was only a few miles to his own home. Doofus had been alone in the house since late yesterday afternoon. He was hoping the dog had not been bored, because bored usually equalled mischief, or worse. He was praying the dog had not had much food in his bowl. He was wrong on both counts.

He pulled into the muddy trench he called a driveway and opened the sliding door on the front of his house. Walt sometimes wondered what kind of a builder would put a sliding patio window on the front side of a house, but he'd grown to love the oddity. It gave him a better view of his front yard, and it made life very convenient when it came to letting the dog in and out. There was traditional door on the back side of the house, but Walt seldom used it. He wasn't going to enter his own home by sneaking in the back way.

Doofus was nowhere to be found when Walt first entered. That was never a good sign. A good sign would be Doofus sitting at the window, wagging his tail and waiting patiently for his master to arrive. Barking maybe, overflowing with joy that Walt had finally arrived home.

"Doof, come here boy," he called out. He was greeted with utter silence. He tried again. "Doofus, come on pal!" He slid off his shoes, took two steps toward the kitchen on his right, and immediately got a foot full of warm dog crap. "Doofus, you idiot! Get down here!" he screamed in anger. The dog came scurrying down the stairs, tail between his legs. He hesitated as if considering whether or not to greet the hopping man. Was this a trick? He knew what he'd done probably wouldn't be rewarded. There was more damage upstairs that the man could not have even seen. The dog decided to play it safe. Doofus saw his opening and shot straight out the open door and into the neighbor's yard. "Bastard," cursed Walt, as he hopped on one foot toward the bathroom.

When he reached the bathroom, the wastebasket was overturned and garbage was strewn everywhere. Doofus was a sweet dog, but not when left alone for extended periods of time. That's when his destructive streak came out. He needed to run and he needed to hunt, and Walt provided him only sporadic opportunity for either. If the dog got bored, well this is what you got.

Walt had owned Doofus since he was a pup. Back when he was first married to Dora, having a dog seemed like a good idea. Walt's job often took him to far reaches of the state for days on end, and Dora never felt secure spending long periods alone in a back woods home. Doofus was both a security system and a friend to his wife, but Walt wasn't around with enough consistency to do Dora or the dog much good. Eventually Dora found her own security with some guy from Coldwater, and took off for greener pastures. Coldwater didn't work out for Dora either, and she eventually headed back to their old hometown of Providence. Dora was never what you'd call a 'long-term' kind of woman. Walt kept the house, the dog, and the occasional load of free fertilizer.

He hopped over to the tub, stripped down, and got in the shower. The water that trickled out of the shower head was tepid at best. The house needed a new water heater. The one he had was well past its life expectancy, and the water never seemed to get up to full temperature. It was one more thing on the growing list of things that were falling apart in his life, things that would have to wait for better times. He soaped and showered in the cool water, waking up a little bit more as his skin turned bright pink from the chilly blast. Walt stayed under the water for a good fifteen minutes.

The house had seemed empty since Dora left, though Walt had done his best to fill it up. For a while he'd reveled in his new found freedom. A few drinks could go a long way with the right sort of woman. Walt, despite his temper and his quick mouth, could almost be considered "a catch." He had a steady job, which was a rarity in these parts. He drank some, but not often and not much. He had his own hair and teeth, and there were no kids to support. He even owned a home, though he was upside-down on his mortgage, but then who wasn't nowadays?

In his first few days of being single again, Walt entertained a steady parade of women, none of whom stayed in his life for more than a few nights. Sometimes it was his fault, sometimes it was theirs. Sometimes it was what it was. Word spread quickly about some of his less redeeming qualities, and a few bridges got burned along the way. Lately he'd been through what he described as "a dry spell." In a small town, even where standards were never too high, you could eventually exhaust the supply of women who were willing to play house.

Walt got out of the shower and put a single ash log in the wood stove. The house was chilly, but he didn't mind. He didn't have money to refill the propane tank, that could easily run five hundred dollars or more. And he didn't want to burn more wood than absolutely necessary. If he could keep the house at fifty-five degrees, he was happy. One log on the fire would take the bite out of the air. He put on a fresh pot of coffee and looked in the refrigerator. Two sticks of butter, half of a moldy english muffin, and a jar of grape jelly stared back. He gently scraped the mold off the muffin, threw it in the toaster, and filled the dog's water bowl. There were two apples on the counter. He took a bite from one of them. He'd have to find something for the dog to eat later. He was barely feeding himself these days, but Doofus needed food. The dog was skin and bones as it was. He sat down in the recliner and waited to hear the "ping" of the toaster.

What was it Elvin had said in the canoe yesterday? Something about Hoffa? That guy could be such a wise-ass. Why was he hanging around with some wise-ass, anyway? He looked over at the clock; nearly seven in the morning. It was Sunday. No work today. He could head back to bed. Then again, what was the point in that?

The thought of finding that body in the river gnawed at him. Walt wasn't necessarily burning for adventure. He wasn't burdened with overarching curiosity, either. If anything, he yearned to know many things out of *spite*. The temporary disruption of his life, caused by that one chance discovery, was like every other disruption in his life. Walt viewed it as an imposition. It was as if someone was crowding him out of his own personal space, his own life, forcing their way into his territory. Someone needed to be held accountable, blame needed to be placed. One-upping the sheriff's department, that would be a bonus for Walt. For a man with seemingly bottomless depths of anger and energy, that wayward hip bone had pointed him in a clear direction. It was calling to him: "solve the riddle, and you will be respected." Walt heeded the call. Every missile needs a target.

He got up, retrieved a cup of black coffee and his muffin, now slathered in jelly, and slipped his clothes on. A drive up to the Bitch River and a hike in the woods would do him good. Look around, see what's what. Get some sun, if the sun was ever coming out today. There was still dew on the grass and a haze in the air, but it would probably lift within a couple of hours. It might be nice to get out of the house for the day, walk around in the fresh air. He'd pick up a bag of apples on the way, maybe a stick of summer sausage for protein. He'd find his dog, load him in the Samurai, and go. It was a plan.

An hour later man and dog were driving north together, looking for answers to questions unknown.

A SNAKE IN THE SAWGRASS
9

The mist and haze were beginning to clear around nine o'clock, just as Walt was pulling off the freeway onto Wolverine Valley Road. It was shaping up to be a clear day, and the temperature might even sneak into the low sixties. Walt passed a few cars on his way to the Sparrow River, probably campers up for the weekend driving into Sturgeon to buy coffee or forgotten essentials. It was Memorial Day weekend, after all, the official kick-off to summer in the North.

The guys with the big Winnebagos and campers went elsewhere, where there were showers and running water with drains and electrical hookups. Those big campers sought out park rangers teaching crafts to the kids, and swimming pools. They would park their aluminum-sided forts within spitting distance of each other, roast smores by the campfire, and at night retire inside to the comfort of a warm bed and Leno on the satellite television. *Those* campers, they were still on the interstate heading elsewhere to the bigger campgrounds. They would spend a night or two parked shoulder to shoulder, drive their ships back to the city by Sunday night or Monday morning, and regale their coworkers with tales about how they "roughed it" all weekend.

It was a busy weekend for the smaller campgrounds, too, at least busy for this area. There were six state campgrounds all within a five mile radius of each other, most accommodating between ten and twenty sites. A few were on tiny lakes, boats permitted but no motors allowed. All had pit toilets, smelly wood-sided vaults that got hosed down and sucked clean a few times each season. None offered showers. If you wanted water you pumped a well by hand. Most sites were designed for tents, although you could squeeze a small pop-up or teardrop trailer into a campsite, if you were careful. These were the folks of the Sparrow River Valley.

There were times when a person could be the sole camper at Rattlesnake Lake or Dead Indian Bridge campground, the least popular of the state units. Memorial Day weekend was not one of those times. The big holiday weekend generally meant that even the most remote sites filled to capacity.

This year, however, the cooler temperatures and predicted rain meant that a handful of spots remained vacant.

A blue Volvo station wagon passed Walt heading in the opposite direction, a solitary woman at the steering wheel. Walt stared hard as she went by. The driver did not notice him, as she focused on the winding road back to Sturgeon. Walt turned his eyes back to the road.

“Probably another yuppie freak,” Walt informed his dog. “We hate Volvos, don’t we boy?” Doofus did not answer. He did not pass another vehicle for the rest of his drive.

When he finally reached the pullout, the two-track looked completely different from when Walt had been here in April. The snowbanks were gone, though an occasional white mound still cringed in the shelter of a large tree or depression in the ground. The last of the snow wouldn’t disappear until the middle of June. Fiddlehead ferns had sprung up on the forest floor, sheltered by the jack pines and what hardwoods the lumbermen hadn’t felled a century before. In a few weeks the ferns would be waist high and tip-to-tip, creating a floating subfloor of green beneath the canopy of trees that danced with the wind. The ferns were growing rapidly, but not yet in full bloom. You could still see the ground in places.

The road itself was no longer sheathed in ice. The Sparrow River Valley was largely made up of sand, and sand drained quickly. Dust trailed behind the Suzuki as it jostled its way toward the trailhead. A perfect imprint of its mismatched rear tires lay in its wake.

“Wanna go for a walk, Doof? Do you want to go for a run in the woods? Well, do you?” Walt was cranking the dog up, hoping Doofus would burn some energy once they got to their destination, run himself into exhaustion, and stay out of trouble for a few days thereafter. “Who’s a good boy? Find the birds, Doofus. Find the birds.” By the time Walt stopped his little tin can of a vehicle, Doofus was practically bouncing out the window with excitement. When Walt turned off his engine and opened the driver’s side door, the dog hurled himself across Walt’s lap and out into the wide space.

Walt grabbed the bag of apples and two venison sticks he’d picked up at the Speedway, dropped them in a small backpack with two plastic bottles of water he'd refilled from the tap at home, and set off toward the Sparrow. It was a great day for a walk.

"Come on boy, find the birds."

He knew he shouldn't be letting the dog run free near nesting birds, but Doofus needed the exercise, and nesting season was just about done. It was good practice for the fall hunting season, and might prevent the dog from chasing deer and other "trash" species when it mattered. The dog flushed two ruffed grouse and one woodcock before they even reached the CCC bridge.

"Good boy, Doofus. Come here, boy."

The dog healed on command, then raced off, galloping first left and then right, all the while keeping his master in the corner of his eye. Once they reached the Sparrow River, Doofus plunged into the pearlescent liquid and paddled around in circles. Walt stood at the base of the bridge and looked out at the river that, two months previous, was another world from the one he observed now. The river was nowhere near its summer lows, but was nonetheless almost serene. It was hard to believe how vicious this flow had seemed, only a short time ago.

Walt looked around the area, at the Sparrow's eroded banks, and at where the banks *had been* during April's high water. The police had done a good job of cleaning up after themselves. A wrapper from a Sweet and Salty bar and a tiny can from one of those instant three-hour energy drinks lay near the high water mark. There were few signs that the police had trampled this area for the better part of two weeks searching for clues. In the shallows downstream from the bridge, clinging to the river bottom, lay two empty blue containers the size of small margarine tubs. They hadn't been here in April, didn't show the grime and algae that accumulated from long-term exposure to the elements. Walt could tell that someone had been fishing this spot recently. The containers from Blake's Bait seemed to be found anywhere there was fishable water. Idiots fishing with night crawlers, too lazy to take their trash out with them, in Walt's estimation. The plastic containers would last forever. Along the shore lay a pair of empty beer cans.

"I'd drown 'em all if I could." Worms or fishermen, it was hard to tell which Walt meant.

Another path from the one Walt trekked paralleled the river. Its dirt was hard packed and no wider than a bicycle tire. Knee-high sawgrass on both sides of this line parted ever so slightly. Decades of hikers and fishermen had taken this trail, probably centuries of Native Americans before them, so that even when not in frequent use, nothing grew on the hard brown strip that marked its center line.

Walt began following this path upstream, whistling once sharply. Doofus heard the signal, followed alongside, traipsing through the tree line to the left with his nose to the ground. The sawgrass grabbed and tore at Walt's legs as he hiked. It reminded him of why he rarely wore shorts, even in the hottest weather. Sandals were out of the question. He was glad that he'd chosen to wear jeans and boots this day.

At some point Walt came to a low spot just off the trail, where the high grass was flattened even to the ground. Generally this would indicate a deer bedding down, but on closer inspection Walt spied a pile of garbage in the swale just behind. Bleach bottles, plastic jugs, an empty five gallon bucket, and small cardboard boxes filled the depression. They couldn't have been here long. The boxes were weathered, yet their labels were still legible. Sinus medications, household cleaners.

"Meth heads," he realized. Crystal meth, once the scourge of the inner cities, had quickly found a foothold in rural America. Anyone with a handful of chemicals and a working knowledge of high school chemistry could create their own batch of poison for fun and profit. Toxic piles like this were becoming more and more common in the north woods. Sure, there was still the occasional plot of marijuana growing somewhere on state land. But the short growing season and the risk of getting caught couldn't rival a low cost drug that can be cooked anywhere, at any time. Outdoor marijuana growers were going the way of moonshiners. Meth was quickly taking over. It was almost enough to make Walt sympathize with the pot heads.

Walt took mental note of the spot, though he wasn't sure why. He'd tell someone over at the Conservation Department, but their budget had been cut too, and there were more piles of junk in this county than there was time to clean it. If it wasn't this stuff it was an old washer, bedsprings, roofing shingles. People found it easier to dump their crap on state land than to haul it to the landfill and pay a nominal fee. Maybe the feds could just declare the whole damn forest a Superfund site, and send some real money this way.

"Come on, Doof!" he yelled. The dog bumbled along.

Fifteen minutes further up the trail, Walt heard a single shotgun blast from somewhere downstream. It was hard to pinpoint the location, as sound echoed along the river valley. He stood still and waited.

"What the hell. Heal!" Doofus stepped to his side and stood at attention. It wasn't hunting season, wasn't even close to hunting season. Maybe someone was just sighting in their gun, but who sighted in a *shotgun*, for crying out loud? A rifle, sure, but a *shotgun*? You pointed and you shot. Walt stopped and waited, hoping to locate the shooter if he fired another round. After ten minutes of listening for a second report, Walt decided it was just some yahoo that liked to hear his gun go "boom." He continued his pace east, Doofus matching him step for step. Doofus' boundless energy had run its course, and the dog was now content with a leisurely stroll at the knee of his master.

GETTING TO THE POINT
10

He approached the first of the two big river curves with a wary eye. Walt was trying to imagine what this stretch had looked like back in April, when the water was high. He was seeking a deep hole, a cut in the bank, anything that might have hidden a dead man's body for years. He stopped and stared, squinting into the late morning sun. There was nothing obvious, nothing out of place. He kicked around at a few downed logs, thinking maybe they disguised a hidden hollow. Nothing. A rabbit spooked from under one stump and ran in ever widening circles, looking for cover. A few woodcock took flight, startled from an aspen thicket. Walt munched an apple as he waited and watched. After a while he gave up, pitched the apple core into the woods, and continued walking upstream.

At the second curve, or the first curve if one had been walking downstream from the dam, the story was much the same. There were downed limbs, a multitude of rotten stumps, a few beaver slides, an undercut bank, but nothing to suggest a hiding place for a corpse. Walt stopped to think about what he was missing in this picture. "What do you think, boy? Am I barking up the wrong tree?" The dog looked back inquisitively, trying to understand what was being asked of him. Walt continued to gaze at the bend, until he was startled back to the present when Doofus leaned into his leg, growling quietly. The hair on the dog's back stood on end. Walt listened intently, but couldn't figure out what was putting the dog on edge.

"Who the hell are you?" a voice eventually came from behind Walt. He jumped in surprise. It only took him a second to regain his composure.

"I know who I am. The question is, who the hell are you?" Walt fired back, before slowly turning around to look at the man behind the voice. The man who had come upon him silently was leaning against a tree, not twenty feet away, casually holding a 12 gage Winchester pump shotgun draped over his left forearm. He was about five foot eight, lean build. He was wearing torn jeans, a black t-shirt, and a baseball cap so filthy Walt couldn't make out the logo on the front. The matte gun barrel bobbed up and down in time with the man's twitching leg. Walt was hoping the gun's safety was on.

"This is my land, and you need to move along," the man snarled.

Walt cautiously appraised the situation. He had no gun, he hadn't told anyone where he was going, and there was little chance anyone would notice if things went south. He wasn't even sure that anyone would *care* if things went south. He knew he was standing on public land, knew that this man, whatever his reasoning, was in the wrong. But Walt also knew that it was less important to be right than to be alive. The stranger held all the cards here, or at least the one big card. This guy might be full of shit, but this guy might also shoot him. Restraint, never Walt's strong suit, won out nonetheless. Self-preservation overrode his fighting instincts. He took a deep breath and tamped down the rising anger.

"I'm sorry, I thought this was state land. I must have gotten turned around. Didn't realize we were trespassing. We're staying up at the ranch and just thought we'd take a little hike, me and my dog. Which way is it back to Sparrow Lotus?" Walt hoped he wasn't laying it on too thick. He also hoped this nut-job wasn't with the yoga camp, because then he'd know that Walt was lying. Walt was fairly sure this wasn't some guy on a sabbatical to "find himself." The "we're staying up at the ranch part," well, maybe if the guy thought Walt wasn't entirely alone, he'd be less prone to doing something stupid.

The stranger silently pointed the gun's barrel upriver. He was pointing the way, giving an order. Walt knew where the damn camp was, and it was taking all of his resolve to continue playing the fool. "Sorry again, I'll just get going," he told the man as he began again with cautious strides. It was painful for Walt to turn his back on a man with a weapon, but it seemed like his best bet. Doofus was still growling softly, but moved in lock step with his owner as they started moving up the shoreline.

Ten paces later, the gun went off. Walt went rigid. A laugh came from behind him, and the stranger eased himself into the woods. The stranger hadn't shot at anything in particular. He'd probably just shot into the sky, but Walt couldn't know that with his back turned. It was meant either as a warning or as a sick joke. Either way, Walt kept right on moving.

A FINE HOW DO YOU DO
11

She was in her mid twenties, but looked ten years younger. She couldn't have weighed much more than a hundred pounds, her dark brown curls pulled into a ponytail that reached halfway down her back. She wore pants made of some kind of stretch fabric, a spandex/lycra blend, clinging to skinny legs that belonged on a teenager. Her shirt was loose and billowing in the breeze, light cotton fabric. The rising sun was quickly heating the pond behind her, creating a haze which hovered a foot above the water. The only sound was that of the river gurgling beneath the dam's spillway. She sat motionless at the apex of the berm, legs crossed and hands stretched outward as if awaiting two gifts to be placed in her open palms. Her eyes were closed tight.

Walt approached cautiously from the west. He was still frazzled from his encounter with the man with the shotgun. He didn't know what other surprises lay ahead, and felt he'd had more than his share of excitement for one day. Doofus still stayed close by as he trudged his way upriver. When Walt stepped around a small tangle of tag alders, he was only twenty yards or so from the dam.

The sun shone brightly behind her. It looked as if the girl, the sun, the haze on the water had all been placed there just for Walt. Her silhouette was visible through the light cotton shirt. Walt was sure he'd never seen anyone more beautiful than this particular girl at this particular moment. It was a feeling Walt had experienced only twice before in his entire lifetime.

"Hey, how's it going?"

She didn't answer right away, though Walt knew she must have heard him.

"Excuse me. Miss? Excuse me."

Her eyes gradually opened. She slowly lowered her arms, unfolded the spindly legs beneath her, and rose to her feet in one fluid motion. It was like watching a cheetah awaken from a nap. Taut, sinewy muscles stretched over a compact frame. She was fluid.

"I'm sorry, I didn't notice you for a minute. I was doing a little midmorning meditation. Can I help you?" Her voice became a song on the breeze.

"Yeah, hey, I'm sorry. My dog and I were hiking, and then there was this whack-job with a shotgun, and, I don't know, are you with the camp? I could use a ride back to my rig."

"I'm just staying here for the week, but if you want to walk back to the main lodge with me, we can probably figure something out. You need a ride? You're a guest then? You said something about a person with a gun?" The look on her face didn't suggest suspicion or distrust, more a thirst for knowledge and slight confusion about what she was hearing. Walt realized he was rambling.

"No, I'm not a guest or anything. Look, I know this sounds crazy, some guy and his dog walking up out of nowhere and asking for a lift. I work for the Geological Service, and I was just up here for a walk on my day off. Some guy with a gun tried to chase me off state land about a mile downstream, and I don't want to pass him again on the way back to my truck. My name's Walt Pitowski, and this is Doofus, by the way."

"JoAnn. Nice to meet you, Walt, Doofus." She nodded towards the dog. Doofus, hearing his name, ran up to her and sat at her feet, waiting to be pet. She knelt down and obliged. "I hope you treat your dog with more respect than his name suggests."

"Doofus is just his name. He's actually really smart." Shit. Here was this knockout going to give him a lift back to the truck, and he was getting waylaid by his choice of dog names. These granola heads could be touchy. "In fact, Doofus and I are best friends. The name is more of an inside joke." It was hard to tell if she was buying what Walt was selling.

"Well, I'll give Doofus a ride to wherever he's going, and as long as *he'll* vouch for *you*, you can come with."

"Thanks, I appreciate it." Walt wasn't sure what to say next. He was dumbstruck in the girl's presence. "Rambling or speechless, feast or famine," he thought to himself. "You're an idiot, Walt."

The pair started hiking the quarter mile back to the main building, with Doofus in happy pursuit. All the while his eyes searched the pond and surrounding area, wondering where a body might have once been concealed. The pond was deeper than he'd originally thought, probably eight to ten feet in spots. It's bottom was buried in black silt, and vegetation had taken root in this slower current. In some places the surface was covered with an impenetrable mat of weeds. A person could remain buried in that muck for a long, long time, Walt thought to himself. But why was he worrying about a dead body, when he had this beauty standing beside him? Nice place, this camp.

"Have you been here before?" It was the best conversation he could come up with, under the circumstances.

Before she had an opportunity to answer, they crossed paths with a man from camp, who was strolling back towards the dam.

"Walt, this is Anton Kalinik. He manages Sparrow Lotus Camp. Anton, Walt Pitowski. Walt got lost hiking and needs a lift back to his car."

Anton was a string bean at six-foot-three and probably no more than a hundred and sixty pounds. He had long brown hair, feathered and well past his shoulders. He had a lithe, liquid stride. He wasn't particularly good looking, but the kind that could pass himself off as an 'interesting artist' or some other baloney. Walt had met plenty of his kind. Another hippie a little too full of himself. Walt was sure women at the camp loved his schtick: "Are you centered in your being? Here, let me help you with that...."

"Pleased to meet you, Walt. You're a long ways from town. Are you familiar with our facilities?"

"I am, sort of, thanks. My dog and I were just out for a little walk, and got turned around is all. This young lady is kind enough to be taking me back to my vehicle." Walt knew he sounded a bit brusk, but screw this guy, he thought. It's not as if he was going to have a come-to-lotus moment. Walt just wanted to get back to his truck without getting shot.

"Well, good luck to you." Anton dismissed them, continuing down the narrow path.

"What brings *you* to Sparrow Lotus?" Walt asked JoAnn, as they resumed hiking towards the compound.

"Every year for the last six, I come up here for a week or two. It helps me cleanse my mind and my soul. My friend Amy usually stays with me, but she had to get back to Tinley Park. She had some deadline to meet at her office, so she cut it short this year. She left earlier this morning."

"She wouldn't happened to have been driving a green Volvo, was she?"

"As a matter of fact, she was!" It was a small world after all, her voice squealing with delight. "How did you know that?"

"I passed her on Wolverine Valley Road. You don't look old enough to have been coming here for six years," Walt suggested. Things seemed to be moving a bit more smoothly.

"I'm old enough to have heard that line more than once, I know that," she answered. "And what brings you, Walt of the Geological Service and his faithful companion Doofus, hiking to Sparrow Lotus? I mean, it's not as if you didn't know there's a private camp here, you being in the river-survey business or whatever it is you do. Were you panning for gold?" Her tone was playful without being flirtatious.

Walt forged ahead. "Well, to tell you the truth, I was the guy who found a dead body in the river last spring. I'm guessing you heard about it?" He wasn't sure how much the camp had shared this tidbit of information. He *was* sure it wasn't going to help Sparrow Lotus drum up new business if word got around, so it was possible people around here didn't know.

"I heard a little something about it. A man I believe, he'd been in the river for quite some time. He hasn't been identified yet?"

"Yeah, well, I was just, you know, sort of poking around. I thought maybe I'd notice something the cops hadn't. They haven't identified him yet. Plus it's a nice day to be out walking. I don't know what that guy with the gun back there was about. Look, I ran into you, so something good did come out of today."

"Thanks for the compliment, but I'm not looking for a boyfriend." She seemed sincere, *genuine*, and had a way of letting a man down, all the while him thinking she'd done him a favor. It was hard to be insulted by a woman like that.

"No, hey, sorry if I sounded like I was hitting on you. Not that I wouldn't or anything, you're really attractive." God, he was sounding like a dolt. Time to change the subject. "Has anyone ever mentioned a person gone missing from the camp, you know, disappeared? Any customers that just left in the night unexpectedly or anything?"

"Not that I know of. But I'm not here all that often, and it doesn't seem like the kind of thing you'd bring up, even if it were true. Here's my car." They came to a grey Civic hatchback, battered but serviceable. "Let me clear off the seat for you." She took a small pile of papers, an empty coffee cup, and a half pound of sunflower nuts from the passenger side and slipped them behind the driver's seat. "Hop in, Doofus. You, too, Walt, if you still want a ride. If you really want answers about the camp, you should probably talk to Anton. He's been here since it first opened."

"Thanks, maybe some other time." His response sounded a lot nicer than what was going through Walt's head. Walt didn't like Anton, didn't like guys that looked like Anton. "He looks like a prick" probably wouldn't get him far with this young lady. It was better to just keep his mouth shut.

Doofus leapt into the back seat and Walt eased himself into the front passenger side. Just as JoAnn started the car, Walt looked to his right and saw the two women he'd encountered at the Deer Track, entering one of the smaller cabins. "Do you know those women?" he asked JoAnn. He hoped he sounded casual.

"Those two? Not really well. I think they're just here for the weekend. They're from Marquette, in the upper peninsula. I haven't seen them around much. Are they friends of yours?"

"I ran into them at a bar last night. They forgot to say goodbye."

"Did you buy them a drink or something? I got the impression they were, you know, *together*, not exactly your type. I can stop if you want to say hello," she offered.

"Nah, thanks. I got the feeling they were *together*, too." Walt almost spit the words. "I'll say hello some other time."

The rest of the short ride passed mostly in silence. The two miles by river turned into six miles by road, but it still beat walking. Walt thanked her when she dropped him at his vehicle. It had been an interesting morning, but he wanted to get back home and think. Who was the guy with the shotgun, and why'd he chase Walt off? That JoAnn was a ray of sunshine, but he knew he didn't have a shot with a young thing like her. And what were those other two women doing at Sparrow Lotus? It didn't make sense, if they were really a couple of earthy-crunchy lovers, that they'd have been drinking beer at a dive like the Deer Track. It wasn't like the Deer Track was a short distance from the camp. Why wouldn't they have taken the quick trip to Sturgeon if all they wanted was a drink? Something wasn't adding up. Then again, they were women, a species Walt never fully understood.

"Come on, boy, let's go home."

THAT'S THE WAY THE WORLD GOES ROUND
12

"Did you get your windshield fixed yet?"

The last thing Walt expected, rolling into the office on a Sunday afternoon, a Sunday afternoon on a frickin *holiday weekend*, to be precise, was to find Bill Fourshe standing out front shooting the breeze with that jawless wonder Matt Amberson. The deputy's question caught Walt off guard.

"I fixed it myself," he managed to sputter.

"Nice duct tape," Fourshe chimed in, noting the hillbilly repair job.

"I couldn't find a new gasket, and the old rubber was dry-rotted. I found the glass at that big junkyard in Bellaire. I just popped it in and taped up the old seal with duct tape." Walt was antsy. He knew the repair was slipshod, but he didn't need people pointing out his flaws for him. Running in to Fourshe outside his own office, well that was one thing. Running into Amberson? What was that jerkweed doing here? Walt knew that Fourshe and Amberson were casual friends, but the sight of the sheriff's deputy was enough to throw Walt off. "Shouldn't you be out looking for jaywalkers or something, Matt?"

"Wow, I've never heard that one before, Pitowski. You should be doing standup in Vegas. However, I do need to get back on the road." He began to step toward his cruiser.

"Hey, Amberson, before you go, I need to talk to you. I was just up on the Sparrow, and some guy pulled out a shotgun and threatened me. Anything you can do about that?"

"Now that is a shame," the deputy mused, pausing in mid step and turning to face Walt.

"I know, can you believe it, pulling a gun on me for no reason?"

"No, I mean it's a shame he didn't shoot your dumb ass. What kind of an idiot would pass up an opportunity like that? I should investigate and make sure he's not a danger to himself. Imagine, depriving society of the greater good and letting you live."

"I'm serious, Matt. This idiot pulled a twelve gage on me on state land, told me to keep moving. Scared the hell out of me."

"Really? And you didn't do anything to provoke this?" the deputy was having a hard time believing there wasn't more to this story than Walt let on. He screwed his face up tight, trying to imagine the myriad of ways in which Pitowski could have ignited a bad situation.

"Nope. Just walking around, getting some exercise."

"Just getting some exercise?" the deputy repeated. That was highly unlikely. "Do you have a description?"

"Wiry. Five-seven, five eight. Maybe in his late thirties, kind of hard to tell. He could have been a little older or a little younger. T-shirt, jeans, a ball cap. Just a guy."

"I'll write, 'half of northern Michigan' down as your official description. And you don't recall having met him before, no words exchanged beforehand, nothing?"

"I swear to God, Matt, never seen him before in my life. I was just out hiking with Doofus. This guy came out of nowhere and threatened me."

"Bill, this sort of sounds like a Conservation Department issue to me," Amberson stated to his friend. Maybe he could pawn the problem off on Fourshe. "It did involve a gun, out of hunting season, on state land." It was possible his friend would step in to save him. Anything would be better than a wild goose chase with Walt Pitowski.

"Varmint hunting's legal all year long, Matt. Nope, sounds like a case of criminal assault to me" Fourshe surmised. "I'll see you two later," as he rapidly retreated to his office. It was hard for Walt to blame Fourshe for being both quick *and* smart.

"Well, I guess we've got to take a look around, then," admitted the beaten Amberson. He felt the foreboding of a doomed man: doomed to yet another day wasted. "Get in the cruiser, Walt. Do you need to do something with that dog of yours?"

"He can wait in my truck. Let me crack the windows and get him some water. I'll be ready in a second."

Within a matter of minutes, Walt found himself heading to the Sparrow for the second time that day. He was not cheered by the fact, but he knew he'd brought it upon himself.

"Is there some remote chance this was a jealous boyfriend or a husband, Walt? Someone followed you up there to settle a grudge?" It was still unimaginable to the deputy that some schmuck had accidentally stumbled upon and threatened the most deserving man in the county.

"Nope. I've been keeping it dry and clean. I heard one shot before I saw this guy, but I thought it was just someone dinking around. You know, kids, or someone just bought himself a new gun, sighting it in."

"Not to be judgmental, Walt, but you can sometimes be, how should I say this without hurting your feelings, 'an asshole.' Is there any reason you can think of, that someone would want to shake you up? Besides the fact that they've met you, of course."

"Matt, seriously, I've got no idea. There was some junk up there by the banks, like someone was brewing meth and left their trash behind. I don't know if that has anything to do with anything. Maybe the guy is delusional. Maybe this all ties in to that body I found in the river. Maybe I'm getting close to something."

The deputy turned his head from the roadway with a look of mock surprise. "Close to something! Why didn't I think of that! You must be getting *close to something!"* His smile disappeared as quickly as it had arrived. "Walt, you've been watching too much Law & Order." His eyes were quickly back on the road ahead.

"Christ, Matt, you don't need to be so touchy."

They retraced Walt's steps silently, but they didn't encounter a soul, and they didn't find a thing. Walt showed the deputy the refuse from the meth lab, but otherwise it was a fruitless trip. The sky was dark by the time they finally returned to Walt's office. Doofus was sound asleep in the back seat of the Suzuki, waiting for the two men.

THE GOOD DETECTIVE
13

Matt Amberson liked to consider himself a good guy. Not a great guy, but a good guy. He was a cop, after all, and he knew that most people he met, even law-abiding citizens who had nothing whatsoever to hide, were always a little guarded in his presence. He saw that as a positive sign, that people knew he'd do his job, no matter what the circumstances. He was unlikely to let somebody slide just because they were acquainted with each other. But Deputy Amberson didn't consider himself a hard-ass, either. He was smart enough to realize that not everything in life was black and white, and that, in a town where you knew practically every single individual, some things just weren't worth pursuing. If he wrote up every traffic violation and civil infraction that occurred in this county, there wouldn't be anybody left to run the town. They'd all be sitting in jail, hoping one guy might get paroled so he could pick up lunch for the rest of them. No, Matt knew he probably wasn't a great guy, but he was certainly a good guy, and an above-average cop. He was honest, and he was good at reading situations.

Unlike a lot of people who went into law enforcement, he hadn't always wanted to be a cop. He hadn't even grown up in Rasmus. His hiring defied the usual pipeline for restocking one of the infrequent openings on the sheriff's patrol. More often than not, a full time deputy's job with health benefits, a rarity around here, would go to a local boy, a relative. If a relative wasn't handy, the job went to a kid who'd either been a star on the high school football team, or one who'd done his four-year stint in the army and had come home looking to settle down. If he came from an influential family, all the better.

Amberson was none of the above, an outsider. He'd been born and raised in the small town of Niles, nestled in the far southwest corner of the state. He'd met his future wife, Carol, while they were both attending Michigan State University. It was Carol who originally hailed from Rasmus. Matt had never had a clear vision of what he was going to do with his life. He was bouncing around from department to department at MSU, having a hard time deciding on a major, and well en route to a generic liberal arts degree. But when he spied that mousy brunette girl from the back row of Egyptian History 403, he knew whatever it was that he was destined to do, he was destined to do it with her at his side. They began seeing each other that first week of junior year, and never stopped seeing each other.

Carol had first gone away to Michigan State vowing never again to live in Rasmus or any town that remotely resembled Rasmus. She intended to major in Art History, and was going to work at some of the world's greatest museums. Paris, London, Seville were all whispering in her ear. But then her parents got sick, and her mom died three days prior to graduation. It was Carol and Matt that came back to take care of her father. She was an only child, and it was the right thing to do. She didn't mind, really she didn't mind. That's what she told people, and they almost believed her.

And she really didn't mind, at least not at first. Losing her mother made her appreciate how supportive a small community can be when you need them the most. The couple thought they'd help dad get back on his feet for a few months, then they'd move to the coast (it didn't matter which one, as long as it was to a big city with a world class museum). Carol told everyone who asked, and some who didn't, about how the pair were going to travel the world together. Maybe someday they'd get married, have kids, but they weren't thinking that far down the road, and besides, that whole scene, it was all so *bourgeoisie*. They had plenty of time.

Carol's dad passed away six months later, and Matt was by then scraping by on a part-time job at the video store and another part-time job delivering pizzas, living in a small apartment over one of the barbershops downtown. Carol was depressed, having lost both her parents in less than a year. She felt lost, overwhelmed. Matt once again did the right thing, and married the girl. He wasn't going to leave her alone in this world. And she acquiesced. The loss of both her parents had suddenly changed her, and Rasmus seemed somehow *safe,* at least for the time being.

Amberson stumbled into his job with the sheriff's department: it happened to be an election year, and then Sheriff Hoolihan was fighting accusations of nepotism. Hoolihan had been sheriff for twelve years, and had gradually built a department that was composed completely of family and friends of family, so he wasn't entirely sure how the nepotism complaint was suddenly relevant. If it wasn't important in the last five elections, why in the hell was it so important now? In any event, he offered Matt Amberson, the job just to prove that the nepotism charges weren't true. It was an unexpected decision, to say the least. A bolt from the blue for Matt, who eagerly took the position having no idea what to expect, other than a steady paycheck for a change. It was a grand move by the Sheriff, but it didn't play well with the voting public.

Matt's hiring managed to anger almost everyone, both pro and anti-Hoolihan. His usual supporters were angry that a job that should have gone to "one of theirs" was given to a virtual outsider. His opponents rallied around the fact that, after years of being denied any opportunity to work within the department, they were still being denied the opportunity to work within the department, if only for different reasons. And the handful of independent voters, who usually wouldn't have cared either way what the sheriff did or didn't do, thought it downright stupid that Hoolihan would hire a 23-year-old kid with a bachelor's degree in an unrelated field, no long-standing ties to Rasmus or this part of the state in general, and who hadn't even played high school football. No offense to Matt, of course, who seemed like a nice enough guy. It seemed proof positive that Hoolihan was getting crazier than his detractors had already accepted. The only ones happy with the decision were Matt and Carol Amberson.

Sheriff Hoolihan lost that November election by a landslide, but by then Matt was on the force. Somehow he survived the housecleaning that ensued under the new sheriff, and by this point in his career, was considered a reliable, dependable member of the community. He wasn't "from here," could never really be "from here," but fifteen years on the force bought him some credit with the townsfolk. That was fine by him. He wasn't really sure that he wanted to be "from" Rasmus. He only knew that he wanted to be *with* Carol.

Carol became president of the local historical society, a thankless, volunteer position that required significant amounts of time spent begging for donations. The historical society was trying to refurbish the old train depot, but the funding wasn't there. A town like Rasmus had a lot of needs, and memory lane was low on the pecking order when it came to financing. At first she figured they'd stick it out for a few years, with Matt finally having a real job and all, and then get on with fulfilling their dreams. She did a little substitute teaching at both the middle school and the high school, and found a myriad of other things to do with her time. But none of this was what she had originally planned for her life. As Carol began pondering her thirty-eighth birthday, now only months away, she'd begun to feel her life slipping through her fingers.

Matt sensed his wife's restlessness, and it was starting to weigh on everything that the couple did. She wouldn't state it outright, but he knew the clock was running. Matt was beginning to wonder whether there was time for any of it to happen at all; living in the city, kids, the travel. More and more Carol had been dropping hints about pulling up roots, moving to the coast. He wasn't sure if he had the energy for starting from scratch once again, but he was still madly in love with his wife, and he knew he'd do whatever he had to in order to keep her. It was a lot to think about. All of this was running through deputy Matt Amderson's mind when he pulled the police cruiser off the pavement and in to his own driveway. The porch light was on, and Carol was going to be mad that he was running this late. And that asshole Pitowski had asked him why he was so cranky.

EXODUS
14

The rain started to fall before dawn that morning, a cold soaker that wormed its way into every nook and cranny. Memorial Day weekend was always hit or miss when it came to the weather. Mother Nature frequently forgot to check her calendar, and you were fooling yourself if you thought the last of May equalled summer. By Monday morning most of the campers were breaking down their tents, getting ready to join the stampede of everyone else southbound. Get an early start and beat the traffic, went the logic. The only real way to beat the traffic was to leave late at night, or better yet, to not leave home at all.

The freeway was snarled for one-hundred and eighty miles in one direction. Everyone was heading south to the cities. Now and then the congestion would ease without warning, as if someone pulled a cork from a bottleneck ahead. Cruising speed would shoot up to fifty or so for a mile or two, only to quickly settle back to a stop-and-go twenty or thirty miles-per-hour. The customary three hour drive soon became five, six, seven hours. McDonald's made a killing. Families reminded one another that it was nice to get away from it all. "Nice."

Walt found himself at loose ends. He'd called Pam three times, left two messages for her. She hadn't called back. She probably had something better to do on this dreary holiday Monday. Fishing was a lost cause. With this weather, he'd spend more time bailing water than paddling. Elvin was doing something with his wife and kids. Walt and Doofus sat on opposite ends of the couch, watching Elmer Gantry on the Zenith console television. "Burt Lancaster was cool, boy." It was still early afternoon. The rain showed no sign of letting up. He sipped a cup of coffee. He thought about Pam, and got a little agitated that she wasn't waiting around the house for his call.

The Zenith sucked, but at least it was his to own. When Dora left, she took most of the furniture with her. The old beast of a television and the sagging couch weren't worth her time or effort. Burt Lancaster was preaching up a storm on the screen. Walt had the sound down to where he could barely hear it. He'd seen the movie before, he couldn't remember exactly when. He knew how it would end. Fate always gets you in the end. People are full of themselves. End of story.

Dora, now there was a piece of work. He met her down at the shore, on a Fourth of July weekend. He and his pals were hanging around the waterfront, hoping to pick up the rich girls who spend their summers in Providence. Dora wasn't one of those rich girls, she was more of a gypsy beachcomber. She always seemed to be around, though no one could quite remember who had invited her in the first place. Elvin would have called her "ubiquitous," a ten dollar word where a five cent word would do.

Walt's two closest friends at the time, Rick and Don, took an instant disliking to Dora. Sure, she could be fun. But she was a bit too wild, even for those guys, and it made them nervous. She'd be the life of the party one minute, then put everybody's hide in jeopardy pulling some stupid stunt. Like the time they were all sitting around drinking, and she decided to hang from her knees beneath the Henderson Bridge. They were all goofing around, and the next thing you know there she was, dangling upside down like an oversized, drunken bat. It took all three of them to reel her back in, and they were shaken for days thereafter. They all got the impression that she would have been just as happy had she fallen. Even Rick and Don knew she was a train wreck waiting to happen.

One thing about Walt, if you told him he couldn't do something, he was certain he had to do it. The fact that everyone seemed to hate Dora made him love her that much more. "She's effin' crazy, Walt," Rick told him. "She'll be an albatross around your neck," his dad warned him. Those seven words from his father sealed the deal. Walt and Dora eloped the following weekend, and when Walt graduated from Rhode Island College in the spring, the couple moved to Michigan. He wanted to put as many miles as he could between his new family and the naysayers back home. His time with Dora had indeed been a train wreck, but it was one glorious ride.

Elmer Gantry was winding down. Sister Sharon died in the fire, and the movie credits were flashing across the screen. Walt must have been lost in his thoughts. He got up, set his empty coffee cup in the kitchen sink, and looked out the window at the side yard. The rain hadn't let up. The woodpile needed attention. He and Elvin had brought in three loads of red oak this spring, but Walt hadn't gotten around to splitting the wood. He hadn't even stacked it properly, and the logs lay scattered every which way. "Not today, not in this weather," he thought. There was one beer left in the fridge from the six-pack he'd bought last night. He opened the last bottle and settled back on the couch.

'Sorry, Doofus. Not much fun today, is it?"

The dog lifted his left ear, sighed, and ground his body deeper into the couch cushions. One good thing about living alone was that no one could complain about the dog being on the furniture.

Walt was thinking about his dad, about Providence. The old man would probably love for Walt to move back there. The whole family could be together, the old man, mom, his sister and her family down in Kingston. There was no way he was going to give them the satisfaction. Walt was many things, but he was not a quitter. No way would he come home with his tail between his legs. Moving back to Providence would be admitting defeat.

Dora had long ago moved on, without looking back for as much as a second. Walt hadn't spoken to her since she'd left, but the Friend of the Court still took a healthy slice out of his check every month to remind him of his mistake. He wasn't even sure where she was living, though someone told him they'd seen her around Providence a year or so back.

His folks had given up on him a long time ago, too. They still talked once in a while, usually by phone when Walt needed to borrow money. He'd skipped his sister's wedding, told them he couldn't afford the airfare or the time off work. His parents had offered to pay for his airline ticket, but he declined. Judy and her husband hadn't spoken to him in the four years since. He meant to send them a wedding present, as soon as he got some money together.

Another old movie was playing now, something starring Andy Griffith. He'd missed the beginning and wasn't quite sure of the plot. Griffith wasn't lovable sheriff Andy from Mayberry. Here he was playing a loud rube from the Ozarks or somewhere down South. Walt turned the sound up a bit and went back to his thoughts.

It seemed like people were always *leaving*, turning away from him. His parents, his own sister, Dora, a whole string of women since. He didn't have any friends left from Providence. God only knows what had become of Rick and Don, and Walt didn't particularly care to find out. Once a year the college would send him an alumni bulletin, which he tossed into the wood stove without reading. Why would he want to hear about everyone else's success? They were assholes then, and they were undoubtedly still assholes now.

The guys at work were just more of the same, especially Dewers. It was like some private fraternity, and he wasn't invited to pledge. He tensed up just thinking about it. Private fraternities, that Sparrow Lotus camp was another one. Man, would he like to take them down a notch. Maybe not sweet little JoAnn, she was a cutesy pie. But the rest of them, they could rot in hell. He had to remember to speak with Anton if he ever got a chance. Anton probably knew all about that body in the river. Anton and those two butch girls from the bar, they were probably in on it together.

He'd totally lost track of the movie. Andy Griffith was yelling into a microphone in a recording studio somewhere, looking wild-eyed and full of himself. Patricia Neal was busy working some sort of double-cross. Walt got up and turned the Zenith off. You could just tell that none of it was going to end well.

FOR FUN AND PROFIT
15

"Hey Pam, long time no see."

"Hello Ray. What can I get you?"

"Not much of a greeting for an old friend. How have you been?"

He wore a smile, but she could tell it was not a friendly kind of smile. It reminded Pam of a grin she'd once seen on a cartoon snake. "Ray, I'm sort of busy. Would you like something to drink? 'Cause this is a bar, and that's what we do here, we serve drinks." Her tone was meant to say "I mean business" without being outwardly hostile. She knew Ray, a small-time local drug dealer, no more or less than any other semi-regular who came in here for a drink. This one would probably die either from smoking his profits, whatever he was currently selling, or owing someone a lot of money from having smoked *their* profits. Either way, she didn't want to make an outright enemy of the twitchy little addict. Druggies could be unpredictable. It was always better to let them think you tolerated them, while letting them know where you stood.

"I guess I'll have a beer, then," the thin man said. "Hey, any chance you know anyone looking to score a little something?"

Well isn't that wonderful, she thought. The little weasel thinks he can come in here and deal whatever crap he's selling. "Ray, we don't go for that shit around here. If you want to peddle your trash, do it somewhere else." She hoped that would put him in his place without leading to a scene. Either way, she dropped her right hand below the bar and out of his sight. Let him decide whether to do something stupid or not, she thought. Her left hand silently slid to the .45 caliber Sig Arms pistol underneath the bar. She had never had to shoot anyone: usually the sight of the small cannon was enough to head off major trouble. Pam had no qualms with pulling the trigger, should the need ever arise.

"Jeez, Pam, sorry. I was just asking, you know. I'm sure people come in and ask once in a while. I thought I might be doing you a favor, helping keep the customers happy and all."

"Keep your favors, Ray. I don't need you hanging around here. You're done. Get out." The last thing the Deer Track needed was cops hanging around because some small-timer was trying to peddle his pot or whatever to the clientele. Shit, she was hardly making a go of it anyway. Like she needed to borrow trouble.

"Fine, fine, I'll go. Hey, you haven't happened to see my dad around lately, have you?" He was half way to the door. Pam's hands were back above bar level, once again polishing glassware.

"He was here Saturday night. Why don't you ask him yourself?"

"The old man and I aren't talking so much lately. If you see him, tell him I stopped by," as he stepped toward the threshold.

"If I see him, Ray, I'll tell him what I just told you. I don't need you or the crap you're selling anywhere near this place. As far as I'm concerned, he can run your ass over with that scooter he's riding." She was hoping Ray would get the message, loud and clear.

The screen door yelped and slammed shut as Ray slipped away.

SNICKERS ALL AROUND
16

Tuesday morning might have been any other Monday, for all Walt cared. He was running late, as usual.

He'd gotten up early enough. The rain had stopped sometime during the night. It was still cool and damp, but not uncomfortable. Walt arose around six, and he and Doofus took a three-mile jog through the woods on the path behind his house. The woods were quiet in the early morning. Most of the trees and shrubs were just beginning to bloom. It was Walt's favorite time of the day. He liked to break a good sweat and get his body's juices flowing.

He got back to the house, where he showered and had a cup of coffee, wearing nothing but his bath towel. It's not like anyone ever stopped by unexpectedly, and neighbors weren't close enough that you had to worry about people peering in your windows. He'd left the television on. Matt Lauer was talking to some "expert," probably some liberal do-gooder, about the growing drug epidemic in America. "What a load of horse shit," Walt sighed as he finally got up and get dressed. By then he was running fifteen minutes behind schedule. He'd have to hurry if he wanted to get to work on time.

He stopped at the Speedway, said hello to Trish behind the counter, put ten bucks worth of gas in the Samurai, and picked up two Snickers and a Pepsi for the road. Trish was chatty as usual. Walt listened for a while, just happy to have the human companionship. It's not like there was a line forming behind him or anything. Mostly Trish talked local gossip. She was still dating the same guy, but things had been rocky. Walt figured that sooner or later she'd be single again, so he let her prattle on. Fifteen minutes late was now twenty-five minutes late.

Walt rolled into the office parking lot to the sight of Tom Dewers getting in the last of the Ford trucks. "Son of a bitch!" Walt cursed. Dewers started the truck, cranked up the heater, and went back into the office to get his gear. Dewers and his partner always got the easy run, heading over to the western side of the state. Theirs was only a forty-five minute drive, the terrain was scenic and isolated, and they'd be back to the office before five. Walt had a higher pay grade than either of those two, and by all rights should have gotten the easier run. Instead, he was driving down to Flint for two days, were he'd be sampling rivers that weren't much better than urban sewers. If he was lucky, his truck wouldn't be stolen or vandalized by the time he got out of those streams. If he was really lucky, he wouldn't come down with hepatitis from incidental contact with water.

"Walt, these guys have wives and kids. You're just you. It's better if you do the overnighters, no one is waiting for you at home," his boss had reminded him. Walt couldn't wait for Marcus Washington to retire. Things were too buddy-buddy around this place, and Walt felt he was always getting the short end of the stick. Maybe Walt would take Washington's place, and then there'd be some changes. He knew one thing he'd change: whoever had the two hour drive and spent the night away from home should get the better truck. That should be written in stone.

He grabbed his backpack full of spare clothes, the Pepsi and a candy bar, and set them in the back seat of the Astro van. Walt went back to the Samurai, got some toilet paper that he kept for emergencies out of the glove compartment, and carefully unwrapped the other Snickers bar. He placed the candy bar in the wadded up toilet paper, warmed it gently between his hands, then set it directly in front of the defroster on the dashboard of Dewer's idling truck. That would give the idiot something to think about when he came back out. There was a light kick in Walt's step as he went into the office. It truly was the little things that made life worthwhile.

"Where have you been?" Washington caught him as he came through the door.

"I had to get gas. I'll be on the road in a few minutes," Walt shot back. He hurried back to his desk and tried to look as if he were rushing. Maybe if he kept moving Washington would leave him alone.

"You should have been on the road a half hour ago. You need to get this done in two days. We're not paying for a second night at the motel, you know." The boss wasn't going to let him off easily.

"I'll get it done. I'll be back by tomorrow night."

"Your dog's not with you, is he?"

Walt had gotten into trouble last month for taking Doofus with him on what turned out to be a four day trip. Apparently the USGS wasn't happy having employees treat every day as "take your pet to work day." Walt suspected it was someone in his own office that ratted him out, claiming to have pet allergies. Washington claimed it was about "liability" and dog hair in company trucks, but Walt was certain it was about co-workers that were out to get him. What did they expect him to do, leave his dog alone at home all week? Fortunately, an elderly woman down the road, Mary Ellen Berner, had promised to let Doofus out a few times between now and tomorrow night. He hoped she came through, or there would be a hell of a mess waiting for him when he got back to the house.

"No, he's at home. I told you it wouldn't happen again." This was a truthful statement on Walt's part, if "it wouldn't happen again" meant Walt not getting caught. Doofus was still spending time in the truck, but Walt was being more cautious about it. He kept a lint brush with him at all times so he could wipe down the upholstery at the end of the day. On overnight trips like this one, though, Walt wasn't going to press his luck. Someone at the motel might complain about a dog barking all night. "My neighbor's watching him, Marcus."

"Well good. Have a safe trip. And remember, keep the expenses down."

"Sure," Walt thought, "Heaven forbid I get a good meal and a couple beers at the end of the day. It might come out of your paperclip budget," but he kept those thoughts to himself. Things were getting tighter and tighter with the economy the way it was, but dinner on the company dime was about the one thing he looked forward to on these trips. "I will," he answered instead. It seemed as if every year the budget got leaner and leaner, death by a thousand cuts.

When Walt finally made it back outside, Dewers was just pulling out of the parking lot and on to the road. Dewers flashed him a one finger salute and yelled something behind the glass that Walt couldn't quite make out. The sentiment was clear, and Walt laughed. That candy bar on the dashboard might have been the best ninety-five cents he'd ever spent.

SHIPS IN THE NIGHT
17

"I'll have the prime rib, medium rare, baked potato no sour cream, dinner salad with blue cheese, and bring me another Labatt's, please." Walt smiled at the waitress and leaned back on the cushioned chair. This was his favorite part of any trip. The Steak and Hooch was no Morton's or Carl's Chop House, but it sure beat anything available back in Rasmus. The fact he could expense the whole thing? Even better.

"Sure, Sweetie, I'll be back in just a minute." She was pleasant enough. "I'm Lindsey if you need anything." Walt watched Lindsey's backside as she returned to the kitchen. Man, this was the life.

The day hadn't gone badly. Walt got to the river a little later than expected, and the overgrown ditch was every bit as ugly as he'd remembered it. Instead of the wide open fields and dense woods of the Wolverine Valley, Davison Creek ran through urban back yards and the blighted industrial districts of a collapsing city. You were more likely to find shopping carts and tire rims in these streams than otter or mink. Flint, Detroit, it was all the same. Cities built in a hurry on the promise of good wages and boundless opportunity, only to be gutted and abandoned when both the money and the jobs left for greener pastures. The remaining people gave up caring a long time ago. Solvents, hypodermic needles. The stuff that got poured into those streams, he hated to think about. He was glad his job was mostly about flow and velocity, not water quality. He'd seen toilet bowls in gas stations with better water quality.

Walt had gotten his day's work done quietly and efficiently. The van was still where he parked it, a miracle unto itself. It still had four tires, another stroke of fortune. By seven he was on his way back to the hotel to get cleaned up. Eight o'clock found him sitting in this restaurant, checking out the clientele and sipping a beer. He'd have to get an early start tomorrow, and if he hustled he could be back home before ten. The rest of tonight was Walt's to enjoy.

"Here's your salad, and the gentleman at the bar sent you another drink."

"What gentleman at the bar?" Walt didn't expect to see anyone he knew in these parts. He was a long ways from home, and he didn't have that many friends to begin with. He looked across the room seeking a familiar face, but came up empty. There were about six gentlemen at the rail, none looking Walt's way. Eventually a man seated at the far end of the bar got up and began walking towards Walt. "Ah," Walt thought, "that hippie from the yoga camp." But what were the odds they'd bump into one another here, of all places? As the man approached the table, Walt stood up and reached out a hand.

"Anson is it? From the camp?"

"Anton. Thank you for remembering. You got my beer, I see."

"Thanks, yes," he answered, tipping his glass to the visitor. Walt didn't know where to go from here. Should he offer the man a seat, something he didn't really want to do, or ask him what the hell he was doing following Walt around the state? Maybe it was better to start slowly. "Want to sit down, join me for a few minutes? I haven't eaten yet. I just ordered."

"Sure, if you don't mind. Just for a moment. I noticed you across the room and thought you looked familiar. You're the guy that got lost hiking with his dog, right? Miss Blue gave you a ride."

"Guilty as charged. She's a sweet girl, by the way. She didn't know me from Adam, but she still helped me out. She said you manage Sparrow-Lotus?" Walt asked as he shoved a forkful of salad into his mouth.

"I do. I've been the primary caretaker since we took responsibility for the facility. It's a beautiful place to get in tune with the Earth and the Spirit. How about you? JoAnn said you're some kind of surveyor and have some questions for me about our dam?"

"Not exactly. I work for the US Geological Service. My work has more to do with stream runoff and things like that, but that's not what I wanted to ask you about. I'm curious, though. How is it you happen to be in a Steak and Hooch in Davison at the same time as me?" Walt thought coincidence was unlikely, but he'd let the guy fend for himself.

"I had a meeting with our board of directors down in Ann Arbor. They're considering some capital upgrades to the physical property, and wanted my input. I was on my way back north, but even a caretaker has to eat once in a while. This area isn't teeming with sushi bars, in case you're wondering. I was just grabbing a salad and a beer."

Walt stuffed another load of salad in his mouth, chewing and ruminating on what he'd just heard. It sounded plausible enough, but still didn't sit right. On the other hand, why would yoga boy want to follow Walt around? It's not like Walt had been stirring up trouble with the camp customers or anything. He decided to take Anton at his word and play it straight, at least for the time being.

"Well, my real question is, do you remember the big run-off we had this spring, when the first melt waters hit? Around the first week of April? The water was near an all-time high."

"I remember it," Anton answered. "It nearly washed out the whole dam. It would have been bad news all around had that happened."

"Did you change anything with the dam to alleviate the heavy flow? Did you pull a board or two from the top to relieve hydraulic pressure or anything? I'm just asking. Unofficially. I'm not Department of Environment or anything, I'm not going to bust you if you did do something illegal. It's not my job, not my area of expertise I'm just curious." Walt stuffed the last bit of cucumber in his mouth and chased it with a swig of beer.

Anton paused, looked down at his hands, then up at the ceiling for a second. It was obvious he we weighing whether or not to continue this little chat. Finally he chose to proceed. "Off the record, agreed? I pulled two boards and lowered the pond depth by a foot. I know I'm not supposed to do that, not without the state's permission, but I thought the whole thing was going to blow out. It seemed like the right thing to do at the time."

Walt took another gulp of his beer and pondered that answer. "Did it draw down a load of sediment or anything when you did that? When the initial rush went downstream, did you notice anything *unusual* in the flow?"

"Like what?" Anton didn't look entirely comfortable with Walt's line of questioning. He wanted Walt to *say it*. "Like a *body* or something? That's what you're asking, right?" At least he wasn't hiding the fact he knew about the dead man.

"Yeah, like a *body* or something." Walt didn't realize, but he was now standing at the table. He couldn't remember getting up, but he towered over the seated man. The smarmy puke with his smarmy tone of voice, he made Walt livid. A few other customers were staring in Walt's direction, wondering what was about to happen.

At this point the waitress arrived with Walt's steak. "Is everything o.k.?" she asked.

Walt caught himself and sat back down quietly. He'd have other opportunities to straighten out Anton, if needed. What Walt didn't need was to have the cops called over to a disturbance in a restaurant and word get back to the office.

"Great, thank you." He looked back to Anton. "I'm sorry. I get excited. Did you notice *a body* going over your precious dam?" Now it was Walt with the snarky tone. He began cutting his meal into small chunks.

"Look, I don't know who you are, or what this is about, but no, I didn't see a body go over the dam. There was a thick layer of ice on the pond, and it was breaking up all over the place. The water was pretty agitated. I'm not sure I would have noticed a submarine going over the dam as black as that water was. Do I think that man they found came from the Sparrow Lotus Camp? Impossible."

"Impossible why? Nothing bad ever happens because instant karma's gonna get you?" shoving a big gob of beef into his mouth.

"No, impossible because I've been at the camp since it first opened. We haven't had a single guest disappear in that entire time. I'd have noticed. It's what I do. I'm responsible for what goes on up there. You're crazy if you think otherwise. Whatever you're looking for, I can't help you. I'm sorry I've disturbed your dinner. Good luck with whatever it is you're trying to accomplish. And be careful, that red meat will kill you." With that Anton sidled back to the bar, paid his bill, and eased out the side door.

Lindsey the waitress returned to the table, asked if Walt needed anything more. He thanked her, no, he didn't need another beer, and she left him to finish his meal.

Anton seemed like a guy telling part of the truth, but Walt felt like there was more to his story. Walt sliced off a piece of filet and chewed methodically. How could anybody trust a guy with hair like that, any ways?

SECOND HELPINGS
18

The following day seemed endless. No single thing slowed Walt down, yet he was inundated with work. At least it was honest work, thought Walt. His shoulders ached from the heavy lifting. He'd waded in and out of various rivers and creeks, in and out of the van all day long, all the while packing his equipment. He focused this entire time on the tasks at hand, and was grateful once he finally called it a day and was headed back north. The drive was peaceful, and Walt let his mind rest as he settled in behind the wheel.

He rolled into town around ten thirty that evening. It was still warm out, the temperature working its way subtly downward before night time cooling had a chance to settle in. His windshield was plastered with the remnants of dead mayflies. Somewhere along the way he'd passed through a swarm of the little pests in the fading sunlight. The glass was a collage of translucent carcasses and bug guts, impervious to wiper fluid, and would have to be scrubbed clean when he stopped. Walt was too tired to fight with it this evening. He'd get to the office, swap the government van for his own vehicle, and head home. The bugs could wait until morning.

Back on familiar turf, driving through his adopted hometown of Rasmus, Walt's thoughts wandered back over the events of last evening. Who did that Anton think he was, offering to buy Walt a drink? Anton acted as if they were buddies or something. Hell, Walt barely knew the guy. If it weren't for the long hair and ponytail, Walt would have a hard time picking him out of a lineup. It didn't pass the smell test. The more Walt stewed upon it, the more certain he was that Anton was up to no good, and that it had something to do with that dead body in the river. It seemed as if the body in the river was going to haunt Walt one way or another.

He took the long way home, driving down the business loop and through the town proper. There was no real reason for his detour, sometimes it just felt good to travel a different road. The north end of the city consisted of three blocks littered with strip motels, overnighters that sprung up in the fifties and sixties when the national guard base was going great guns, only to slowly falter as they aged into oblivion. Many now offered weekly rental rates for the area's burgeoning low income and soon-to-be homeless populations. A room with a kitchenette was becoming the new American dream. Walt eyed the beat up cars and rusted trucks speckled across the various parking lots, lives held together with nothing more than faith, prayers, and the occasional roll of duct tape.

As he approached the downtown core, if one could call it that, Walt slowed down. There was no pedestrian traffic, but Walt didn't need to attract the attention of a bored police officer. Hell, Amberson might be short on the budget this month, passing out tickets to boost county revenue. Downtown was a speed trap if ever there was one. The speed limit was twenty-five. Walt figured anything up to thirty was probably safe, but faster than that was trouble.

Most of the remaining retail stores, novelty shops, really, catering to a nonexistent tourist trade, had closed at five o'clock. The grocery store was still functioning, surviving on a sporadic clientele with an insatiable thirst for alcohol, tobacco, and lottery tickets. Two teenage girls were sitting in their Dodge Shadow at the far end of the grocery lot, trying for all the world to look like they weren't doing anything wrong. "Can you buy for us mister?" was more than likely their refrain. Kids didn't necessarily grow up faster around here, but they seemed to lose hope at an early age.

Walt stopped for the red light at Michigan Avenue. The county seat was a block and a half to his right, with two or three businesses on either side of the street that had thus far refused to give up the ghost. The majority of the storefronts were empty, either for sale or for lease. The big hotel and restaurant at the far corner had been vacant for over a decade. Its weathered sign still paid homage to a time when dining, dancing, and cocktails marked the heights of sophistication.

When he peered to his left, Walt glimpsed a shadow of a man sliding into a faded red seventies Chevy pickup truck. The man had just left the front of the closed Rasmus State Bank, probably getting cash from the twenty-four hour ATM in the building's foyer. The bank was one block to the east. Walt didn't get a great look at the man, but something set the hair on the back of his neck on end. He'd met this man somewhere before, and Walt was sure it hadn't been a pleasant experience. Who was this guy? Walt needed to know.

When the light turned green Walt accelerated hard through the intersection, swung the Suzuki quickly left at the first alley, and left again at the next street. He immediately arrived at a stop sign directly facing the bank. The red Chevy truck was now to Walt's left, having left the front of the bank, and was turning off Michigan Avenue south onto the business loop. Walt made two more lefts and followed the truck from a distance. Like so many decisions in Walt's life, it was a decision driven by impulse. The Chevy turned again at the next light, heading east away from town. Walt stayed a half mile behind, close enough to observe without being spotted. He'd have to drive this way to get home, anyhow. When the Chevy passed the turn off to Walt's house, eight miles outside of town, Walt kept steady behind the truck. Why hurry home to an empty house?

Not long thereafter the truck veered off the left side of the road, crossing the gravel shoulder and rolling to a stop in the parking lot of the Deer Track Inn. Walt kept driving on past. A half mile further down the highway, Walt spun the little Suzuki around and made his way back toward the bar. Now he'd see what was what.

He parked the Suzuki along the side of the building, where it would be less visible from the road or from the front entrance. He could see Pam's car parked around back: that was a good sign. Walt opened the screen door and let it whack shut behind him. "Never let them think you're scared," his dad had always told him. It was one of the few useful things his father had ever taught him.

Walt strutted in to the Deer Track like he owned the place. On this night he pretty much could have owned the place. Pam glanced up from behind the bar and acknowledged him with a nod. She was setting a highball glass full of something in front of her one and only customer. The man hadn't bothered to look up from his seat at the bar. Even from behind, Walt knew exactly where he'd met this man before. Even without a shotgun in the man's hands.

HERE'S MUD IN YOUR EYE
19

"Hey Lick-knob, how's it going?" Walt decided to take the offensive, come right out with a verbal assault and catch the man off guard. It should be enough to get his attention.

The man looked up slowly, as if awakening from a long nap and confused by his surroundings. He appeared older than Walt remembered him, his eyes slightly sunken, his face sallow and ashen. At first he didn't seem to recognize that Walt was speaking directly to *him*, and his eyes searched the empty bar for a phantom customer. Walt looked the scrawny figure over once more. There was no doubt this was the man that had threatened him by the Sparrow River. He'd appeared more alert, more imposing at the time, but it was still the same person. He seemed to gradually absorb the idea that Walt was addressing him and him alone.

Walt was trying to egg him on: "I'm talking to you, asshole. Don't you remember me? The last time we met you were holding a twelve gauge and staking a private claim to state land. I was walking my dog. Ring any bells?" Walt wasn't backing off. He was looking forward to mopping the floor with the little bastard, now that the man was disarmed and they were on equal footing. Walt had a world of rage swirling inside of him, and this was the best opportunity he'd had to share it in a very long time. Pam stood behind the bar silently, one arm leaning atop the counter and her other arm resting casually beneath the countertop. Walt paid her no mind. It was no fun if this guy didn't put up a fight.

The slim man still looked dumbfounded. He slowly began to ease himself up off his stool. "Now that you mention it, I do remember you. My apologies. Must have been a mistake. Here, let me get you a drink."

It only took a second. The man had quick reflexes, the stupid look and slow verbal responses all part of his act. In one swift motion the man flung his drink, glass and all, squarely into Walt's face. Walt was so unprepared for the assault that he didn't react. The whiskey hit his eyes first, stinging and burning on contact. The highball glass shattered against the bridge of Walt's nose, opening a small gash that by itself was no big deal. The whiskey dripping down into the open cut on his face, now that hurt. Cheap whiskey in his eyes, that went *beyond* hurt. Walt was temporarily blinded, in pain, and not sure where his assailant now stood.

"Shit, Pam, get me a towel," he howled, all the while wildly swinging his fists and hoping to connect with any part of the other man. His nose was bleeding profusely. He could taste the blood and whiskey as it rolled down his face and into his mouth. "I'm gonna kick the shit out of you, you worthless puke!" Walt was a raging windmill of anger. He couldn't see a damn thing, but that wasn't going to stop him from pummeling the little jerk. Walt still hadn't landed a punch, but that wasn't going to stop him from throwing as many as possible. Maybe he'd get lucky. This continued for all of twenty seconds before Pam spoke up.

"He's gone, Walt," she screamed, trying to settle him down. "He ran out the back door the minute he threw that drink. Here's a towel." She handed him a white cotton cloth from behind the bar.

"Son of a bitch," he yelped. "How'd he get away so fast? Couldn't you stop him or something?" Walt still couldn't see, and was hesitant to quit pumping his fists. Why couldn't he have landed at least one good blow?

"Yeah, Walt, sure. I love getting in the middle of two grown men trying to kill one another. Has anyone ever told you that you have a special way with people? I mean, think about it, you've come in here twice lately, and both times someone felt obliged to kick your ass. You're a piece of work, did you know that? What do you have against Ray, anyway? He screw you on a dope deal or something?"

"You *know* him?" Walt was incredulous. What were the chances that the man from the river, the man whom Walt just happened to notice while passing through town, the man who, on the spur of the moment, Walt decided to follow, would end up at the Deer Track Inn? It didn't help that he'd suckered Walt with that flying glass. And then what were the chances that Pam would know that very same man? It seemed like an awful lot of coincidences. "Ray *what*? Does he have a last name?"

"Just Ray. I don't know his last name. He comes around every now and again. He's a small time dealer. He and his dad live somewhere around here.

I threw him out just the other day when he was trying to peddle his junk. Why, what did he do to get you riled up?"

"He threatened me up on the Bitch River, ran me off state land with a gun." Walt had settled down, but only slightly.

"Well be careful. He's a little squirrelly, to say the least. Too much drano got in that brain of his, and it doesn't always work right. His dad's an old drunk, and just as crazy as he is. What were you doing up on the Sparrow, any how?"

"Just looking around. It's state land. I've got a right to go anywhere on state land, don't I? Your good friend Ray doesn't own the forest." Walt was feeling defensive.

"Here, let me see that." Pam tried to gently take the blood soaked towel away from Walt. He resisted, before reluctantly giving in. The towel was saturated with blood, tears, and alcohol. The wound was still bleeding, and it hurt like hell. Pam took a pitcher of ice water from behind the bar. "Tilt your head back. I'm gonna flush your eyes for you." Walt obeyed. Pam carefully trickled the cool water across his face. "Here's a clean towel. It's gonna need a couple of stitches, I think. You know Walt, not everybody is out to get you. Ray's no friend of mine, he just drinks here sometimes."

"Ah, Jeez, this sucks. Sorry about the mess." Walt became aware of the broken glass and amber liquid that coated the Deer Track's floor. He was also becoming aware that Pam was the closest thing he had to a friend over this past week, even if she did disappear over the holiday. Once again, things weren't going the way Walt had planned. "I'll help you clean it up." Someone once told him that a little contrition can absolve a world of sin.

"No, you won't. I'll take care of it later. Here's a clean towel. Keep the pressure on that cut. Let me grab my coat and keys. You need a trip to the ER, and you can't drive if you can't see the road. I'll only be a second." Pam stepped into the back room to get her things.

"Pam?" he called.

"Yes?" as she stepped back into the room.

"Does this count as our second date?"

A STITCH IN TIME
20

The new emergency room at the hospital was state of the art, at least as far as small town hospitals go. Two years previously a large donor had stepped forward and put up enough money to start the total renovation of the then antiquated facilities. The town rallied to raise matching funds, the state and feds kicked in with a few grants, and it all came together. The hospital was now one of the largest employers in this impoverished county, and its central location attracted patients from many of the surrounding communities. "Give us your sick, your pregnant, your wounded, your stupid, unlucky and unfortunate," should have been inscribed in the cornerstone. Everyone came to rely on the new facilities, from well-to-do weekenders to the Amish farmers that lived twenty miles to the east.

Walt sat on a table in one of the many small examination rooms off the main corridor, wearing a white cloth gown with blue polka dots, tied loosely in the back. Most of his back and buttocks were exposed, and Walt didn't care in the least. If anyone complained, they could kiss his chilly and exposed behind. Pam sat quietly in a leather and wooden chair leaning against the wall. The room contained a counter with a hand sink, cabinets above and below holding various medical supplies. On the wall was mounted a plastic box for needle disposal, and three dispensers with three different sizes of latex gloves.

The nurse at the front desk had led them both to the room, taken Walt's vitals, and given him a clean towel to press against his injury. She promised that the doctor would be in shortly. That had been fifteen minutes ago. Apparently no one thought Walt was going to bleed out in fifteen minutes or less. At least that was good news. Walt dangled his legs off the edge of the table and stared up at the ceiling. The gash on his face bled less if he kept his head tilted back. He began counting ceiling tiles, but quickly got bored.

"This Ray character, do you know where he lives?" Walt tried to sound nonchalant. They were the first words either Walt or Pam had spoken since the two had left the bar. The words sounded forced.

"It's not a good idea, Walt. You're not even stitched up yet and you're already looking for more trouble." Pam kept her voice on an even keel, as if she were a teacher talking to a slow student.

"I'm not looking to *do* anything Pam, I'm just asking if you know where he lives." Walt hated when people talked down to him. He believed Pam was treating him like a child. This thing between him and "Ray," that wasn't over with. Not by a long shot.

"Why don't you let the police take care of it? It's why we pay taxes, you know." Pam's eyes drifted to a poster affixed to the back of the door, a cartoon tutorial on the proper methods of hand washing and coughing into the crook of your arm. Were people really so helpless that they needed to be taught how to *cough,* for heaven's sake? The next thing you know, they'd be posting *breathing* instructions on the walls of the lobby. "Step one: inhale. Step two: exhale. Repeat." There were other posters on the wall, two with inspirational messages and one with information on wound care.

"I'm not getting the police involved. Are you kidding? They'll probably make this out to be my fault. I'd rather shoot myself than give those clowns at the sheriff's department the satisfaction. Screw them."

"Walt, you're a sweet guy. A little thick sometimes, but sweet. Nobody's shooting anybody. Let it go." She could tell this was a losing battle. Why did she always find herself with men who had fundamental blind spots for common sense? Walt would do just what he wanted to do, as had every other man she'd ever known. There was little point in arguing the matter.

"I'd love to let it go, Pam, but I'm not done yet. For all I know, Ray's killed some man and threw the body in the Bitch River. Why else would he be trying to run me off state land at gunpoint? I'd bet money he killed the guy over drugs, and he's worried I'm close to nailing him."

"Correct me if I'm wrong, but a week ago you were sure the culprits were from that yoga camp, part of some lesbian love triangle gone wrong. Now it's the local drug dealer that killed that guy? Ray's a small timer. He fried half his brain cells years ago, and probably would have a hard time knowing which end of that gun goes 'bang.' He's an idiot, but I doubt he's a killer. Pick a theory and stick with it, Columbo." Pam sounded sure of herself.

When she spoke like that, Walt almost believed it possible that she was right. Almost.

"All I'm saying is that I was up by the river looking around, and right before I ran into Ray, I stumbled across a big pile of drug paraphernalia. The next thing I know Ray is introducing me to Mr. Winchester. If he killed someone, even if it was a long time ago, that would be a good reason to chase me away." It all sounded so *logical* to Walt when he spelled it out this way. "I think they were partners, Ray and the dead guy. The dead guy was a buyer from the city and Ray killed him, or he overdosed and Ray panicked. Ray buried the body up there where he keeps his stash, and now he's ticked off that it turned up all these years later. Ray's the killer, for sure."

"Well, I guess your two girl friends from the bar last weekend will be glad to hear you've cleared them of all previous charges." Pam could be particularly sarcastic when the mood struck.

Damn it, Walt had forgotten about those two women who'd clocked him, the two women he'd later seen at the yoga camp. Why would they have sucker punched him if it wasn't tied into the dead man somehow? This was getting complicated. Maybe they were lesbian *and* druggies, and they were friends with Ray. He'd have to stew on it for a while.

Just then the doctor knocked at the door. He let himself in and quickly examined Walt. Thirty-five minutes and seven painful stitches later, Walt was dressed and released from the hospital.

"Do you want to head back to your place?" Walt asked, once they were in Pam's car. He might be down, but he wasn't out. Maybe he'd get lucky tonight.

"I think you'd better get some rest. I'll drop you back at your truck," she answered. Her tone was perfunctory. Walt's face drooped with disappointment.

"Thanks for driving me, Pam." It was never easy for Walt to say 'thank you,' but his face was truly repentant.

"You're welcome, Walt. Call me tomorrow. Maybe I'll let you buy me lunch." Walt thought he heard a touch of compassion in her voice. His eyes lit up. He started to smile, but when he did so, his brow pulled against the fresh stitches in his face. A flash of pain ripped through his head, converting his smile into a contorted grimace. "Really?" he whimpered.

"Our third date," she answered. Pam had always had a soft spot for lost puppies.

A RAY OF LIGHT
21

The sunlight streamed through the dirt streaked window, concentrating a beam of heat in the middle of Walt's forehead. His face was crusted with two rivulets of dried blood. Though he'd attempted to clean up when he first got home, he agitated his stitches as he slept, and the blood seeped slowly down both sides of his nose.

Walt could feel the mid morning sun soaking into his brow, slowly arcing across his face and towards his temple. He was in the middle of an intense dream, and the morning warmth was dragging him toward that semiconscious state where he knew his dream wasn't reality, but still resented having to give up on the warm vision. Walt reluctantly stirred and opened his eyes. He'd been sleeping on the living room couch, and the right side of his face bore the distinct ribbed impression of corduroy. He felt a pain at the bridge or his nose, reached up to scratch it, and yelped loudly before remembering too late the events of the previous evening. A fresh droplet of red blood bubbled to the surface of his stitches.

The coffee table in front of him bore a bottle of Yukon Jack, or more precisely bore two fingers worth of Yukon Jack in a mostly empty vessel. Walt sat up begrudgingly, carefully taking in the room. Pam had graciously borrowed the full bottle of canadian whiskey from the Deer Track, before ushering Walt to his own vehicle. He couldn't talk her in to coming along for the ride, but at least she sent him home with a bottle. The cheap liquor helped to marginalize the pain last night, but it was reaping its vengeance this morning.

He couldn't remember leaving the hospital, but he must have driven himself home. The Suzuki was parked at an angle in the driveway, almost even with the front porch. Pam couldn't have driven him *and* his car here, not unless she decided to walk home herself, and that was unlikely. Funny that he couldn't recall the short drive. He knew he wasn't *that* loaded. It must have been fatigue.

The sliding door had been left open. There was a gap about a foot wide, enough for a dog or a slim person to step through. Doofus was visibly sniffing around out by the road, on the scent of some animal or another. Any number of game birds or critters might have wandered through the yard last night, and Doofus was an equal opportunity sniffer. Raccoons, deer, or people's crotches, it was all the same to Doofus. The more pungent the better. The morning was warm, a lucky thing for Walt. Had it been a cold night, with the door left ajar, the house would be freezing by now. It wasn't bad in here, and Walt felt no need to stoke the fire.

Walt's head was pounding inside. He'd have to take something for that, once he got moving. His shoes, shirt, and pants made a visible trail across the floor, from the doorwall to the bathroom. He faintly remembered having a desire to shower when he'd gotten home. Walt couldn't remember much beyond that point, couldn't remember even taking the shower, but the damp towel that clung to his midriff suggested that he'd at least been successful in one endeavor. Walt had fallen asleep with the towel wrapped around his waist, and a faint wet spot marked the couch where his hips had settled for the night. He looked across the room to the kitchen. There were dirty dishes on the counter, something he rarely tolerated. Walt might be a bachelor, but he had his standards. His eyes drifted to the clock on the far kitchen wall.

"Ah, Shit! Washington's gonna kill me. It's almost ten o'clock."

Walt rose to his feet quickly, too quickly. Blood rushed to his head, and the drumbeat that was playing in the back of his brain intensified to a whole percussion section. He was wobbly on his legs, and he sat back down to catch his breath. Walt grabbed the whiskey bottle from the coffee table, sucked down the last inch of amber liquid, and pitched the empty bottle into the trash can adjacent to the kitchen counter. There was a fresh prescription bottle sitting by the sink, another reminder of his nocturnal adventures. Walt couldn't recall if the doctor had said they were painkillers or antibiotics. Either way, his body suggested a need. He shook out two capsules, chucked them down the back of his throat, then drank with his lips beneath the kitchen faucet to wash them down. His legs and back were stiff from sleeping on the sofa, and despite last night's shower, Walt felt crusty all over. This was not a good way to start the day. He stumbled achingly to the phone, and called the one number he knew by heart.

"Hey, Marcus, this is Walt...Yes, I know what time it is...Yes, I know it's a work day...Look, I had an accident last night....No, the van is fine. Not that kind of accident....No, I slipped and fell, split my face open on the bathroom sink....It's not a big deal, but I had to take a few stitches, and I'm pretty beat up. I just need some rest is all, and I'll be fine by Monday....Yes, I know I've used up my p.t.o. for this pay period.....I know it won't be paid....I heard you.....Hey, you too, have a good weekend."

Walt wasn't going to explain the details of last night to Washington, or to anybody at the office. Why make life more complicated than it needed to be? They'd just use it against him if they knew the truth. Walt figured the less anybody heard about his personal life, the better.

He put on a fresh pot of coffee, started the shower, and slipped beneath the cool stream of water. Forty minutes later he was a new man, freshly scrubbed, dressed, and sitting at his kitchen table sipping coffee and scratching Doofus between the ears. "How are you boy? Are you a good dog? What did you do last night?" The dog looked up at the man faithfully, tilting his head from side to side as if trying to better understand the questions. "Thank you for not crapping on my carpet. You're a good boy." The dog didn't understand the words, but the man's tone suggested he'd done something right for a change.

Walt turned his thoughts back to the events of last evening. It was hard for him to recall how exactly a short ride home had been converted into a trip to the hospital. "I *paid* a visit to the hospital." Walt joked to himself. "*Paying* is the right word." Walt could hardly afford to keep food in the house lately. Even with health insurance, the copay for that E.R. visit was going to put one more hole in his already leaky budget. "One more bill collector to avoid" he cursed beneath his breath. At least today was payday. He'd have to make sure his check was direct deposited before he withdrew anything from the ATM. Walt figured he wouldn't be truly broke for another four or five days. Maybe there was a song in that story, somewhere. "I won't be broke, for four more days." It sounded like country blues. He'd have to get his guitar out later and see if he could come up with a tune to match the mood.

Why *had* he followed that guy to the bar? In retrospect, he could have been more cautious. If this Ray character had pulled a gun on him once before, Walt should have expected him to turn to violence. Walt wouldn't make that mistake twice. At least now he knew to be prepared. Pam had said something about calling the cops, but he'd be damned if he was calling anyone. After he'd had a chance to make things *even*, *then* Walt would call the cops. Once the score was settled, Amberson could drive *Ray* to the emergency room. Until then, no cops.

Walt looked up from his thoughts, and the clock read noon. Nearly time for lunch. "Lunch!" Hell, he'd forgotten that Pam had invited him to lunch. He needed to get moving. Walt jumped up and looked around for his cell phone. Where did he put that damn thing? He remembered he'd called in to work this morning. It must be in the kitchen somewhere. Not on the counter. Not on the table. Not by the fridge. He finally found his phone in the cupboard over the sink, next to the coffee. How had he left it in the cupboard? He needed to *focus,* be less distracted. He dialed Pam's number. She picked up on the third ring.

"Pam....yeah, are we still on for lunch?....Great, twenty minutes then.....do you want me to pick you up?....sure, see you here, then." She wanted to pick Walt up. It didn't seem right, a woman picking him up for a date. But he wasn't going to look a gift horse in the mouth, either. It would save him having to pay for gas, if nothing else. By one o'clock they were sitting in Pam's car, with two foot-long submarine sandwiches and two large sodas on the seat between them, Doofus panting merrily in the back seat, heading north for a picnic in the Huron National Forest.

A WALK IN THE PARK
22

"So how are the stitches feeling?"

"Alright. A bit sore, if you know what I mean. They haven't started itching yet."

"That's good. 'Sore' means its healing. You sure know how to liven things up on a Thursday night."

"That's me, Mr. Liven-Things-Up."

It was soothing to be riding along in the car, talking, just having a *conversation* for a change. Walt cracked the rear window on the passenger side by a few inches, and Doofus stuck his nose in the breeze and his head in the clouds. Walt didn't envy anyone in a car trailing behind them, though. They'd probably think it was raining dog slobber.

"Why won't you tell me where Ray lives?"

"Walt, I don't want to go over that again. That man is not stable, if you can understand what I'm saying. I don't know you all that well. I'm not sure you're entirely stable, either. I don't want to be responsible for whatever foolishness might be coming next. You two need to stay away from one another." Walt sat silently and considered what he'd just heard. A less stubborn man might think Pam sounded *reasonable*, but that wasn't Walt's way. "Reasonable" was just another word for weakness. A few miles passed before she spoke again.

"I would really like to enjoy this day and have a quiet picnic," she finally stated. "If you want to spend your time worrying about Ray, you probably should have asked *him* out to lunch instead of me." It was both a statement of fact and an implied threat.

He briefly considered pointing out that Pam had invited *him* to lunch, not the other way around, but knew that wasn't going to win him any points. Walt finally admitted he was licked. "I'm sorry. Where do you want to go?"

"I was thinking we'd take a run up to that bridge on the Sparrow River. You spend so much time talking about it, I'd like to see it for myself. You good with that?"

This was slightly unexpected, but sure, what the hell, it was as good a picnic spot as any. Secluded. Maybe they could get a little frisky after they ate. "Why not? It's a pretty place. I'll show you around."

Pam drove the back route through the forest, two-lane roads that hadn't been resurfaced since the Eisenhower administration. The little town of Spur passed by, nothing more than a general store, long since converted to an antique/second hand shop, and a cluster of three or four homes rapidly on their way toward abandonment. Plywood replaced a few windows, the leaking roof got patched with a "temporary" blue tarp that never became permanent, you could see the decline looming.

On either side of the road was either dense forest, swamp, or some combination of the two. A ruffed grouse pecked at the gravel along the road's shoulder, oblivious to the occasional car whizzing past. Pam jockeyed her vehicle over the divots and potholes. Most people around here believed that if you could just drive fast enough, you could fly above the highway craters. The tough part was keeping it on the road when your car eventually landed. Walt didn't worry, though he could feel the ball joints and tie rod ends on Pam's car groaning with each and every bump.

The road curved sharply to the right three or four miles further to the north. Pam veered to the left in the middle of the curve and turned onto Dead Indian Hill Road. It wasn't much more than a dirt path through the forest. The road commission had long ago renamed it Warrior Way, but the locals were no more likely to buy into that political correctness than they were to call the Sparrow River by its given name. Dead Indian Hill Road it was then, and forever more it would be, or at least until the flatlanders took over the area.

As the car bumped along, Walt stared out the window to where the sun filtered tight beams of light through the forest canopy. Walt contemplated the alternating columns of light and darkness flickering along the side of the road. When Pam sped up, it seemed as if he was peeking through a picket fence. He was trying for all the world to see what lay beyond that fence.

“A penny for your thoughts,” Pam whispered.

“What is that supposed to mean?” he answered back. “Are you saying my thoughts aren’t worth much?” She had startled him. How long had he been daydreaming? Walt hated being caught off guard.

“It’s an expression, Walt, a figure of speech. It means ‘I wish I knew what you were thinking,’ or something along those lines.”

“I’m sorry, I was just drifting away. I was watching the sun cut through the trees, you know, the light so intense where it cuts through the leaves, and then areas so dark you can’t see a thing.”

“Kind of like life, in a way,” she answered.

“You’re right, now that you mention it. Like this thing with the river. That body I stumbled on, that I can see plain as day. That jerk Ray, clear as all get out in my head. Even the yoga camp, I understand why people like going to that place. It’s restful. But I swear they’re all connected in some way that I just can’t yet see, like the dark spots in the forest. I know the pieces are all there. It’s like I have a handful of pieces to a jigsaw puzzle, only I can’t see the picture on the cover of the box.”

“Maybe if you just let it go, it will eventually come to you.”

“Now you’re starting to sound like those people from the yoga camp,” he replied with a smile. “Platitudes. ‘You will meet a tall stranger,’ stuff like that.” ‘Platitudes?’ Hell, he was starting to talk like Elvin.

“You might get lucky if you learn to keep your mouth shut,” was Pam’s.

“Was that an example of a platitude, or an offer?”

“Did you quit listening after I said the word ‘lucky’?”

Walt bit his tongue and smirked.

SPARROW RIVER

After a few more miles Warrior Way ran smack into Wolverine Valley Road. Pam and Walt turned left onto the paved surface. Within minutes they found the two track, turned left again towards the river, parked, and were walking the path to the CCC bridge. They had their submarine sandwiches, a couple of bottles of Rock & Rye, and a blanket in the backpack. Doofus ran point in front of them. The sun was high in the sky and life was good. At least for a few more minutes.

A BIRD IN THE HAND
23

They were lying on the blanket, hidden behind the tall weeds and basking in the afternoon warmth. He lay flat on his back, with Pam's head nestled on his chest. She was dozing lightly, mouth slightly agape. She snorted quietly when some trace of pollen tickled her nose. Walt, unable to snooze, stared up at the shifting clouds as if they were tea leaves waiting to be read.

They were about a hundred feet downstream from the bridge, a few yards back from the river's edge. They'd chosen this spot because it was both level and dry. Closer to the riverbank there were mud holes and beaver slides. Further back and they wouldn't be able to see the stream for the weeds. They'd enjoyed their lunch, taken a short hike, and then settled in for a short nap. There had been a little kissing, and Walt was feeling relaxed and happy. He was content for the first time in a long while. The purling stream was hypnotic, and Pam had drifted into slumber about twenty minutes ago. Walt's gaze was on the sky, his mind trying to decipher how he had come to this point in his life.

His father had never been particularly encouraging. "You'll never amount to anything" was as close to a pep talk as anything he'd ever received from his parents. And it was understandable. His parents were from a different generation, a different time. They had grown up at the tail end of the depression, and the memory of onion sandwiches for lunch every day had left an indelible mark on their psyche. The war, the only *real* war, in their eyes, because it encompassed the globe and helped to define an entire generation, had taught them that life was often brutal and fleeting. As if they hadn't already learned that lesson, having survived a Depression childhood.

These were the people that had brought Walt into their world, late in their lives. His mom was forty when she had him, his dad forty-two. Walt always believed that they should have named him "Oops." He was sure they would not have deliberately brought a child into the world as they saw it. They lived a life that, rightly or wrongly, was a life spent in fear. Fear that the next thing to go wrong might be the thing that took them all down. Fear that the next paycheck might not come, that there would be another war, fear that they'd left the iron on and the house would burn down while they were attending church. You will be hit by a bus, it's dangerous outside, bats would bite you if you were out after dark. No risk was worth taking, any cost was too high. This was the world view that shaped Walt's upbringing.

By the time he was in his teens, Walt was as lost and rebellious as a kid could be. If life was going to be short and miserable, as his parents predicted, or worse yet, long and miserable, why not live as if nothing mattered? Throw the dice and let them roll. And for years that's how Walt lived, as if nothing he did had any bearing on himself or on anyone else. If something was risky, stupid, or dangerous, Walt would be the first person to give it a try. His dad had told him he was doomed to failure. Walt figured he might as well enjoy the scenery, and he'd spit into the faces of the gods along the way. He was always in trouble at school, and it didn't matter. His dad would chew him out, ground him for weeks at a time. The lectures would have no impact on Walt. He would get a part time job, show up late one too many times or not at all, and get fired. It didn't matter. He could always find another job. And he would go right on living, because nothing really *did* matter, did it? Right up until he met Dora.

Dora was all the things that Walt wasn't. She was beautiful and free, the kind of girl that turned heads. The only heads Walt had ever turned had been those of wary shopkeepers and Providence policemen. Men were drawn to Dora without knowing why. She brought a lightness with her, an airiness that made Walt feel that, just by being in her presence, standing at her arm, he was somehow *better* than himself. Walt knew why he was attracted to Dora, though he could never quite figure out what Dora had seen in *him*.

Walt felt that he had finally found his purpose when they first got together. He became Dora's protector, both from others and from herself. There were things that had drawn Walt to her, beyond her frail beauty. He loved her unbridled spirit, her sense of whimsy. Even her thunderstorms of emotions, she could instantly switch from ecstatic to morose to casual, were a joy for Walt to watch. She was a living artwork, and Walt marveled at her depth and colors. It amazed him that a girl so slight in stature could have such monumental impact on everything and everyone around her. Sometimes they would fight, tooth and nail. Dora would be vicious, and try to wound Walt as deeply as possible. Hours later all would be forgotten, and making up was that much sweeter.

She had that same reckless streak that Walt had shown throughout his teens, but Walt rapidly learned that Dora's need for danger came from a darker place. Whereas Walt had acted out in response to hopelessness and despair, Dora's passion for risk was an unquenchable thirst. She needed to test the limits of life at each opportunity, constantly walking the boundary between *enough* and *too much.* Occasionally she appeared to breach that demarcation line of life and death, only to have Walt reach across and snatch her back. Instead of tempering her behavior, it only fueled the fire inside. How far might she take things before Walt could no longer drag her back? And what were these demons that drove her? Walt never really found out.

In the meantime Walt became more hesitant and cautious, as if in direct response to Dora's extremes. He was suddenly afraid of heights, of slippery mountain foot paths, of driving in bad weather. It frustrated Walt, and it drove a wedge between him and the woman he loved. The seeds sewn by his parents were slowly taking fruit, a crop of unfounded fears and phobias Walt hadn't even known were planted inside of him. He was being sucked to the ground by gravity, just as Dora was spiraling further and further out of control. Walt finally believed he had something to lose. In Dora's eyes, he was no longer keeping up the pace.

And then Dora vanished. The woman who could seemingly light up a room at will disappeared before his very eyes, making Walt second guess whether she'd ever really been there at all. She folded inside herself, shut down. Suddenly the life of the party became one more wallflower, until she evaporated completely. It was a trick that served her well. Now you see me, now you don't. It made it easier for when she decided to chase that next shiny bauble, that brass ring on the carousel. She was standing in front of Walt, and then she wasn't. Where did she go? Hiding in the dark spaces, or chasing rainbows? She'd be gone for a few hours, four days, two weeks. And when the shine wore off that bauble, that brass ring, Dora frequently found her way back to Walt, her safe haven. Until that last time, when she didn't.

Pam stirred. Her head lifted slightly off Walt's chest. A small wet spot, about the size of a quarter, marked his shirt where she had inadvertently drooled in her sleep. Her face bore temporary creases from pressing against his wrinkled shirt. Combined with the crow's feet and smile lines that Pam had earned in her lifetime, she looked as if she had been sleeping on a barbeque grill. "What are you thinking about?" she asked, groggily.

"You," he lied. "Thinking about how beautiful you are." How could anyone honestly answer a question like that?

THE SOUNDS OF SILENCE
24

The first thing he noticed was the silence. The river still percolated, a pulse in the background, but the songbirds had stopped singing. Walt knew that sometimes, just before a storm, birds would suddenly stop singing. Usually a storm was preceded by a drop in the barometer, though, a tangible drop in air pressure. The sun was still shining, the air didn't feel any different, there was just this deafening silence. Doofus, lying off to the side of the blanket, lifted his head and stared upriver, ears twitching like furry radar antennae. The dog could hear something, sense something, that couldn't be heard on Walt's frequency. Walt put one finger to his lips, signaling Pam not to make a sound. His other hand he laid upon the dog's collar, warning Doofus to lie still.

Footsteps cutting through the sawgrass, another set from a different direction, then the sound of two pairs of feet walking to the middle of the bridge from opposite ends. Walt, Pam and Doofus remained flat against the blanket, listening attentively.

"Hey man, you got it?"

"Yeah, I've got it. Did you bring the cash?"

"Right here. Let me see the proof. A little evidence, if you will."

"You sure no one followed you? I've got enough trouble right now, without you leading somebody straight back to me."

Walt could tell there were two men, but was afraid to lift his head enough to see who those two men might be. If Walt could see them, they'd be able to see Walt. They'd be able to see Pam and Doofus, too, and Walt wasn't sure he was up to fighting two against one if it came down to that. He still felt pretty banged up from his run in with Ray at the Deer Track. The wound on his nose itched like crazy, and was seeping yellow liquid. His headache was gone, but the back of his neck was stiff. His shoulders ached. Better to stay low, act like a fly on the wall. The voices sounded faintly familiar.

“Who’s gonna follow me? I just want to see what you have. I’ve got faith, but it isn’t necessarily in you. I could use a little evidence. Show me what I want to see, man.”

“Hand over the cash, I’ll show you what you want to see. That’s the deal. That’s always been the deal.”

Walt wasn’t sure what these two were up to, but he was sure they weren’t selling Girl Scout cookies. Why meet way the hell out here, like some secret society or something? He knew he’d heard the first guy’s voice, the guy with the cash, somewhere before. But where? Some kind of transaction was going on. Bastards. It must be dirty, illegal. Too much crime going on in this part of the county, he might as well be living in the city. You couldn’t even picnic in the woods without running into grief nowadays.

“No need to get all hostile, brother. Center yourself. Want to fire one up, smoke the peace pipe?”

“I learned a long time ago never to get high with a customer. I’ve got a job, you pay me. That’s how it works.” The second voice again, the one who wants the cash.

Shit! Walt recognized the first voice now. “Center yourself.” Anton, from the yoga camp. Him and his new-age, Yanni loving bullshit. Talks a great game about inner peace and all that, but yeah, all the time he’s out here smoking his ‘peace pipe’! Can’t quite figure out who the other guy is, though. And what’s Anton buying? “Proof.” Proof of what? “Evidence.” Another legal term, as if they were talking in code. Something’s not right here. Pam lay alongside him silently, taking in every word spoken by the pair. Doofus remaining obedient, pressing flat against Walt’s leg.

“Business, man, it’s all business to you. That’s fine. But it will come back on you some day. It’s a bigger universe out there, you should get in touch. Expand your horizons.” It was Anton’s voice again.

“Five grand. Five grand and you’ve never heard of me, never seen me. I’m a ghost to you, that’s all. An angel of deliverance. Anything comes back on me, *I’ll come back on you* some day. Comprende?” The second man, whoever he was, sounded agitated. And what was with the "Comprende?" It was beginning to sound like a spaghetti western.

"No discount for making the world a better place?"

"No discounts for my grandmother, my mother, not even my brother. Five grand, cold hard cash, *friend*."

"Fine, here's your blood money. Watch out for karma."

There was a brief rustling noise, and nothing more said. A long pause, maybe five or six minutes. It was hard for Walt to keep still that long. Walt thought back to deer hunting, how you had to be perfectly still, lest the tiniest little movement give you away. Then the sound of boots on timber, two sets of feet retreating to opposite sides of the bridge, before disappearing through the sawgrass from whence they'd come. Eventually a bird trilled in a bush nearby. Other birds quickly joined in. The spell was broken.

Walt finally felt safe enough to sit up, just in time to see the backside of Anton's striding purposefully toward the Sparrow Lotus Camp. Anton appeared smaller and smaller as he marched to the horizon. Eventually the long grass swallowed him up completely. Walt looked across to the far side of the river. The other man was long gone.

25

"What do you think that guy was selling?" Those were the first words that Pam had uttered in a long while. "Dope?"

"I don't think so. At first I thought it might be dope, but then all that crap about 'proof' and 'evidence'? I think there's more going on than drugs. We need to get out of here, in case they come back."

"Did you recognize the voices?" Pam sounded as if she knew more than she was letting on, as if she had a secret and she was feeling Walt out, to see if he too knew the answer.

"The first one, Anton, he manages the Camp. I've met him twice now. He was doing the buying, or the payoff, the whatever. The second voice seemed familiar, too, the guy collecting the money. I just can't place him." Pam said nothing.

Walt and Pam arose cautiously. Walt had a leash in his backpack, which he carefully clipped to Doofus' collar. He didn't want the dog running off, alerting people to their presence. He quickly folded the blanket and stuffed it into the pack. He did one final check of the area, making sure that no wrapper, no napkin, no indicator remained that they had ever been to this spot. Then, wordlessly, they hightailed it back to Pam's car.

"What do we do now, Sherlock?" They were safely in the car, cruising Wolverine Valley Road back to the freeway.

"I don't know what we do now. I hate to say it, but I'm guessing I talk to the cops, tell them what I heard."

"I can't see as they're going to do much. We heard one guy talking to another guy on a bridge in the middle of the forest. The only thing we really know is that Anton is paying the other guy five grand. He could be buying a used car." Pam had a way of stating things as if they were fact, as if she and she alone understood how the universe worked. It wasn't deliberate on her part, and by no means was she smug or arrogant. She just had a certain *confidence* about her. It annoyed the living hell out of Walt.

"Really? A used car? That's what you got out of this?" Walt was getting slightly pissed, and the volume of his voice was creeping up a notch or two with each word. "A used car?" He stared at her in disbelief. How could women be so utterly dumb?

"Calm down, big boy. *I* don't think he's buying a used car, I'm just suggesting what *the police* are likely to say. We didn't see any cash change hands, didn't see anything that was *technically* illegal. We don't know who the second guy was, or what he was selling. So far you've got a whole lot of nothing." Maybe she was a bit smug, after all. But her tone of voice was consoling, and Walt managed to simmer down.

"Well something dirty was going on out there. Anton looking for 'proof' and 'evidence.' Like it was a payoff for a murder." A bulb went off in Walt's head. A murder! This was a payoff for a murder, that corpse Walt had found in the river! The second guy on the bridge, he was a hit man! The only problem was, that body had been lying around somewhere for eight or ten years. It was a little late to be paying for a hit man now. Then another thought came to him. Hush money! Anton was paying hush money to cover up the killing. Anton killed the man, the second guy found out about it. He was blackmailing Anton. That had to be it!

"Walt, you look like the cat that swallowed the canary. What's going through that skull of yours?"

"I think I've figured it out." The smile stayed pasted to his face. Pam pulled onto the exit ramp and they rolled back through town.

"Well let me know when you want to share your wisdom." She dropped him off back at his house. It was nearly five p.m., and she was already an hour late for her shift at the Deer Track. "I'll be done around two-thirty if you want to see me tonight."

"Can't, I'll be busy." With that Walt gave her a quick kiss and skipped into the house.

RECONNAISSANCE
26

He was nestled beneath the trunk of a gnarled oak, the army surplus sleeping bag wrapped around his legs. Walt wanted a cigarette, *really* wanted a cigarette. He'd quit smoking over a year ago, switching to smokeless tobacco. Not that he'd done it for his health or anything. That governor, she whose name he couldn't even bring himself to mention, she's why he quit smoking. She'd jacked taxes up so high that smokes cost over five bucks a pack, and that's when Walt drew the line. Trying to balance the state budget on the backs of the little guy, that's all she was doing. Trying to dictate what type of life everyone should live. So he'd switched to snuff, and he had a tin in his back pocket, but it wasn't really the same. Snuff had nicotine, but he felt cheated out of the rituals of smoking, tamping down the fresh pack, carefully pulling on the little white strip and removing the cellophane, finding a light, and sucking that initial burst of hot air deep into his lungs. He could *really* use a cigarette right about now. Thinking about smoking wasn't making things any easier.

Walt looked at his watch. It was a little after one in the morning. He'd been here since shortly before dusk. In the distance Walt could see the faint outline of Sparrow Lotus Camp, with its great lodge and a smattering of smaller buildings behind it. From this angle it looked like there were five separate guest cabins, but Walt knew from his previous visit that there was another row of four guest cabins behind that first row. Cabins two and four, as Walt numbered them in his head, still had lights on. No noises came forth, just a pair of reading lamps illuminating their windows. He tried to imagine what was going on inside of cabins two and four. Was there a single woman reading a thriller? A fat guy meditating naked? A young couple hovering around a hookah? Maybe the two women who'd assaulted him back at the Deer Track were involved in some Tantric love ritual or something. It helped him to stay awake, visualize these little scenarios. His imagination couldn't be bothered with cabins six through nine, the invisible row in the back. No lights shining, nothing to see there.

What was he doing out here, sitting alone in the woods? Walt wasn't entirely sure himself. He was certain that Anton and the man Anton had met on the bridge were up to no good, and that the only way Walt was going to learn anything more was by observing the yoga camp. He didn't think he'd learn much during the daylight hours. During the daylight hours Anton would be busy with guests, taking care of the needs of the resort. If he was going to show his hand, it would be after hours, on his own time.

So Walt had gone home, put together a sleeping bag, some snacks and a few bottles of Powerade, a thermos full of coffee, a mini maglite and some binoculars, and parked his butt under a tree with a good view of the camp. Thus far he'd been sitting beneath this tree for a little over five hours, and all he'd manage to observe were a few SUVs full of guests rolling in for their weekend retreat. People checked in at the main lodge, then retreated to their assigned cabins. Cabins one through five were full, and at least two women had stepped around to one of the cabins in the back row. Nothing suspicious in that. He assumed the back row was full, too, he just couldn't see it.

At one point a man crept out of his shack long enough to retrieve a brown paper bag from the trunk of a Buick Acadia. Probably a bottle of good booze. Walt was regretting not having brought a bottle of something for himself. It would make the time pass more quickly. He wondered if alcohol was permitted at Sparrow Lotus. Probably not, that's why the man had to sneak out to his vehicle in the darkness.

The night was cool but not cold. Fireflies put on a show in the tall grass by the river, but they'd stopped an hour or two after sunset. The sky was partly cloudy. The moon remained bright, and did a reasonable job of shining through the gaps in the broken sky. It wasn't "I can walk around in the darkness without breaking an ankle" light out, but Walt could discern structures and shapes, and the camp was visible. A large mercury vapor light broadcast down from the entrance to the main lodge building, and a second lamp illuminated its back side. From where Walt sat, he had a prime view of the main lodge. It would be impossible to enter or leave the main building without being spotted. Walt waited. "It would help if I had any idea what I was waiting for," Walt whispered to no one in particular.

The lamp in cabin two clicked off, someone apparently deciding to call it a night. The window in cabin four was still brightly lit. Insomnia? Passion? What kept people up at night? Walt looked at his watch again: three o'clock. What was keeping Walt up at night? That was a better question. He had to wonder why he wasn't in a warm bed with Pam instead of sitting out here all night. He took another sip of coffee and leaned back against the rough bark of the tree. Maybe if he shut his eyes for just a minute, it would all make sense. That was all it took.

Walt awakened with a start. He could hear something moving rapidly towards the camp. A deer? An elk? He listened intently. Sawgrass pulling against pant legs, definitely a man or a woman walking near the river. Walt tried not to move, tried not to give away his position. The low gnarled branches of the oak tree masked him from sight. He blinked the crust out of his eyelids and strained to see. A lone man walking purposefully in the dark. There was a lumpy shape on the man's back, a bag or a package. He was carrying something. The man bent slightly forward to help bear the weight of whatever it was he was hauling. The man's back was turned to Walt. He must have passed within twenty yards of the oak, and hadn't noticed Walt, watching from the base of the behemoth tree. Walt was glad he hadn't been noticed. Dozing in the inky shadows, he would have been particularly vulnerable.

Walt stole a glimpse down at his watch. Nearly four a.m. How long had he been asleep and what had he missed during that time? He hoped nothing. He must have been out for nearly an hour, though. His eyes traced back to the hiking man. The man was maybe two hundred yards from the camp.

The door at the front of the main lodge opened, and a lanky figure stepped into the bright floodlight shining from above. Anton. Anton peeked around the right side of the building to the cabins behind him. The light in cabin four was now out. All was quiet, with the exception of the main lodge. Anton seemed satisfied with the situation, returned to the front entrance of the building, and leaned casually against one of the great timber posts that supported the mammoth overhang. Old growth timber, the posts were at least three feet in diameter. The overhang extended out twenty feet in to the driveway, enough to allow two cars to pull up at the entrance, side by side if it were raining. Anton didn't appear to be in a hurry. He must be expecting the hiker. Why else would he be standing around outside at four in the morning?

'Walking Man,' that's who he was in Walt's mind. Walking Man was now within fifty yards of the lodge, and Anton silently hailed him with a raised right hand. "How, me big Indian." That's what Walt imagined Anton saying, if this were an old western movie. It reminded him of something, the 'old western' thing, but he couldn't quite say what. Walt couldn't tell if Walking Man nodded or otherwise acknowledged the motion, but Walking Man was set on a direct course for a powwow. Walt got out his binoculars so he could better watch what was going on.

The two men were talking with their faces close together. Walking Man still had his back to Walt, and Walt couldn't get a clean look at him. The shadows from the overhang weren't helping. The back of the man's head partially obscured Anton's face. Walking Man set his package, what looked like a burlap bag full of flour, at his feet in front of him. The width of the package was all that divided the two men. Anton was talking, leaning tight to the other man, bobbing left and right as he spoke. Anton nervously pointing down at the bag, then appeared to listen as Walking Man spoke. He pulled something, Walt couldn't tell what, from his back pants pocket, and handed it to Walking Man.

Eventually Anton took the sack in his hand, turned, and went into the lodge, closing the door behind him. Walking Man looked up at the sky for a second, and Walt looked up too. The Milky Way was intense, enough to make anyone quickly respect their own insignificance in the greater scheme of life. Walking Man gazed back at the ground, hesitated, and turned back in the direction from which he had come. He was strolling right back in Walt's direction. Walt knew something more now: Walking Man was Ray. Walt slipped the sleeping bag up over his head and slumped back into his hollow at the base of the tree. Ray passed by without noticing, and Walt, content that he had another piece of his puzzle, slowly drifted back off to sleep.

THE CAT OUT OF THE BAG
27

In his dream, Walt was seated at the head of a large banquet table. It was in the main dining room at Sparrow Lotus Lodge. It was night time, and crystal chandeliers provided a warm glow to a room that bespoke of bygone elegance. The table was set before him with fine bone china, and each porcelain place setting was off-white, with elegant gold trim. Gold paint traced the contours of its scalloped edges. In the center of each plate was a single lotus, painted in the very same exquisite gold leaf. Crystal goblets, stemware, and water glasses, each filled with liquids of various hues, sat before each and every chair. Some of the glassware contained less fluid than others, an indicator that the participants had indeed been drinking. Walt could sense that this party had been going on for some time.

The room was filled with hundreds of guests draped in their finest formal wear. A man in a silk top hat and morning coat with tails stood in front of Walt, speaking to a buxom matron in a shimmering emerald gown. Walt could not make out what the man was saying, though the grey-haired woman appeared to be laughing raucously at something the man had just said. There was a jazz band playing in one corner of the room, six or eight men including a small horn section, couples swaying merrily on the parquet dance floor. The voices in the room were indistinguishable from one another, joining together as part of one single, ambient chorus. The volume would swell and then decrease, an audible, sonic pulse that modulated with the excitement of the moment.

A waiter drifted through the room with a small tray of canapes. Another passed by carrying flutes of champagne. The second waiter drifted across the floor, with such fluidity of motion he might well have been on wheels. Walt tried to see the waiter's feet, to see if there actually were feet. The bottoms of the waiter's legs were obscured by the mingling crowd. Walt would have to remember to ask the man if he had feet, should the opportunity ever present itself.

Across the room stood Dora, his ex, flirting with a man of about twenty who was obviously captured by her charms. "You're too old for him!" Walt wanted to scream, but he could make no sound. Dora lifted a glass from the waiter's tray, curtsied and raised her champagne in mock salute to Walt, then turned away and faded into the crowd. Walt wanted to cry out to her, to stop her from leaving, but still could find no voice.

After a few minutes a contortionist came to the front of the vast hall, seating himself on the floor directly in front of Walt. He stretched a soft mat out and twisted himself into the most unbelievable positions. A dozen or so people formed a half circle around him, watching his every move. A second man, shorter, possibly even a dwarf, placed a card on the floor naming each of the performer's poses. "The War God," "Scorpion." With the placement of each new placard the contortionist would change positions, and his audience would cheer and applaud before awaiting the next.

Walt realized that none of the guests was speaking directly to him, that he was essentially invisible to all party goers. He wondered how this could coincide with his place of prestige at the head of the main table. He looked down at his own clothing, and realized that he was still wearing the black pants, black turtleneck, and camouflage jacket that he'd worn in the woods last night. He hurriedly checked beneath the table, was relieved to find no sleeping bag wrapped around his legs. Why was he at this party? Who had invited him? And why was he the only person still seated at the main table? At least he wasn't wrapped in a sleeping bag.

When Walt tilted his head back up, the guests had all vanished. The residue of the party, half eaten pieces of chicken, lipstick stained wine glasses, confetti strewn across the floor, all remained, but the party guests had evaporated. All excepting Walt. Was the party in Walt's honor? If so, why had everyone deserted him?

As Walt pondered these questions, the main entry doors to the dining hall opened. Anton Kalinik stepped into the room bearing the burlap bag that Ray had delivered into his hands only last night. Anton was wearing the same jeans and shirt he had worn the previous evening, as well. Walt was briefly embarrassed for Anton. He must not have been informed that this was a black tie affair.

"Hello, Walt, good to see you." Anton was polite, almost formal.

This was a relief to Walt, that Anton could see him. Because Walt couldn't actually be invisible to other people, could he? Camouflage clothing was only so good, after all. It might hide you in the woods, but he didn't think it would be effective in a ballroom. Being invisible might have its benefits, but Walt suspected it also would bring entire layers of grief that he'd yet to even consider.

"Hey Anton, what's in the bag?" Walt was trying to remain calm, sound relaxed. But the disappearing guests and the fact that he was, at least intermittently, invisible to others, were weighing heavily on Walt's mind. He was excited to hear the sound of his own voice at last.

"I've been waiting for you to ask. A present for you. The answer to a riddle, as it were."

"A riddle? What's the riddle?"

"What's in the bag. Isn't that the riddle, Walt? Isn't that what you want to know? You want to know what's in the bag." Anton slowly approached the table.

"The bag that Ray gave you last night." Walt was a little slow in understanding what Anton was getting at, but now it was coming together in his mind. The bag that was worth five thousand dollars to Anton. "You tell me. What *is* in the bag, Anton? Why are you playing games with me?" Walt was beginning to feel more like himself, and thus a little anger was rising inside of him. He tried to rise, but couldn't stand up. It was as if he were affixed to his seat.

"The money I paid Raymond was a finder's fee for property of Sparrow Lotus L.L.C., property that was lost, but has now been returned to its rightful place." Anton was now standing only three paces in front of Walt. Walt hadn't notice him moving closer, but here he was, directly in Walt's face. And for some reason, Walt was no longer certain he wished to know what was in the bag. Something in Anton's tone of voice didn't seem right, and Walt was fearful of what he might learn.

Walt considered the situation carefully. A small part of him *did* want to know what was in the bag. On the other hand, whatever it was must be something fairly important that Anton would pay five grand for it. The words 'proof' and 'evidence' came to Walt's mind, and all Walt could think about was murder. But what kind of proof would be transported in a burlap sack? No, Walt didn't really want to see the contents of that bag. He could only imagine what was inside, and his imagination was running wild. The space between Anton and himself suddenly seemed inadequate. Walt felt penned in, his eyes frantically seeking any avenue of escape. Still his legs refused to move.

"Don't you want to know, Walt? Inquiring minds want to know, after all." And with that Anton turned the sack over and emptied its contents onto Walt's pristine dinner plate. Walt stared at what was placed before him. A human head, the waterlogged head of a corpse. At first he was repulsed, but then curiosity took over. Only upon closer inspection did Walt discover that the head on the plate was Walt's own. Walt couldn't make sense of it. How could that be? You can't really look yourself in the face, can you? He stared for a full minute or more. He thought maybe he should ask Anton what this all meant, but when he finally looked back toward Anton, that man, too, had vanished. Walt was all alone in the hall.

Then Walt was transported. He could see himself drifting through the air, a spirit untethered to the earth. This spirit had a head, at least. There was a joy in the weightlessness, and Walt was relieved to know that at least his spirit self had both a head and a torso.

This other self was whisked outside, riding a brisk wind into the great vacuum that was the natural world outside. It was traveling faster and faster, and the increasing speed made Walt almost nauseous. And then Walt was swimming, swimming with all his might in the cold clear waters of the Sparrow River, swimming madly downstream to escape the stagnant, oppressive warmth of the pond above the dam. The warm waters of the pond were chasing him, trying to overwhelm and drown him. Walt knew his one true purpose was to hurtle himself towards the cool depths of the Great Lakes. The footbridge flashed past him in the air above, a fleeting shadow as his spirit hurtled downstream.

The current was now Walt's home, the entirety of his world. He no longer needed air to breath, no longer needed other people. He was both free and lost, a homeless entity driven by the endless flow of the river, and that sudden realization set him to panic. He tried once again to suck breath, to be more than just a small fish in the universe, and was all the while taking more and more water into his lungs. "Just keep swimming," he thought. Swimming to the inland sea.

Walt woke up shivering in his sleeping bag. Disoriented, he slipped out of his burrow, a groundhog seeking his bearings. The sun was high in the sky. It must be damn near eleven in the morning. Saturday, he thought. That had been one hell of a dream. He was glad to once again be a man, rather than a fish. Christ, he must have spent the entire night sleeping beneath that tree. One hell of a dream.

He stood up and stretched his arms wide, bent over and touched his knees, loosening the cramped muscles of his lower back. His hip was sore from where he must have been lying on an acorn or a stone during the night. What did it all mean? Walt stared off into the distance, letting his eyes adjust to the harsh light of day. He saw people milling about the grounds of the yoga camp. No one had as yet noticed Walt, standing a half mile away in the meadow. The guests at Sparrow Lotus were going about their daily business, whatever that might be. Walt pissed against the trunk of the massive oak, watched the steam rise in the late morning sun. He then gathered his things and hiked back to the Suzuki.

THE ALUMINUM HATCH
28

He was still a little groggy when he got behind the steering wheel. Walt turned right when he reached Wolverine Valley Road, and drove four miles east before realizing his mistake. The road ended abruptly at the water's edge, the bridge at Sparrow Crossing Campground removed for a summer-long, total reconstruction. That would suck for campers on the far side of the river, who'd have to drive eight miles north and then twelve miles west, via dirt roads, to get back to the main highway. He looked down at the river for a moment, a sluice of water dividing the roadbed as cleanly as any incision. Nature went where it wanted. Walt turned the Suzuki around and headed back to Rasmus.

His house was just as he'd left it. The air smelled musty, confined. Walt experienced a temporary sense of desolation, coming home to this perpetually empty nest, as if everyone had died and he were there to clear out their possessions. He'd have to get Doofus back from the neighbor later today, but it wouldn't hurt to wait a few hours. The dog was probably enjoying Mrs. Berner's company. He opened two windows, allowing a cross breeze to clear out some of the stale air. What Walt needed, more than anything, was to clear his head and to stretch his body. He could think of no better way than to get in a canoe and paddle.

He realized that it was already June, and he hadn't done any serious paddling in over two weeks. Not a good way to train for a marathon. The big race was the last weekend in July, not that far down the road. He had yet to find a partner for this year's event. Last year he'd been thrown together at the last minute with another stray dog, some French guy from Quebec. It wasn't unusual for a few solitary competitors to make their way from across the country, or further, to race in the legendary Limoneaux River Canoe Marathon. Most were French-Canadians, where paddling is a way of life. Some folks would come from the east coast, guys that raced scull in New Hampshire or competed in college at Ivy League schools. Occasionally paddlers would arrive from Seattle or Portland, where there were fewer opportunities to test one's prowess against top-notch competition. Usually these racers travelled in pairs, old friends from college, a husband and wife team from Minnesota, kayakers trying to spice up their relationship. You had to be fairly hardcore to make the trip alone, taking your chances partnered with whomever might be available.

He wasn't a bad paddler, "Rene" from Quebec, but it was only his second time in the race, and the two men had pulled out of the competition due to exhaustion shortly before dawn that Sunday morning. Rene was younger than Walt, mid-twenties, but green. It hadn't helped that they'd gotten lost in the fog on Mioe Pond for well over twenty minutes, or that they tipped and got soaked when they hit a gravel bar in the darkness. Both errors meant time and energy wasted. When they dragged their sorry, wet bodies out at Polk Bridge that Sunday morning, forced to quit the race because they could no longer continue, Walt lay down on the weedy bank and wept. Wept for exhaustion, for pain and borderline hypothermia, for all the things he had lost in the last year or so. And then he got up and walked silently to the truck. Elvin and D.J. were waiting there with Powerade and sandwiches, and retrieved the canoe for a pair of men who could barely stand on their own two feet. Walt slid into the back seat of the borrowed extended cab truck, didn't say a word for the entire ride home.

Walt desperately wanted to partner with a local this year, someone with experience, so that they could train together year round. The day of the race was not the day to first meet someone you were expecting to synchronize with for sixteen straight hours. So far he'd been unable to find a consistent partner. He'd had a couple of offers, guys who thought about running the marathon as a lark. Walt didn't want to run with another novice. Walt wanted to get with someone *good*, someone who could propel them into the top forty or so teams. Once he'd established himself as a serious paddler, he'd be part of that tight fraternity of racers, those who'd fought the river and won. And once you were part of that core group, it was easier to get a top-tier racer in your boat.

In the meantime, Walt needed a training buddy, *anyone* to pull a few hours on the water and help him work on his conditioning and his technique. He called Lefty McGoo, an old timer with whom he'd gotten in some river work over the winter. No luck. Lefty was in Mississippi visiting his daughter. Mikey Babcock was a good paddler, but he was racing with his kid this year, a high school junior who also played varsity football and basketball. The kid was a horse. They'd finished twenty-second last year, and were hoping with enough practice to move up into a top ten finish. Mike had no interest in getting into a boat with anyone other than his son.

Walt ran through a few other numbers in his address book and came up empty. He was out of ideas for "serious" paddling partners today, and was quickly working his way to the bottom of the barrel. He thought about Beth Woody, a local schoolteacher who'd competed successfully for more than a dozen years. Beth was a good paddler, had finished in the top twenty a few times as part of a mixed team, one male and one female in the same craft. She was always looking for a few more hours of training, knew what she was doing and wasn't too fussy about who she ran with, but Walt couldn't bring himself to phone her. He'd be damned if he was going to let some *woman* tell him how to get downstream.

"Elvin, how the hell are you?" He knew it was a long shot, but at least it would put another butt in the boat. He was hoping his friend would make it worth the phone call.

"Alright, what's going on?" Elvin was always a little leery of unsolicited friendliness from Walt, and hadn't been expecting the call.

"You want to make a quick run down the river, say Primo's Landing to Rusty Bridge and then back upstream? I could use a light workout." There was silence on the other end of the line for a good twenty seconds. Elvin was thinking.

"Did you just say *upstream*?" Elvin finally replied. Walt should know that Elvin wasn't a competitive paddler. Sure, he'd gotten in the Wenonah racing canoe a few times, just to mess around and keep his friend happy. It was fun to pretend he knew what he was doing once or twice a year. The sleek little rocket was thirty-some pounds of fiberglass and cedar, designed for speed, but not for stability. The nose of the craft tapered quickly to a sharp point, as did the tail of the boat. There was barely room for your legs once you were seated. It had a narrow beam. The slightest mistake by a paddler, leaning a little too far left or right, wiggling at the wrong time, could easily send both men for a quick swim in the river. It was fifty-fifty whether Elvin was going to tip the canoe going *with* the current, let alone *against* the current. And while it was early summer and the water was gradually warming, getting abruptly dumped in the river was never as fun as it sounded. "I'm going to have to pass on that one, Walt. I don't feel like doing the breaststroke today."

"Come on man, just an hour or two. I need to get some time on the water, and everyone else is busy. I promise we'll take it easy."

Elvin knew what "take it easy," meant. If things went well he'd break a good sweat, get lightheaded, wish he were dead for at least five minutes, and then feel marginally better, though exhausted for the remainder of day. That was a best case scenario. It was more likely he'd be vomiting and wet within an hour, with Walt cursing him for being out of shape. Elvin also knew, somehow, that he was probably Walt's last resort. If there was a "real" paddler available, Walt wouldn't be calling *him*. It was a call of desperation. They were friends, after all. Against his better judgment, he gave in. "Sure, just don't kill me."

"You won't regret it."

"I already do."

"Half an hour?"

"I'll be there."

At two-thirty the two men were standing at Primo's Landing, cautiously lifting the Wenonah racer off the top of Walt's Suzuki. It was a good time to be starting on the water. The "aluminum hatch," as the fly fisherman referred to it, was mostly done with for the day. An armada of rental canoes launched in the late morning of most summer weekends, clogging the Limoneaux's narrow arteries with downstaters who could barely navigate a shopping cart down a crowded aisle at WalMart. The slow moving recreational paddlers would drift along, chugging beer or soda from a cooler, crashing into every deadhead and overhanging branch along the way. Then they would stop off and swim at the whirlpool, before making their bucolic way downstream to where the vans from the liveries were waiting to pick them up. From the late morning on, they provided an amazing obstacle course for a fragile racing craft, even a relatively slow one.

By early evening the river would populate with fly fishermen, slow wading men, standing chest deep in the current, casting little wads of hair and hook to fish they couldn't see. They were easier to avoid than the rental canoes, more like safety cones randomly placed throughout the river. They called this stretch of the river "The Holy Waters," but Walt thought had forever thought that the fly fishermen were a holy pain in the ass.

Walt and Elvin were arriving in the middle of the afternoon, a 'sweet spot' when the majority of the rental canoes were off the water and done for the day, and most of the fly fisherman were not yet on the river.

"Don't drop it. These things cost two grand and they're about as puncture resistant as wet toilet paper."

"Shit, Walt, I'm not an athlete, but even I can lift half a canoe."

"I'm just saying. Don't drop it, *please*." Like 'thanks,' it was another word that didn't come easily for Walt.

They gently placed the boat on the graveled edge of the stream. Should he take the bow or stern? This was always a tough question for Walt when he was boating with Elvin. If this were serious training, and Walt considered *any* time spent on the water serious training, Walt would take his usual position in the front of the craft. He knew the bow was a more crucial position, and Walt liked to practice in what he deemed his 'natural spot.' It was a place that commanded respect, a place for leadership. On the other hand, he outweighed Elvin by a good eighty pounds, and if Walt took the bow, the lighter man was paddling stern. The canoe would lurch forward, the front half-submerged and the back end cresting out of the water. It made Elvin even less effective of a paddler than he otherwise might be, which was saying a lot. Elvin had *significant* trouble steering from the rear. If, on the other hand, Walt put Elvin in the front, the two generated no real power. Six of one, half a dozen of the other.

Walt was leaning toward taking the stern. At least with Elvin in the bow, Walt would know whether his friend was paddling, puking, or swimming. Should Elvin fall out of the *rear* of the boat, Walt might not notice for a quarter mile. "Take the bow Elvin," he finally decided.

"Yes, captain!"

They started hard, each stroke thrusting them farther and faster than the meandering current. Ten minutes in, they had achieved a reasonable rhythm, switching sides whenever Walt called "hup!" Elvin misread the flow once or twice, and Walt had to brake hard with his paddle to correct course. That would never work in the race, he knew. Any time you dragged a paddle in the water, you forfeited momentum. It was clear his friend didn't know what he was doing, but at least they were working up a lather. They passed a couple of rental canoes in the first stretch, stragglers that had fallen behind a much larger group.

Twenty minutes on the water and Elvin was spent, saturated in a clammy sweat, and calling for a break. This was not the workout Walt hoped for, but sometimes you took what you got. "Take it easy. You can't afford a heart attack. I'll keep paddling solo for a while," Walt told his pal.

"Thanks, man. I just need five minutes to catch my breath." A fall overboard was looking more appealing by the minute. At least the water would be cool.

Walt admired the day. The sun was shining brilliantly, the temperature near seventy degrees. A few wispy cirrus clouds drifted across the troposphere. Walt increased his stroke rate. The good paddlers averaged fifty to eighty strokes per minute for the duration of the marathon. Walt silently kept time in his head, trying to synchronize the paddle in his hands with his heart rate. He only seemed to be averaging around fifty strokes per minute, but he also knew that each paddler was different. He might not be as fast as some men, but his swath generated better than average power. With the right partner, he'd be plenty fast enough.

The Wenonah flew past a pair of mallards bobbing around an eddy, seeking food. A great blue heron waded along the shoreline, taking flight only when the canoe got within thirty yards. A mink saw them coming, and scurried up amongst the red cedars that line the river's banks. It was a great day to be on the water.

"You alive up there?" he finally asked. Walt was beginning to wonder if Elvin would live through the afternoon.

"Barely, but I'm coming back." Elvin had resumed paddling, at least sporadically. He seemed to be recovering some of his strength. When he turned to look back toward Walt, he didn't look nearly as ashen as he had ten minutes before.

"You need to learn to pace yourself, not burn yourself out so quickly. Try not to be so quick out of the box. You do that every time, you know."

"You sound like my wife on a Saturday night," he retorted.

"Now that's funny," Walt answered back.

"Did you find a partner for the marathon yet?" Elvin hadn't seen much of Walt in the last couple of weeks, didn't know what his plans were.

"No. I've been busy with work. I've been seeing a woman once in a while, the bartender from the Deer Track, Pam. And then there's that thing up on the Sparrow, I'm still working on that."

"Did you find Jimmy Hoffa yet?"

"Not Hoffa, but some other things that don't add up." Walt's body was on autopilot, and the synchronized paddling of the two men resumed, though at a significantly slower pace. "The guy that runs that yoga ranch is involved in drugs, I think." It was hard for Walt to adequately describe his tangled suspicions.

"There's a novel concept, a hippie that smokes pot. I'm guessing at the hippie part. You think this has something to do with that body in the river? Drugs aren't the same thing as murder, Walt, if it even *was* a murder," Elvin offered.

"There's more to it than pot. But where there's drugs there's money, and where there's murder there's usually money, too. Could be they're connected. I just need to connect the dots."

"Could be. Just use the right crayon." Elvin was starting to feel sickly again, and wasn't up to arguing. He thought about pointing out that Walt still didn't know how the man had died. Was it a murder? Maybe it was, maybe it wasn't. He'd learned long ago to let Walt think whatever Walt wanted to think. It was foolish to try and convince the man otherwise. "Rusty Bridge, coming up. Ready to turn around?"

"Sure thing."

"I need a break before we head back upstream."

"Don't worry about it, I'll paddle." Walt spun the Wenonah around, dug his paddle in deep against the current, and picked up the pace, going back against the flow. He was straining hard, the muscles in his shoulders and arms bulging from the work, and he felt great. He was now pushing seventy strokes per minute, and the canoe lurched forward with each and every effort. Elvin joined in sporadically, but knew he wasn't making much of a contribution towards their progress. The real power stemmed from Walt.

"What do you think?" Walt asked, when they finally dragged the canoe up on shore at Primo's Landing. Their vehicles were right where they'd left them. Walt was just feeling warmed up. Elvin looked like he might need a doctor.

"I think you'd have to be insane to do this for one-hundred and twenty miles straight."

"That too. Do you think I'm getting any faster? That's what I meant."

"It's hard to tell, Walt. Maybe I'm just getting slower. I haven't done this in a while. You could put a clock on it, but you're not going to learn much racing with me. Got anything to drink in your car?" Elvin was once again coming around, now that he was back on dry land, but he was a long ways from feeling good.

"There's some bottles of water in the back seat. Grab one for me while you're at it." Walt sat down on the wooden timbers that reinforced the stream bank and rested. Elvin returned with two water bottles and sat next to him.

"Back near Rusty Bridge, you said 'that thing on the Sparrow.' What are you hoping to learn, poking around up there?" Elvin had long ago tempered his curiosity when it came to Walt. Some things you just didn't want to know. Yet this piqued his interest, whatever it was that Walt was attempting to accomplish.

"I need to know who it was I found dead in the river this spring, and how he died. I *need* to know, Elvin." Walt was emphatic. There wasn't much more he could say by way of explanation. "I'm sure he came from the Yoga Camp, and I'm sure he's dead, whoever he is," as if that explained all.

"You mentioned someone at the camp is using drugs, and you think that has something to do with a ten year old death?" Elvin was sounding out the idea, more than anything. The concept seemed less plausible when spoken than it did as a thought bouncing around in his head. Maybe if he said it out loud, Walt would realize how preposterous his theory actually was.

"Not *using drugs*, Elvin, *dealing* drugs. At least I think he's dealing, because the package he received last night was too big for personal use. It was big, big like a basketball."

"Where'd you see this package delivery? Maybe he's got glaucoma, and it was just one big ol' prescription for medical marijuana. He's probably got a card from the State allowing him to officially get high in the name of medicine. And who the hell is this 'he' we're talking about?"

"Anton, the guy that runs Sparrow Lotus. He got a package from a drug dealer named Ray in the middle of the night. I was watching them from the meadow by the river. Last night," he added, almost as an afterthought. When he said it like that, it even sounded stupid to his own ears.

"Don't know him. Seems like a good way to get yourself killed, spying on people in the middle of the night." Elvin *didn't* know Anton, and he probably wouldn't have admitted it even if he did. His interest in this subject was rapidly waning as he recognized the likelihood of getting sucked into yet another of Walt's conspiracy theories. This was looking more and more like one of those times when curiosity becomes a liability. Elvin decided to keep quiet.

After a few minutes, a few pulls on the water bottle, Walt broke the silence. "There's something else going on, and I'm going to find out what that is. It's more than just drug dealing, it's big. I was watching the yoga camp all night. I might head back up there. Want to help me?"

"Thanks, but I think I'll sit this one out." Elvin could smell trouble, he had a nose for trouble like a wharf rat on the Titanic. "It was a good workout." Change the subject, he thought. The canoe marathon was a much safer topic, less likely to get you beaten up, or worse.

Walt let it drop. He hadn't really expected his friend to sign on for nocturnal reconnaissance work. Elvin had a wife, kids, things to tie him down. He had a *life,* Walt realized, with a touch of jealousy in his heart. "It *was* a good workout. Thanks for coming out. Do you want to go again Tuesday night?" He was hoping his pal had a few more runs down the river left in him.

"I've got kid's soccer practice, I think." Elvin had no idea if what he was saying was true, but it was an excuse that usually worked, got him out of things he didn't want to do. It sounded plausible at least. "I"ll let you know."

"Alright. Give me a ring if things change." Walt knew it was unlikely that his friend would call. The two men left it at that, and once again parted ways.

Walt slid behind the wheel of the Suzuki. Now what was he going to do? It was late afternoon, almost time for dinner. He was ravenous. He started humming to himself without even realizing it. Pam would be working at the Deer Track tonight. There'd be no sense in calling her until closing time, or a little before. If he showed up before last call, he could get a snoot full on the house, and maybe something more afterwards. He decided to head into town and grab a bite to eat. The words finally came to him, and he sung quietly to himself.

Another Saturday night and I ain't got nobody...
I've got some money 'cause I just got paid....

THE RED EYE SALOON
29

He came through the door of the Red Eye with a lilt in his step. It was early for dinner, not quite six, but the restaurant was filling up quickly. His eyes quickly swept the dining area. Right away he spotted Mikey Babcock, sitting at the table closest to the door. Babcock was snugged up close to a woman who was not his wife. He didn't seem to mind who knew it, either.

Babcock was a good looking man in his late thirties, salt-and-pepper hair and an "I forgot it's not the seventies" mustache that he dyed brown. It seemed stupid to Walt that Babcock would dye his mustache but not the rest of his hair to match. To each his own, Walt figured. It didn't seem to be hurting him in the romance department.

Like any good paddler, Babcock had the sculpted upper body of an athlete. Walt had met Mikey's wife, a hard woman who had put in twenty years raising three kids. She was nothing to look at, seemed hard around the edges, but something told Walt she hadn't started out looking that way. She must have been fairly attractive not too long ago, before life with Mikey ground her down. Walt was fairly certain that Mrs. Babcock didn't know that Mr. Babcock was currently hanging around the Red Eye with another woman. He was sure she wouldn't appreciate it if she knew. Walt figured he'd say "hi" to Mikey and dig a little dirt, all at the same time.

"Hey Mikey. Who's this young lady?" She wasn't really young, and most likely wasn't a lady, but Walt wasn't one to back down from an opportunity. In Walt's mind, this was a fact-finding mission *and* an opportunity to needle a rival.

"Walt Pitowski." Babcock said it with disdain. He could have just as well been an anthropologist announcing the appearance of a new species. "Asian Dung Beetle!" he might have asserted. "Northern Michigan Son of a Bitch!" Instead, he followed up with the obligatory introduction. "This is my friend Cheryl." Walt took a closer look at the woman. She was younger than Babcock by a few years, probably had been something special not too many years ago herself. She had a nice figure, but beneath the flashy dress and the plaster of paris makeup, cracks were beginning to show. She wasn't that far behind the absent Mrs. Babcock in the early-aging department. Maybe it was being around Mikey Babcock that did that to a woman, maybe it was just living in the North. "Pitowski works for the United States Geological Service," Babcock offered by way of explanation.

"Really? You don't look like a doctor," interjected the moderately surprised Cheryl.

Walt stood silent and confused, thinking maybe he'd misheard her. It wasn't *that* loud in here. He might need to get his hearing checked. What in the world was she talking about? Mikey also looked stunned, but only for a moment, then smiled when he figured out what his date was thinking.

"*Geo*logical, sweetheart, not *Gyneco*logical Service," Babcock corrected her.

"Well, that would be different, then," she answered, blushing slightly.

"Not as interesting, though," Walt chimed in. Now it was Babcock and Cheryl's turn to look dumbstruck. "It's a joke, Mikey. Being a Gynecologist would be more fun than what I do." It always annoyed Walt when people couldn't tell that he was kidding. "Christ," he thought, "what kind of a woman thinks the government has a Gynecological Service? What would they do there? Does she think it's part of Obamacare or something?" People were idiots, he was more certain of that every day of his life. They certainly seemed to lack capacity for humor.

"If only your jokes were funny," Babcock deadpanned. "You on your way somewhere?" A more observant man might take his hint. Walt showed no indication that he noticed.

"Just coming in for dinner. Are you paddling with Keith again this year?" Keith was Babcock's oldest, now a junior in high school. The father-son team had raced together the previous year and done fairly well. Walt was hoping that Babcock's boy might not feel like racing the marathon this year, maybe the kid had found a girlfriend or a hobby that was burning up all of his youthful energy. Maybe he had something better to do that weekend, or had decided that paddling with dear old dad might not be as cool the second time around. It couldn't hurt to ask.

"Yeah, we're racing together." Babcock was growing visibly annoyed by the minute. Walt mentioning his teenage son in front of 'the other woman' wasn't doing him any favors. It wasn't as if Cheryl didn't *know* that he had kids, but he didn't need Walt to broadcast a reminder. Who knew how that might sit with a woman though she had baggage of her own. Babcock was beginning to wonder if the idiot was going to next ask him how his wife was doing.

"Well let me know if anything changes. I'm still looking for a partner."

"Did you try Beth Woody? She's good." A conversational peace offering from Babcock.

"Not my type."

"She should be. She's a good paddler. Your loss if you're unwilling to admit it," Babcock answered.

"Thanks, but no thanks. I'll take my chances." Walt finally took the cue and headed to an empty table near the kitchen entrance. He eased his body into the cane backed chair, closest to the wall. This way he could see who entered and left the big room. A few familiar faces drifted through. Others, less familiar, were sitting down eating an early meal or catching a quick drink. Most of the customers were downstaters, fisherman up for the weekend, or people who owned cabins on the big lake so that they could "get away from it all," whatever the hell that meant.

Walt resented those lakefront property owners most of all. Locals, working men like himself, couldn't afford a house on the water. People with big salaries from the big cities had driven the price of waterfront real estate up so high that it was only a privileged few who got to enjoy a dock on the water, a view from their breakfast nook. And then the bastards blocked the road endings, deeded easements for all, as if they owned them. Public access points clearly denoted by law were rendered useless, cordoned off so that you couldn't even drag your canoe down to the shore for a little evening respite. Instead, you had to drive around the far side of the lake to the one and only public boat launch, where you'd be lucky to find a parking space. Downstaters were for sure the worst that mankind had to offer.

He thought about all the arguments he'd had with those arrogant bastards, how they were always proselytizing about how their good fortunes were good for everybody, because they came up north on weekends and bought gas and beer at the local party stores, and how really they were providing a huge benefit to the entire local economy. Trickle down economics, they'd call it. He wished they'd take their benefits and stick them where the sun didn't shine. "Take your tank of gas and your twelve pack, your gift of a few minimum wage jobs, and go the hell back south," Walt thought to himself. "I'll be happy to swap that for a cheap house on the lake, and better access to the river."

"Ready to order?" the waitress asked.

Walt snapped to attention. He hadn't noticed her standing in front of him. How long had he been lost in his thoughts? Had anyone noticed? Probably not, since the waitress was just now asking if he was ready to order. He needed to watch himself, though. People might start thinking he was going crazy, not that he cared all that much what people thought. Still, you don't want to be known as the crazy guy in a town this size. Labels could stick with a person, and Rasmus already had its quota of crazy.

"Give me a Leinenkugel and a Red Eye Burger with the works, please."

"Fries with that?"

"Sure. And can I get a glass of water?"

"Coming right up."

Walt looked around the room once again. Pretty much the same faces as the first time he'd looked around. Mikey Babcock and his friend Cheryl were just getting up to pay their tab. He threw a half-hearted wave in Walt's direction. Walt gave him a half-hearted wave back. "Moron," Walt muttered under his breath. "Like I'd ever paddle with a woman."

And if you asked him, Walt would have a hard time telling you exactly *why* he refused to paddle with a woman. He had met a few of the better women paddlers, and he knew that they were good athletes. None had ever *won* the race, and maybe that was part of it. But very few paddlers, male or female, really had much of a shot at *winning* the marathon. That wasn't the point.

The thought that, if you were in a boat with a female partner, you were *settling,* somehow admitting you had no chance of winning before you'd even begun to race, *that's* what didn't sit right with Walt. Not that he had high expectations, at least not this year. But if he was racing with another guy as a partner, at least the *illusion* that he might win still existed.

More importantly, though, Walt couldn't stand to take directions from a woman. He liked them fine, mind you, in the appropriate time and place, he just didn't want one telling him what to do. And if he was to spend sixteen straight hours in a canoe with some woman, *any* woman, he was assured that, at some point, she'd begin telling him what to do. They all did. It was in their nature. He knew he didn't need that crap.

The beer and a tall glass of water were on the table in front of him. As he mulled things over in his mind, the waitress, "what was her name again?" brought him his burger and fries. Lots of protein was important when you were training for the big day. By the time the actual race came around, you couldn't take in as many calories as your body burned. It didn't matter how much you shoveled down your throat, it wouldn't equal energy expended. As far as cholesterol? Walt had bigger things to worry about than cholesterol.

"Pitowski, how are you?" County Sheriff's Deputy Matt Amberson was leaning over the table, an unexpected guest if ever there were. Yes, they knew one another, but they weren't exactly buddies. "Mind if I sit down for a minute?"

"Sure, go ahead." Walt shoved a few more french fries into his mouth. "What's up?"

"I just got some information back from the State Police, thought I'd fill you in. Word is you've taken a bit of an interest in that body you discovered up on the Sparrow River."

"Whose word would that be?"

"Don't get defensive, Walt, it's a small town. Stuff gets around. You know as well as anyone you can't swing a dead cat in Rasmus without hitting somebody that knows you. There's not much to do around here, unless you're the outdoorsy type. Folks eat too much and gossip between bites. Some of 'em even go to church on Sundays. People talk, that's how they are.

How anyone thinks they can get away with having affairs and shit, I'll never know."

"You're right about that." Walt was thinking about Mikey Babcock and his 'friend.' "Affairs and shit." It was hard to admit it, but Amberson was right on that account. You couldn't get away with much in Rasmus, not without *somebody* taking notice along the way. "So what did you learn?"

"The body you found was a male, but then we already knew that. Age eighteen to twenty-five, they couldn't narrow it down any more than that. He was in pretty rough shape by the time you got to him. Caucasian, which shouldn't come as much of a surprise, either. We don't have too many visible minorities kicking around northern Michigan, although it's not completely unheard of. The deceased had a broken left tibia at one time, an injury which occurred prior to death and had fully healed. The tibia is the shin bone, in case you didn't know."

"I know what a tibia is, Matt, I'm not an idiot." He'd heard the word "tibia" before, but he couldn't remember if it was bone in the leg or the arm, and certainly couldn't remember *which* bone in the leg or arm was the tibia. Either way, Walt didn't want Amberson talking down to him like some middle school science student. He knew what a tibia was as of now, anyways, so it wasn't really a lie. All the while "The shin bone connected to the knee bone....." danced through the back of Walt's mind.

Amberson continued. "We know he had a broken tibia because there was still a tibial rod in place, suggesting this guy had a fairly serious break at one time. It was healed over, not fresh. Possibly from a car accident or other serious trauma. Sometimes they leave the rods in place for life, from what I hear, so it might have been there a while. I'm no expert, so anything more than that and you'd have to ask an orthopedic surgeon. No internal organs remaining, so it's not as if we got a lot of information off this one. Soft tissue decomposes or gets eaten by critters pretty quickly. He'd been deceased somewhere between five and ten years when you first got to him. He was probably buried most of that time, high water flushed him out from wherever he was buried. Or he was buried and someone dug him up and through him in the river. Somehow I doubt that's the case. No visible signs of trauma, other than what the river did to him, a lot of chips and scrapes on those bones, all after the fact. Cause of death undetermined."

"Any luck matching him to missing persons reports?"

"You'd think. It's hard to believe that someone in his age bracket could fall off the face of the earth without family or friends noticing, but nope, no luck. We searched local and state databases, even asked the feds for any missing persons reports that fit the description, but again, no luck. There's tens of thousands of them out there, kids that ran away as teenagers and lived on the streets, young guys that couldn't find a job and just dropped out on life. We don't have enough information to narrow it down. He could be anyone from anywhere."

"Yeah, but Matt, *the Bitch River?* If you were a runaway kid, would you really run to rural northern Michigan? Seattle, L.A., New York, that I get. But *northern Michigan?* Where it's thirty below in January and there's no shelters, no soup kitchen, no Walmart? Get serious."

"I thought about that, and you're right. We've got our share of runaways, but they're always locals. No kid from New Orleans is going to come up here to escape his rotten childhood. There's better choices available out there. Remember, he was probably between eighteen and twenty-five years old. An adult. He was most likely here for a reason. Maybe his folks have a cabin nearby, maybe he was on a camping trip, maybe he had a girlfriend in the area. Who knows."

"Dental records?" he mumbled, through a mouthful of fries.

"Not a lot of dental work, and no matches so far. We're not exactly CSI up here. You never know, we might get something on that somewhere down the road, but I wouldn't hold your breath."

"So you've got a white guy who once had a broken leg, eighteen to twenty-five, good teeth, and nobody in Michigan noticed him missing? And you don't know what killed him?"

"Pretty much."

"Where's that leave your investigation?"

“Where do you think? Still screwed, like you’d expect. Yet another reason to call that river ‘The Bitch.’ I thought you’d like to know, anyhow. I’ve got to get moving along.”

“Thanks for telling me, Matt. Good luck.”

Amberson started to leave, began to turn towards the door, then stepped back to the table for one last word. He was hesitant, unsure whether the advice he was about to dole out would do any good. “Yeah. Hey Pitowski, be careful where you poke your nose. And let me know if you stumble across anything that might be useful. If there’s a pile of crap sitting somewhere in the middle of the forest, I’d put money on you somehow setting your foot in it.”

“I appreciate your vote of confidence.” Walt enjoyed the chance to be smarmy.

“I’m just saying be careful. I hear you’ve been skulking around the woods looking for I don’t know what. You never know when you might piss off the wrong guy.”

“It hasn’t happened yet. Thanks for your concern, but I can handle myself.” Walt raised his glass in mock salute, and the deputy, choking back the temptation to offer one last word of caution, trundled out the front entrance of the Red Eye. With no one left to distract him, Walt attacked his dinner like a starving wolverine.

SEVEN YEARS AGO
30

Henry cast his eyes on the river's current as it riffled across a shallow gravel flat, bumping and leaping across the uneven surface below. At the tail end of the run lay a large granite boulder. At least three feet in diameter and jutting a foot or so above the water line, is was a friendly reminder of the last ice age that had scoured the northern lower peninsula, only to eventually retreat. Henry had taken a geology class at Wayne State last summer, but couldn't recall the official name for those big stray rocks that the glaciers had left behind. "Irregulars?" No, that wasn't it. He'd aced the course final, had known the correct word at that time, but like most things you picked up at school, if you didn't use it you'd lose it. He wasn't a geology major or anything, the course had just been an easy way to fulfill a mandatory science requirement. The answer would probably come to him in three or four days, when he was doing something completely unrelated. He knew that if he didn't remember the word, it would gnaw at him until he did.

The river split and embraced the big rock, swerving to either side, before permitting a small eddy to form in the dark depression immediately behind the stone. This is where the big brown trout should be, lurking, while the roiling waters brought a gusher of food on the currents both left and right.

Henry stood on the bank in his canvas waders and lit a cigarette. Downstream from the boulder, the river straightened itself once more and ran deep and true for about one hundred yards. After that it slowed again, a lazy snake meandering across the valley. He inhaled deeply and looked up to the mid-morning sun. Laura hated that he smoked, though he didn't smoke all that much. He'd usually have a few cigarettes if he was fishing or camping, both things occurring less often than he'd like. Not with a girlfriend that always had plans "as a couple." Hell, he was only twenty-three years old, he'd smoke if he wanted to smoke.

"You're still finding yourself," Laura had told him sometime during their last argument, which wasn't true at all. Henry knew exactly who he was. He'd known since sophomore year of high school, when he spent six weeks of his summer vacation hiking the Appalachian Trail on his own. He doubted very much that he was going to change a whole lot in the next fifty years. He certainly didn't need to "find himself."

What Laura meant, but didn't realize herself, was that Henry hadn't "evolved" into the type of Henry she wished he'd become. She'd thought the backpack trips, the fishing and hunting, were all part of some youthful phase that Henry would eventually outgrow. She was waiting for him to become the guy that wanted a starter home, a better car, more time on the couch cuddling and watching reruns of Friends on television. When she finally managed to put that into words, more or less, Henry realized that Laura herself was the 'youthful phase' that he needed to outgrow. And he didn't need one last fight. She wanted to hash it out. "I'm going fishing," he'd told her, and got into his Jeep. That had been three weeks ago, and he hadn't looked back even once.

He'd thrown together his sleeping bag, bivy tent, fly rod and waders, a few cans of food from the pantry and a small Coleman cooler, and hit the road. If he needed anything else, he could buy it along the way. He'd graduated last month, didn't need to be anywhere special until the cash ran out. And with more than ten grand in the bank and the lifestyle that he lived, ten thousand dollars could last a very long time, maybe more than a year. He'd spent the time since skipping around the state, fishing all the streams he loved and the ones he'd yet to explore. He started in the far western corner of the Upper Peninsula, zigzagging his way back to the northern Lower. Three days ago he'd crossed the Mackinaw Bridge southbound.

Yesterday he'd fished the upper reaches of the Black River, conceivably the best pure brook trout stream in the state. The Black had a spongy silt bottom. Tag elders lined both banks, forming a virtual tunnel over the narrow channel. The river was no more than ten feet across in spots. Wading was at times dicey. Some of the better holes were chest-deep. Some were even deeper. Though the trout were small, the experience was unbeatable. He'd even spotted a black bear, a small sow waddling not twenty feet away, oblivious to the solitary man standing quietly in the water. It didn't get any better than this.

This morning he was fishing the Sparrow. Henry inhaled the last breath of tobacco smoke, bending down and gently snuffing the cigarette out in the crisp water babbling at his feet, before placing the filter in one of the small pockets of his fly vest. Leave no trace behind, he thought. Your vices were your own, as long as you didn't impose them upon others.

He was once again studying the river. This was a place he'd fished hundreds of times before, one of his "go to" spots when he wanted to get away from the city and all that it entailed. The Sparrow was a lot wider than the Black, thirty feet across in spots, with a bottom that was more sand than silt. The deep spots didn't run as deep as the bigger holes on the Black. The wading was easier, the water a touch warmer. There were more brown trout than their colorful cousins the brookies, although there were a few of those, too, if you knew where to look. The Sparrow held rainbow trout, as well. You could catch just about anything in here. The Black had been fun, but it was also work. Hidden drops and a soft bottom could lure you in to places you shouldn't visit. The Sparrow was a river in which Henry could relax and lose himself completely, without most of the hazards found on her close cousin.

Henry concentrated on the spot directly behind the big boulder. There were no rings on the surface, no telltale signs that a big fish lie feeding in its shadow, but Henry knew it was there just the same. There was a big one there, *had* to be a big one there. The spot just looked "fishy." How to get at it, that was the question. Should he start upstream of the boulder, in the shallow rapids, letting a gold-ribbed hare's ear nymph bumble its way along the bottom? Or should he wade in beneath the point, and cast a dry fly just above the rock, letting his tippet swirl gently into the eddy? Ah, life is full of choices.

He looked at the assortment in his fly box. Some guys were all about the latest and greatest. "A fly for every occasion" seemed to be the motto of the day. He'd been fishing with his cousin Kenny and one of Kenny's friends not long ago, and this friend of Kenny's must have had a hundred different fly patterns in five or six sizes each. He had more fly boxes than he had pockets in which to put them, and spent most of that day searching for "the perfect match." Kenny's friend swore that he had that perfect match somewhere on his possession, but if he did, Henry and Kenny never saw it.

Henry went in the opposite direction: he kept merely a half dozen fly patterns that he knew how to fish well, and which he swore by, in three or four sizes each. Everything fit tidily in the aluminum and glass Wheatley box that his brother had given him on his sixteenth birthday. If it wasn't in the Wheatley, Henry didn't need it. And he'd out-fished Kenny's friend five-to-one that day.

He reached down into the current with his baseball cap and filled its crown with water. A dark brown bug had been drifting along, now struggling to stay afloat in the bowl of the sweat-stained Cubs cap. "A number eighteen Parachute Adams should work," he opined, returned the bug to the current, and placed the wet cap back on his head. He reached into his left front vest pocket to retrieve the appropriate fly. Henry casually snipped off the mosquito imitation that had been on his line, meticulously tied the tiny Adams to his wisp of leader, and put a dab of Gherke's Gink on the fly's hackle to help keep it afloat. He'd put in downstream and work his way back up to the boulder.

Henry climbed up the gently sloping bank, cutting through the waist high saw-grass that lined both sides of the river, careful that he didn't step on a beaver slide and twist an ankle. Fifty or so yards downstream, he parted the taller stream side vegetation and eased himself back into the cool flow of the Sparrow. Just as his foot found purchase on the sandy stream bed, the sky exploded in Henry's eyes, an epiphany of sparkles and fireworks and squiggly little bits of vitreous that floated through the back of his retinas like the times when he'd stared too hard directly into a bright light. It didn't make any sense, this blinding squall. But before Henry could figure out what was happening, he felt icy cold piercing the back of his skull, as if he himself were a fish being hooked. There was no time in which to think. What was happening? Then searing pain, hot and white, and he could no longer see the fireworks or the squiggly lines. Lastly he felt the sensation of cool water filling his lungs. He couldn't move. Maybe Laura was right, maybe he shouldn't fish so much. Maybe he should quit smoking. "Erratics," it finally came to him. The word he'd been looking for was "erratics."

SEVEN YEARS AND THREE HUNDRED YARDS AGO
31

It wasn't that far to go, really. But it was a hot day. Humid. The sun wasn't even high overhead, and already his shirt was wet and sticking to the small of his back and under his arms. Walking through the meadow by the river, it was for sure going to be a scorcher. Good growing weather, though, good for the crop. Another half mile, behind that tree line, and he'd be there. Ray hadn't marked the clearing, didn't wish to draw attention to what was growing there. But he visited often enough that he could find it in his sleep if he ever needed. He was starting to recognize a rudimentary foot path where he'd walked before, and he'd have to be careful about that. If he stayed closer to the river's bank, he could trace the trail that legions of fisherman had already carved, draw less attention to himself. There was no sense blazing a new path to the goods when an old path already existed nearby.

Growing the pot on State land was his dad's idea, and it was a good one. Less chance of getting caught, and even if you did get caught, you could always play dumb. "When in doubt, if anyone questions you, always pretend you can't hear well, act as if you're stupid," his dad had taught him. "It shouldn't be hard for you," the old man always added. The trick usually worked, too. People were only too willing to believe that you were stupid, if you allowed them. Dropped out of high school? You must be stupid. Can't find a good paying job? You must be stupid. Ran out of gas? Idiot. Ray understood how people thought. Sometimes you could work it to your advantage. He rehearsed it in his head, what he'd say if he ever ran into a Conservation Officer out here. "Pot? No, officer, I was just taking a hike in the woods. I've never seen pot. What's it look like? No idea who that plot belongs to." Ray could play dumb with the best of them.

"Never take the same path to your crop twice," that was another piece of sage advice his dad had bestowed upon him. Well how the hell was he supposed to follow that directive? There was a river in the way, for god's sake, which limited your approach options from one entire direction unless you were going to wade across like a Mexican crossing the Rio Grande or something. And there weren't that many pullouts and two tracks within a five mile hike of this area, not many places to park your car at all. So sooner or later you were bound to take the same path twice. Sometimes his dad could be so clueless. Stupid old man. Growing on State land idea, though, now that was a good one.

He'd been questioned by the cops a few times when he was younger, but it was generally over kids' stuff. Like every other teenager in town, he'd been caught with open containers of alcohol at the State Forest Campground. There were about a dozen kids that he knew from the high school who went there for bonfires and revelry. Well what teenage kid *didn't* have a few drinks on a Saturday night? It's not as if there was a mall or a cineplex or anything better to do in this shit town. It's what people did, at least people who were still young enough to have some kind of a life. When Ray and his friends did get busted, the cops would just pour their bottles out on the ground and send them all home. A few times they'd been caught with a joint or two. Again, "Dump it all out on the ground and head on home, boys." Kids' stuff. And when in doubt, play dumb. "Nope, I didn't know Andy smoked dope, officer. Never seen him do it before. I thought he was rolling his own cigarettes."

It turned out Ray had quickly gotten to know *every* kid that smoked dope, in his senior class and the next, and then the next class after that. He discovered that having a consistent supply was as good as gold around here, where you were a long ways from the competition one might encounter in a bigger city. Word of mouth would always prime his flow of customers. On a small scale, it was like having a license to print money, as long as word of mouth didn't come back to haunt you. As far as Ray knew, all of his customers to date had been loyal, or at least discreet. No one had ratted him out, and the cops had left him alone.

What Ray couldn't grow, his cousin from Saginaw supplied. A quick phone call and Randy would run him a load in the trunk of his Cutlass Cierra, charging an extra twenty bucks for the delivery. Ray could make the twenty dollars up in just a couple of sales. He wasn't exactly getting rich, but it was keeping him in gasoline, whiskey, cigarettes, and shot shell. This was his third year of growing a crop by the river, and it was a good one, twice as large as last year's batch. The soil around here was rich, and the river kept it moist. He never had to worry about drought. If this kept up, maybe he could branch out into coke or something that paid even more.

Ray suddenly stopped walking. Something was moving in the river, just around the next bend. Something big. A bear? A hiker? He crouched down, making himself small in the tall grass. He'd been walking silently, a habit he'd developed out of necessity. He was certain whatever it was up ahead of him hadn't heard him coming. Whatever or whomever it was, it/he was milling about slowly in the stream, waiting for something or someone. Maybe it was a bear looking for fish. He'd run into bear around here a few times before, and it was no big deal. Usually they were looking for berries, and if you stayed out of their way, they'd stay out of yours. You didn't want to surprise them, that was the main thing. Especially a mother with cubs. Either way, Ray didn't need to be noticed by a bear or anyone else, when he was this close to his stash.

He duck walked away, perpendicular to the stream, putting about thirty feet between him and the river's edge. There he turned parallel to the shoreline, creeping closer to where he'd pinpointed the noise. The sounds had stopped. Ray peeked his head up, just enough to see a lone fisherman standing in the shallows directly in front of him, smoking a cigarette. It wasn't a Conservation Officer, but this could be a problem nonetheless. Ray didn't need a witness putting him in this area somewhere down the line, should it ever come to that. One clown saying, "yes, officer, that's the man I saw. I remember the date exactly because I took the day off work to drive up north." Something like that could kill you if you ever ended up in a court of law. He'd just lie low until this guy moved along.

The fisherman was a younger guy, undoubtedly a college kid. He had that look of privilege about him, a look that pissed Ray off for no specific reason. The kid probably even smoked dope himself. Ray thought about calling out to him, waving hello and asking how the fishing was going. But he'd never seen the kid before, didn't need to take any chances being friendly with a stranger. He decided to wait him out, that was the smart thing to do. Hopefully the kid would continue fishing his way upstream, and Ray could be back on his merry way.

The guy stood there for what seemed like forever, though it couldn't have been more than five or ten minutes at the most. Ray's legs were starting to cramp from crouching down amongst the weeds, afraid to make a sound. He was sweating heavily now. Why wasn't this clown working or doing something productive instead of wasting time with his lah-di-dah fly gear in the middle of a fucking forest? By the time the fisherman eventually climbed the bank and started hiking downstream, Ray was seething with anger. "Who's got time for this shit?" he cursed under his breath. "Upstream, asshole, go *upstream*," he secretly urged. All the while, he continued to shadow the fisherman, creeping imperceptibly through the tall grass. "I really don't need this crap," he continued in a whisper. He was working himself into a lather.

Now the fisherman was getting back into the river, not fifty feet from where he'd just gotten out. Ray started to make a move, to slink back into the woods, when a stick snapped loudly beneath his left foot. There was no way the fisherman was going to miss that noise. A few minutes later Ray was standing over a lifeless body, wondering what his next move should be.

GOOD LOVE GONE BAD
32

"Now the question," Walt mused, "what to do." His belly was full, his options limitless. "Limitless" might be overstating things a bit, but Walt was a man free to do whatever he felt like doing, within reason. Drive on over to the Deer Track and spend the night drinking and dancing? Take the Bell canoe back over to Shambarger Lake and see if he could nail down a few largemouth bass? The world was his oyster. Maybe not oysters, that would be asking too much of the City of Rasmus. The world was his bullhead or some other bottom-feeding fish. That's about the best you could really hope for around here. It was probably best, he realized, to start his festivities off with a quick nap.

When he finally awoke, it was dark outside, and Walt was once again sprawled out on his living room couch. For a minute it occurred to him that he ought to stop sleeping in his living room, but on the other hand, who the hell cared? It's not as if he had someone special he was trying to impress. What time was it, anyway? Rubbing the crust from the corners of his eyes, he gazed into the kitchen and realized it was already past ten o'clock. Shit. So much for fishing on Shambarger Lake. Maybe the bar was a better choice after all. A little romance would do him some good.

Doofus was sitting by the doorwall, staring Walt down. The dog needed to go out. Why didn't that dog ever bark when he needed to go outside? He'd just sit by the window patiently, silently, as if he was daring Walt to read his canine mind. Walt made a mental note that his next dog needed to be a lot smarter, if there was even going to be a "next dog." What was the point in owning a dog that was too dumb to bark?

On the bedroom floor he located a relatively clean pair of jeans and a button-down, short sleeve shirt. He gave the shirt a quick sniff test, and deemed it acceptable. Good enough for where he was going, anyhow. It's not as if the Deer Track was suddenly going to start enforcing a dress code. A quick shave, let the dog back in, and he'd be out the door. Five minutes later he was on his way.

The place was hopping, at least by Deer Track standards. Walt spotted six cars, two Harleys, and a glorified power wheelchair in the parking lot. When he waltzed through the door, Walt immediately spied Mikey Babcock at a corner table, cuddled up with little miss "not-my-wife." They were engrossed in conversation, completely unaware of others around them. Walt watched the lovebirds for a few seconds. It didn't look like the talk was going too well for Mikey. You could read anger in the woman's posture, and she was doing most of the talking. Mikey was either ignoring most of what she had to say or he was shellshocked, it was hard to tell which. She was giving it to him pretty good. "God, how the mighty have fallen," Walt thought. "Bringing a woman to a shit hole like this."

Walt squeezed himself in at the bar between a scraggly old wood tick and a "lady," such that she was, who was probably in her fifties but had managed to drink and smoke her sagging face two decades beyond her age. He looked around for better company, but there weren't any more appealing options, and he did want to be close to the bar.

"Hey Pam, get me a Jack and Coke, would you?" when he finally caught her attention.

"Coming right up, Charming."

He turned his stool slightly, angling his body away from the wrinkled woman next to him. Walt was not going to encourage banter with that dried-up prune of a woman. Unfortunately, sitting in this new position this gave him a pretty good view of Wood Tick, and an even more powerful whiff of him. Jesus! This guy probably thought getting caught in a rainstorm was fair substitute for bi-weekly bath night. He smelled like wet dog and bad whiskey, and wet dog was winning the battle. Walt winced and took a big gulp of his own drink.

"So what brings you in on a big Saturday night, fella?" Pam had made her rounds and finally worked her way back to Walt, wiping the bar unconsciously as she chatted.

"I thought I'd come and see you."

"Well here I am. Don't take it all in at once, I might overwhelm you."

"I'm only mostly-whelmed. I can handle it," Walt chided back.

"Hold on a second, that table's calling." Pam nodded her head at a spot behind Walt, then slipped around the bar and over to one of the two-tops along the wall. A busy night like this, she could probably use another waitress. The problem was, busy nights at the Deer Track were so rare you couldn't predict them. Most of the time she ran the bar as a one-woman show, and most of the time that was more than adequate.

She was back behind the counter now, handing a Budweiser to a customer at the far end.

"Do me a favor and take this tray of drinks over to that table, would you Walt?"

Walt grunted, took the tray and delivered it to the two-top before returning to his stool. It went on like this for about half an hour before he decided he'd had enough. He hadn't come here to play waiter to a bunch of drunken losers. Pam was too busy to chat with him, and he was feeling both hurt and neglected.

"I've got to get going, Pam, can I swing by your place after you get off work?"

"I'm sorry, honey, that's not such a good idea. I've got to get up early in the morning."

"What, have you got a date?" It didn't take much for Walt to feel insulted, and he was all too willing to take offense.

'Jesus, Walt. Yeah, I've got a date. Guys come in here all the time, some of them millionaires, and they all ask me what I'm doing in the morning, would I like to go to Sunday service with them. They know I look my best in the wee hours of the morning, right after working a twelve hour shift. What do *you* think? You can be a total asshole at times, did you know that?"

A few of the other customers cocked their heads slightly, trying hard to listen in on the conversation without appearing to listen in on the conversation. Old Wood Tick wasn't even feigning at subtlety, leaning hard against the bar alongside Walt and grinning ear to ear. The Deer Track grew silent. Walt and Pam stared each other down, ignoring the rest of the room. All the while Pam wiped the bar purposefully with a towel, in circular slow-motion. They stayed like this for what seemed like forever, eyes locked. It might have been all of minute before she eventually flinched.

"Grow the hell up," Pam finally told him, before turning her back on him and walking to the far end of the bar. She started fiddling with the cash register, deliberately keeping her back turned to Walt. Conversations began to pick up where they'd left off, and it wasn't long before the room was once again alive with the low hum of idle chatter.

Walt stood up, threw a ten dollar bill on the slab surface, sucked down the last of his drink, and walked out the door. "Bitch," he cursed to no one in particular, as he got to the parking lot. "Like *I'm* the one that's got to grow up. Now what the hell am I supposed to do?" Whatever it was, it wasn't likely to be as much fun as his original plan of getting drunk and then going home to Pam. Sometimes women could be so self-centered.

THE OLD MAN AND THE C2
33

They were paddling hard, sweat pouring off their backs in the mid-day sun. Jim Rivard wasn't the best paddler on the river, but he wasn't half bad, either. Walt felt lucky to have him as a partner. Jim had raced the last five marathons with a more experienced partner, but that partner was fighting a serious bout of 'lateral epicondylitis.' 'Tennis elbow,' as it's more commonly called, though Walt had yet to meet anyone who'd gotten it from playing tennis. Either way, it made it damn near impossible to paddle a racing canoe with one arm, and thus Jim Rivard had been scrambling around looking for a new partner as of late June. He and Walt had been training together for almost three weeks now, five days a week, and Walt couldn't believe how much faster they'd gotten. He must be lucky, that's all there was to it.

Rivard and his old partner had finished 53rd, 42nd, 26th, 34th, and 27th in those last five marathons. Not stellar, but it sure beat the hell out of 78th or Did Not Finish. For the first time, Walt felt as if he had a fighting chance at finishing in the top twenty. Why not? He was as good as anybody else. He just needed a competent partner so that he could prove it.

It was now Wednesday, July 20th, and that meant they had less than two weeks until the Marathon. Were they ready? Probably as ready as they were ever going to be, which may or may not be enough. Walt wished he had three grand cash for a faster canoe, or that Jim owned a newer boat, but sometimes you just had to make do with what you had. The Wenonah was a great little craft for what it was, but the damn thing was over twenty years old. Fiberglass over wood construction, state of the art in its time, had since been replaced by new boats of carbon and Kevlar. It might not seem like much, but a few pounds here and a little better design there could make all the difference in the world over the course of eighteen hours on a river. The newer C2 racing canoes, well there was just no comparison. Someday Walt was going to have one to call his own.

"Hup," Jim shouted from the stern, and Walt quickly shifted his carbon bent-shaft paddle to the other side of the boat. "Hup," again, not eight strokes later, and he shifted back again. They were flying downstream, four hours in to a five hour practice run. Walt was "in the zone," as he liked to say, not thinking but doing. His motion came without effort, without thought, he was one with the river. He could think about anything, or nothing at all, his body knowing instinctively what to do at each turn. "Hup."

He had been right to put that shit with the dead body and the yoga camp to rest. That night at the Deer Track, when Pam had essentially told him to get lost, or at least it seemed like it to Walt, although in retrospect hadn't *he* really decided to call it off with *her*? In any event, that night when he left the bar, he decided to focus on the race and nothing but the race. He picked up a six pack and spent most of the night parked down by the old graveyard feeling sorry for himself, of course. But once the beer was gone, his life would be about the Marathon and nothing but the Marathon. He wasn't going to call Pam or set one foot in the Deer Track. She could read about him in the paper after the race was over.

And that next morning, when he woke up and drove into town to fill up the Samurai, who should he run in to at the Speedway other than Jim Rivard, looking for a new paddling partner. It was fate, that was all there was to it. This was going to be his year.

"Hup." They'd just come around a bend, and a small island shelter of logs and gravel faced them down in the middle of the stream. Walt over-corrected and had to pull back, slowing the boat and temporarily throwing off their rhythm. They shot past the island, but lost momentum in the process.

"Can't do that in the race, you know, it'll kill us." That was the first thing Jim had said to him other than "hup" in over an hour.

"I know. I just forgot the island was there. That's why we're training, right? Learning the river."

"Hup. Better learn it faster."

Asshole trout fishermen and their asshole stream improvement projects. That little island hadn't been there last year at this time. The island wasn't big, no more than three feet at its widest and eight foot total in length. But it was big enough to put a hole in your boat if you hit it in the dark of night. Trout groups loved to build these little structures along the river, "habitat" for trout. Rich pricks who acted as if they owned the river, and they pretty much all did. All the prime land on this stretch had been bought up by fifty-year-old assholes that liked to dress in their funny little clothes, wear funny little hats, buy overpriced crap from catalogue stores out east, and sit around smoking ten dollar cigars while bragging about a five inch catch on their three-hundred dollar rods. They called this "The Holy Waters," like it was part of their religion or something. Maybe those islets were their tiny temples, Walt snickered to himself. "All Praise the Holy Trout, now waive the illegal Cuban incense and baptize ye self with the single malt Scottish water!" Sure, Walt enjoyed his fishing once in a while, but *fly* fishermen were a bunch of petty snobs. What a waste of money, and here he was stuck chasing his dreams in a twenty year-old canoe. Well screw the fishermen, screw Pam, screw Dora and the whole lot of them.

"Hup. Pay attention," Rivard chastised.

Less than two weeks, and he'd be in The Club. A good finish in the race, and the whole town would have a different view of Walt Pitowski. He knew it wasn't like he was about to win Olympic Gold or anything, but how could they not respect, him once he proved he was one of the forty or so best paddlers in the world? And so what if it was a relatively small universe of paddlers? They'd have to respect him. What had anyone else in Rasmus ever done, anyhow? Could he and Rivard finish twentieth this year? Yeah, they could crack the top twenty.

"Hup." Only this time it hadn't come from Jim. Another craft was coming alongside, attempting to pass them. Walt stepped up his pace. Man, he hated being passed, even on a practice run. He took a quick look over his shoulder, and damned if it wasn't The Old Man. The Old Man was a living legend, had been running the marathon since the beginning of time, and was still racing well into his eighties. It didn't hurt that The Old Man pretty well had his pick of young and spirited partners. He wasn't winning races anymore, sure as hell wasn't doing it all by himself, but he still finished in the top half of the standings, even at this advanced age. He was a machine, that's what he was. Shit. The Old Man and Billy Burke just blew by them like they were standing still. He looked back again and Jim was giving Walt a dirty look from the stern. The Old Man and Burke were well ahead of them, already rounding the next bend.

"We'll get'em next time," Walt said mildly.

“Next time is coming pretty soon,” Rivard answered. “Hup.”

Forty minutes later they pulled their craft out on a small sandy chute beneath Deeter Bridge. They dragged it up the bank’s incline and began loading it on the ladder rack atop Rivard’s truck.

“Good run.” Walt was trying to pump a little enthusiasm into this tenuous marriage.

“Not good enough. We’re doing fair, but we need to cut down on the mental errors. It’s those little slips that will cost you in the end,” answered Rivard. He was a deliberate man, rarely doing or saying anything without a well thought-out point and purpose.

Walt had to admit that his partner was right, but that was assuming that they would *get* to the end. Technical slips would cost you time and position in any race. He also knew that mental toughness, that willingness to keep going even when your muscles were way past their breaking point, when it was dark and cold and you were shivering from exhaustion and the finish line was still eight hours away, *that* mental toughness was what really decided if and where you finished the Marathon. This new partner Rivard had been to the finish line before, multiple times. He wasn’t worried about Rivard. Walt *thought* he could get himself there, but then, he hadn’t actually done it yet, had he? Walt would always have a seed of doubt about his own abilities until he’d actually finished the race at least once.

“Back to town?” asked Walt.

“Back to town.”

The pair didn’t say another word until they were back alongside Walt’s Suzuki in the livery parking lot.

“Tomorrow night, six o’clock?” Walt wanted to make sure they were both on the same page.

“Tomorrow’s good. Then we pare it back for the week leading up to the race. Muscles need to rest, or you’ll never make it next weekend. Take this weekend off, then we’ll take a leisurely run down river on Monday and then again on Wednesday. Time trials for starting position begin Thursday night.

We've got to be there early Saturday for weighing and measuring the boat. The race is Saturday, nine p.m. sharp. Intros are earlier, I don't know what time yet. Get lots of rest and eat like a wolf, you're going to drop twelve pounds of body weight by Sunday noon."

"I know. I took a week's vacation so I can have time to relax and rest up." Walt loved the week leading up to the actual Marathon, that festival atmosphere, from the youth races to the plywood boats that local businesses slapped together for their competitive sprint on the mill pond. All of a sudden, the town where nothing happened spawned elephant ears, corn dogs, freshly squeezed lemonade and hot popped kettle corn, free sidewalk concerts, the car show and an arts and craft fair. It was the one time all year that Rasmus flooded with visitors. The little town of fifteen hundred people or so would swell to thirty thousand by week's end, and just as suddenly, would shrink back to its normal size by early Sunday morning. Walt beamed with pride for all the community spirit and enthusiasm, the volunteers and the organizers, the people who put on the Kid's Fair and the parade and everything else. And he knew that he and the other paddlers were at the core of it all.

TIME KEEPS ON DRAGGING
34

Thursday might have been the longest day of the week. Sure, it contained the same number of hours as every other day, but these hours were particularly grueling. For one thing, there was no field work to be done, so Walt was trapped inside the office all day. It was unusually hot outside, the temperature reaching ninety-three by mid-afternoon, something that didn't often occur in these parts. And yes, most people would be ecstatic to spend this day in the comfort of a well padded swivel chair and an air-conditioned office. But Walt resented the tedium of inputting data for hours on end, checking and rechecking numbers until his eyes itched and burned, all the while his co-workers quietly going about their own monotonous day and not once asking him about the Marathon. It was very hard to stare at a screen full of numbers when his mind was on the water, visualizing each turn of the river as it would come to him during the race.

By lunch time he couldn't take it anymore. He'd probably gotten up from his desk a half dozen times already this morning, walking the length of the hall to the break room on the pretense of needing a cup of coffee or a glass of water. He'd passed Tom Dewers twice in the hallway, both times saying "hello," and that bastard barely nodded his head in response before returning to his own desk. "Well screw him," thought Walt. "Once an asshole, always an asshole." It was noon, and the hell if he was going to eat his lunch sitting in this morgue with these clowns. So he slipped out to the Astro van, rolled down the front windows, and turned the key in the ignition so that he could catch the last twenty minutes of Right Radio AM. He stretched his body out across the vinyl bench seat, absorbing its radiant heat, and set to work on two bologna sandwiches, an apple, two bananas, and a bag of carrot sticks.

Marcus Washington walked out of the building and to his car, not taking notice of Walt, either. It must be nice to have money enough to eat out every day, Walt mused, as he watched from the front seat of the van. A few minutes later Bill Fourshe stepped from the side door and headed to his Conservation Department truck, more than likely out for an afternoon of looking for people fishing where they shouldn't be fishing. Walt finished his lunch in silence, slipped lower on the van's seat so that his head was resting against the arm rest, and enjoyed the monologue coming from the radio speakers. Right Radio was on a quest to stomp out "big government," a cause with which Walt whole heartedly agreed. Big Government was one of Walt's pet peeves, and the cause of the day, every day, on Right Radio. "Too much tax money coming out of my paycheck," Walt echoed the speaker.

By one p.m. he was back at his desk, anxious for the work day to end. By three he had been to the bathroom twice more and the break room three additional times, and still the clock seemed to be moving in slow motion. Walt nearly skipped out the door when five o'clock finally arrived. He had just enough time to gas up the Samurai, race home and change into his paddling clothes, and grab a few apples for a dinner time snack. By six he was on the water with his new found partner, working up a serious sweat. They made the same run as they had the night prior, and shaved twelve minutes off their previous best time. Things were looking up.

FRIDAY ON MY MIND
35

One more day of work, one more lousy day of work, and then ten contiguous days off in which to be the paddler Walt knew he could be. Fortunately, today he was out working in the field, collecting data on the Jordan River and some of the other streams in the northwest corner of the state. Usually that area fell under Dewer's responsibility, but that dipshit had called in sick today. He was probably off on a three-day weekend with his college buddies in Vegas, or somewhere equally expensive. Dewer's didn't *get* sick, Walt knew that, although the man somehow managed to use all of his allotted sick days before the end of every year. He was undoubtedly off having fun somewhere, dumping his work in Walt's lap. He probably did it on purpose, jealous of Walt's upcoming weeklong vacation. Either way, Walt was happy to be cruising the winding county roads that ran through the Jordan River valley. He was even driving one of the "good" trucks for a change. Walt wasn't about to let Dewers or anyone else screw up his Friday.

The day flew by, and other than the fact that the sky was cloudless, which Walt saw as a major negative because the river was awfully low and badly in need of some rain before next weekend's race, was about as good as a day could get. He even wrapped everything up early on the Jordan, dropped the keys to the truck at the office by 4:20, and was told by Washington to knock off work and enjoy his vacation. Marcus wished him luck in the Marathon, surprising Walt. "That Marcus can be a good guy sometimes," Walt muttered on his way out the door.

With no paddling planned for tonight, Walt had to figure out what to do with himself. Downtown was already starting to hum with a steady influx of visitors. It wasn't really "busy," like it would be in another week, but there were certainly more people on the sidewalks, a few out-of-state license plates parked in front of the Rasmus Restaurant that normally wouldn't have been there, and a palpable electricity in the evening's atmosphere. The air was crackling with mid-summer heat. The bells of St. Michaels Church chimed five o'clock, and the sign on the bank across the street still read ninety-one degrees fahrenheit. Rare heat for these parts. When the mercury hit thirty below in the winter, that wasn't all that uncommon. But anything much over seventy in the summer was considered a hot spell for Rasmus.

Walt cruised Michigan Avenue slowly, watching people congregate in front of vacant stores, their windows freshly dressed to give the illusion of a viable business district. In some case they almost pulled it off. One could forget that the thrilling window display of marathon memorabilia and outdoors bravado, straight from the hand-drawn cover of a 1955 Field and Stream Magazine, was still the old five-and-dime that had been sitting vacant for over six years. Some hung paper backdrops inside to disguise empty space, or soaped their windows and scrawled messages of encouragement to their favorite teams. Most of the remaining merchants were locking up for the night, heading to cars parked in the asphalt lot around the block, or to the diner in search of a solitary meal. Once in a while a pedestrian would trot over to the bank, slipping into the vestibule to use the twenty-four hour ATM, and get enough cash for one more evening's revelry. All in all, it was a perfect picture of a small town going about its daily life, only with more gusto than usual.

Walt stopped off at the Dairy Queen and stood in a line fourteen deep, waiting to order from the teenage girl behind the sliding window. When he finally reached the front of the line, he ordered a small chocolate swirl in a waffle cone, and took a seat on one of the iron benches that were placed alongside the brick front of the four-store strip mall. The Chinese place next door wasn't looking particularly busy. Apparently it was either to early or too hot outside for people to be thinking about dinner. The specialty store on the other side of DQ had closed up a few years back, waiting for a new owner or a new use for the space. A sign on the front said "sold," a rare event in this market. He wondered who had been ambitious or foolish enough to buy the building, in a county full of failed businesses. Walt hoped to hell it wasn't going to be another dollar store. The town had four already, and how many frickin' dollar stores did a town truly need?

The line for the Dairy Queen was still growing, now more than twenty deep, and Walt was glad he'd gotten here when he had. He licked his cone slowly, just enough to keep it from melting all over his hands. This was a good place for people watching. He spotted more than a few faces that he knew, even a couple of folks that he could say he liked, not that they were particularly close or anything. Good folks, though, like the lady that ran the Seven Eleven, and that friendly girl that bagged groceries at the IGA. A lot of faces he didn't recognize, cabin owners that rarely spent time in town except when they needed something, or out-of-town racers and their families here early in order to get the lay of the land and the lay of the river. They might not know it as yet, but they were here, each and every one of them, to see Walt and Jim Rivard in the most important of all canoe races. Of this Walt was certain.

THE SEVEN DAY ITCH
36

He'd been a good boy scout. He'd stopped off at the Red Eye and eaten a porterhouse steak, a big one, blood rare and well over a pound. That came with a baked potato, smothered in butter, real butter, not that fake oleo crap, and lots of sour cream, french cut green beans, and a big piece of pecan pie with whipped cream on top for dessert. That should keep his energy up. He'd washed it all down with two beers and a cup of coffee, and gotten himself to bed by nine that night. Well not the bed, exactly, but gotten himself to the couch. Close enough. He'd watched a little t.v., and still managed to doze off before ten.

Saturday morning he got up at six and took Doofus for a four mile run through the woods. That got his heart pumping. He trotted back to the house, showered quickly, and then drove into town to the Jack Pine Diner and ordered the Lumberjack Breakfast. It wasn't the best food in the world, but it was cheap, and there was lots of it. Three eggs any way you wanted them, a short stack of pancakes, four strips of bacon or four sausage links, whichever you prefer, and hash brown potatoes with toast. And coffee, a bottomless cup of coffee. Walt also tacked on a side order of corned beef hash, just to keep his protein load going, and made sure he ate every lick of it.

By the time that he finished breakfast it was eight thirty in the morning, and Walt was already getting antsy. The Red Eye Challenge canoe race started at nine that morning, but he and Rivard had decided not to compete. A lot of paddlers treated The Challenge as a tune-up before the actual marathon, a short two-hour race against some of the same competition they'd be facing the following weekend. The Challenge only encompassed the uppermost stretch of the river. Jim had advised that they skip this race altogether. It was the stretch of river with which the two men were most familiar, so there wasn't a lot to be learned by revisiting it one more time. The other guys from out of state, some of whom had never even seen this river, well it might do them some good. And then there were the very top paddlers, that handful of elite teams that were like gunslingers with their fingers on their triggers. Those teams were practically dying to see how they stacked up against one another, because, more often than not, whoever led the marathon after the first two hours of paddling was going to be leading the marathon at the very end. Jim was wise enough to know that they weren't living in that stratosphere, either.

For Jim and Walt, the Red Eye Challenge was merely one more opportunity to strain a muscle while showing off, or one last chance to poke a hole in the side of a canoe they couldn't afford to replace. Walt was going to avoid the Red Eye Challenge like the plague. He didn't sneak so much as a glimpse when he drove past the starting line, making his way back home. He went into the house, let Doofus go bounding out the doorwall, and found his spot on the couch for a healthy two-hour nap. When he awoke later that morning, Doofus was resting quietly on the floor next to the couch.

"Good boy, Doofus. Who's a good boy?"

The dog lifted his head long enough to look up at his master, then closed his eyes and went back to sleep. He wasn't falling for it.

"Lazy-assed dog," Walt cursed, as he got up from the couch and headed into the kitchen. He poured himself a cup of cold coffee, placed it in the microwave and set the timer for two minutes. He liked his coffee hot, as hot as possible. Damn near boiling hot. Sometimes he superheated it, and when he'd take his cup from the microwave oven and jiggle it, just enough to break that surface tension on the liquid, a scalding volcano of coffee would shoot straight out of the cup. Once he'd even given himself a burn on his arm through this stupidity. But not today. Today it was just a *really hot* cup of coffee that Walt pulled out of the microwave.

The clock said it was almost eleven. What to do with the rest of this day? The Red Eye Challenge would be just winding down, with a trophy presentation downtown and then paddlers heading back to wherever they were heading to rest or to eat. Town would be crowded for maybe another half hour or so, and then it would be just another slightly-busier-than-normal day in an otherwise staid burg. What the hell was he going to do to keep himself occupied for the next week? Walt hadn't anticipated this problem.

He turned on the television. Apparently the old movie station had run out of every movie ever made by Burt Lancaster and had now moved on to the complete works of Charles Bronson. A short message informed Walt that today's features would include "The Magnificent Seven" and "Mr. Majestyk," then cut to commercials. After a thirty-second ad for the perfect brassiere, followed by a two minute testimonial from some old guy that was about to be permanently placed in a nursing home, but avoided that horrible fate by purchasing a power wheelchair "that even comes with its own cup holder!" the station returned to its current offering from Mr. Charles Buchinsky, a.k.a. Bronson, "The Mechanic." A good film, thought Walt. He'd always been drawn to the vigilante mystique, that lone wolf, outsider tough-guy persona. For a while Bronson seemed to get all of those roles, as if he were a later-day Edward G. Robinson.

In "The Mechanic" Bronson plays an older hit man, and Jan-Michael Vincent a younger becoming his protege. The movie had already started, and some sexy young girl was trying to kill herself, had swallowed a bunch of pills and then slit her wrists. Bronson and Vincent were watching her, chatting with her, but not intervening. The girl was making a cry for help. She was trying to talk Jan-Michael into saving her from herself, proving his love for her, or maybe just testing his humanity. The whole point seemed a little cloudy to Walt. In any event, she wasn't having her desired effect on him.

Women were like that, always fabricating tests to see if you could jump high enough for their liking. Dora sure as hell was like that. Everything was a test with her, in the end. Maybe not in the beginning, but certainly in the end. And Pam, well who knew what she wanted from him. Walt still hadn't figured that out. Walt had seen this movie before, knew the outcome, but still found himself rooting for the sexy girl to die. Jan-Michael Vincent doesn't care what this girl has to say, he's to cool to care. Eventually Jan-Michael flips her the car keys and tells her that if she drives fast enough, she can still get help.

"That was cold," Bronson's character says, as the two men walk out together.

"I knew she wouldn't do it," answers Vincent.

"But, had she done that, would you be willing to pick up the tab?" asks Bronson.

"Fuck yeah," answered Walt Pitowski, as he switched off the television set.

IT ALL COMES OUT IN THE WASH
37

Ray knew what had to be done. The marathon was coming up, next weekend to be precise. And usually, well, who the hell cared? That was twenty some miles away, and Ray didn't give a rat's ass how many tourists and weekenders and assorted other clowns poured into the hick town of Rasmus. In fact, the influx of strangers probably increased the chances that Ray could score a little action off some drunken girl for one weekend each and every year. And his regulars, well the Marathon was nothing but one big party, right? So he'd probably sell more pot, as well. Maybe his buyers would have company in from out of town, share with their friends, and pick up an extra ounce or two. On any other year, Ray would welcome marathon weekend as a boon to both his sex life and his cash flow.

The Sparrow Lotus Camp would be overflowing with people, that was a given during the warmer seasons. Summer was always busy for them, but this week they'd be packed to capacity. The campgrounds around the Bitch River were going to be full all week, too, which made it too risky to check on his crops, but then, the crops hadn't been discovered yet in all the years he'd been growing dope near the river, so this year shouldn't be any different. So none of it, really, was that much of a problem.

Nope, the problem was a hip bone that had washed up by the foot bridge this past spring, and that jerkweed from the government that had found it and brought all kinds of attention to the area. The cops had combed the banks of the river and come up with parts of the skeleton, but not *all* of it. *That* was the problem. Because if *one* bone had washed up from where he'd buried it seven years before, well how long was it likely to be before *the rest* of that dead asshole college kid's bones showed up? Or worse, how long before somebody stumbled across the original grave, and went all CSI on it like they do in the movies? It was possible that the bones not yet found would point a finger in Ray's direction. Or maybe Ray dripped some sweat into the hole while digging that grave, and the state cops would figure out it was him that put the kid there in the first place. Then the shit will really hit the fan.

Ray knew what had to be done. He needed to find the rest of the remains and relocate them to someplace where they'd never be found, someplace that couldn't lead authorities to him or to his cash crops. Hell, he'd be better off if his cousin Randy put all the bones in a bag and dropped them on the steps of the Saginaw County Courthouse. Try and tie that to the Sparrow River, Mr. Policeman. Well, maybe not that, because, as his dad always said, "that Randy could screw up a two car funeral procession." He didn't think Randy was all *that* bad. In some ways he even admired his cousin from the big city. But for once his dad's warnings were right. When you had a major problem, it was better not to bring anyone else in to the equation, not even family. He had to solve this one on his own.

Unfortunately, in order to get rid of the grave, Ray had to *find* the damn thing. He hadn't heard about that first bone washing up until a couple of weeks after the fact, and by that time the cops were pretty much done sweeping the area for evidence. Ray lay low a while longer, wanting to make sure the police were done doing whatever it was they were going to do. Then, once he thought it was safe to return to the Bitch, he figured he'd dig up whatever was left of the dead man and move him. Somewhere. He combed the river banks over and over for weeks on end, trying to locate the exact place where things had first gone awry.

But the river looked different after seven years, twenty-eight season's worth of wind and rain, snow and erosion, growth and decay. He hadn't marked the spot where he'd buried that fisherman, because, well why *would* he? The last thing he wanted to do was call attention to that damn place. Besides the fact that it might implicate him in the kid's death, the grave was on private property. Private Sparrow Lotus property, to be exact. It was on the opposite side of the river from the yoga camp itself, but still, it was on their land. He remembered the place as being only about twenty-five or fifty yards upstream from the dam, and ten yards or so back from the water's edge. Or where the water's edge *used* to be, anyhow. A river's bank isn't a constant.

It was a miracle that the shallow grave hadn't been discovered when he'd first turned the soil with a spade. Now, when he *wanted* to find the spot, he couldn't locate so much as a lump in the ground. It had to have settled and compacted over time. Eventually, the river must have eroded the soil out from underneath her banks, washing bits and pieces into the stream. "Good luck figuring out where it is now," thought Ray. He continued to pace around the living room of his single-wide trailer, the radio droning away in the background. A heavy-metal station out of Alpena was playing all of his favorite songs.

There was that one time, he was not really looking for the grave as much as checking on the crop, that he'd stumbled across the government man, that guy with the Mineral Department or whatever it was. Ray hadn't realized at the time that the man worked for the State, or he would have handled things differently. He probably shouldn't have threatened the guy, run him off at gunpoint, but then, what reason could Ray have given for being out there with a shotgun? And there wasn't a reason, not a good one. He'd brought it on impulse, worried he might find kids pilfering his dope. He'd taken one shot at a crow, just to feel the gun kick. And then, next thing he knew, the government man was standing in front of him. It was a complication, and he'd reacted.

Ray thought hard about the current situation. That dead fisherman's clothes and gear were in that hole, the hole he'd been unable to locate. The kid's wallet, too, less the two-hundred and fifty two bucks it had contained when the fisherman first set foot in the water. The police hadn't reported finding any of that. Yet. Maybe they had found it and they were holding back information. Maybe that stuff hadn't washed out from under the bank. If that was the case, Ray wanted to beat them to the punch. Ray knew what had to be done. Tonight he had to find that damn hole, that idiot's grave. Later tonight, definitely before the day was up. He was running out of time. Sooner or later this was going to come back and bite him on the ass if he didn't take things into his own hands.

He went to the kitchen, opened another Natural Light, returned to the living room, and sat back in the recliner. He closed his eyes as he took a sip of the cold brew, listening to the music. He'd fix everything tonight.

A WALK IN THE WOODS
38

"What the hell do you mean, you're working?"

"What the hell do you think I mean, Walt?" she was trying to contain her anger, making every effort to remain calm and reasonable. Pam silently reminded herself that she was dealing with an emotional child here. "It's Saturday night." She thought that would be explanation enough, a self-standing truth that entailed all the reasons in the world why she wasn't willing to call in sick, but apparently it wasn't.

"Can't you take the night off, for God's sake?"

"Absolutely. I'll call in as soon as you hang up. You'll make my rent payment for me by the first of next week, right?"

Walt paused. She must be kidding, right? Shit, it was hard to tell. She sounded like she might be kidding, but he was no good at this sort of thing. Too bad there wasn't some voice-activated, electronic meter that could detect sarcasm. He had to say *something*, or she'd think he'd gone mute. "So you will take the night off?" he asked hesitantly.

"No, you asshole. I will not take tonight off. It's the Saturday before the canoe marathon, one of our busiest nights of the year. You think I'm going to drop everything, screw up my job because you decided to call me out of the blue after I don't know how many weeks of avoiding this place? Do you remember how we left things last time you were here? And now you're a little lonely, and I'm supposed to blow up my life on your account? I'd say you're dumber than I thought, but I'm not sure that's even possible."

"So.... no then?"

"Goodbye, Walt."

"Goodbye as in, I'll talk to you later?"

"Just goodbye, Walt."

There was a definitive click on the other end of the line, then silence. Walt held the phone to his ear for a good ten seconds more before hanging it up. Finally, a little dumbfounded, he placed the phone back on its cradle. "Well," he mumbled, "I guess I'll just have to find something else to do."

Rasmus was busy, and Walt had had enough of this town for a while. What he really needed, more than anything, was to clear his head. It was a spur of the moment decision when he jerked the Suzuki hard left onto the freeway ramp and stomped on the accelerator. He was heading north, planning to take a walk through the woods and get away from it all. It wasn't long before he found himself meandering along Wolverine Valley Road, pointed back to familiar territory.

"What the heck," he pondered, "it can't hurt anything to take a little stroll along the Sparrow. Maybe I'll even see some deer." He hadn't given much thought to deer season yet, still four months away. But he could still taste that adrenaline rush that had come with killing his first buck, a warm ember from that frosty day last winter, and he thought now about what it would feel like to duplicate the experience. He'd been lucky last year, killing that buck, but you couldn't always rely on luck. The guys who got a buck year in and year out knew the value of advanced scouting, and this was as good an opportunity as any for Walt to check out some spots.

It was late afternoon, but he'd have good daylight for another three hours or more. That would be plenty of time to stretch both his legs and his thoughts. He parked where he usually parked at the head of the trail, and walked the narrow footpath back to the bridge. Grasshoppers were leaping out of Walt's way in every direction, a perpetual wave of motion in advance of the man hiking through tall grass. The hoppers must provide a bonanza for the trout, a never ending feast of protein hitting the river's surface as they leapt to their deaths.

The Sparrow River, turgid in April, significantly quieter in early July, was now absolutely bucolic. "Let it flow, let yourself go, slow and low, that is the tempo..." Walt sang under his breath. Who did that song, he wondered, the Beastie Boys? He stopped at the middle of the bridge and watched the water drifting almost imperceptibly toward him. Walt was amazed that any fish would choose to live in this warm, lazy water. Maybe fish didn't live here after all, he considered. Maybe they were all hiding in the quicker riffles and runs elsewhere, or had moved upstream or downstream towards deeper waters. He looked down upon the water's surface, shielding his eyes with a hand to his forehead to reduce the glare of the sun, and saw a few minnows darting amidst the weeds. "Well, something's still sticking around here." Maybe the fish didn't really *choose* to be here, maybe this was just where they currently *resided.* They might not have a choice in the matter.

He crossed over the bridge to the far bank and began walking upstream, no real purpose in mind. If he could locate those deeper stretches, he could learn where the trout were hiding and cooling themselves. Maybe he could come back and fish for them some hot night, once the canoe marathon was over and done with. Maybe the fish were all hiding in the depths of the yoga club pond, up above the dam. Walt continued walking, his compact stride pushing him at a healthy clip. There were a lot of maybes to contemplate in life.

Eventually Walt came to the dam, stopping to watch the water playfully leaping over the topmost wooden board. With the river this low, the spurts and squirts that managed to make it over the dam became living things, little translucent snakes playing a game of hopscotch with one another. He knew he was trespassing on Sparrow Lotus land, but he wasn't overly concerned. There was no one else around, not a soul to greet the sun or face the downward dog or whatever it was these people did with their time. They were probably busy grilling tofu burgers for dinner, or burning patchouli in their guest rooms in order to hide the smell of whatever else they were burning in their guest rooms. Walt had a hard time understanding what motivated people, people who seemed so different from himself. "Life was simpler in Providence," he thought. "Or perhaps those were just simpler times."

Simpler times included Dora, at least for a significant portion of his life. He didn't think of Dora often. Not anymore, not like when she'd first left. Back then, everything reminded him of Dora. Their home, the smell of the lawn, the sky, the birds in the air. Everything reminded him of the ex that he loved to this day, and of the things they'd shared together. Eventually the reminders had become too much, constantly drawing him to the past, and so he stopped. Stopped thinking about her, stopped doing things that might remind him of her. Stopped cleaning the house, mowing the lawn, or looking at the sky. But when Walt was alone, with no "next thing" to rush off to and no one to distract him, he had to admit that he still missed her. The quiet of this place brought that flood of longing back. He missed having the sense of belonging, the sense of purpose that Dora had once given him. He needed to let it go.

The marathon? Now that was something to strive towards. That represented forward motion, not past nostalgia. And it was only one week away. Once he'd finished the marathon, then what? Pam? Walt wasn't really sure what he desired from Pam. Sex, sure. Companionship, absolutely. Free whiskey at the Deer Track was an unexpected bonus. Did he want an actual relationship? Probably not. It would only complicate his life. He would grow to resent that he couldn't do what he wanted, whenever he wanted, without explanation or excuse. Relationships only tied you down.

It was easier for Walt to know what he *didn't* want from Pam, and what he didn't want was rejection. Pam might be correct that they wouldn't work as a couple, but Walt badly needed to be the one that first arrived at that conclusion. She had no right to leave *him*. Could she really do any better than Walt? He was younger than her, physically fit, good looking. He had a job. Sure, he was broke, but he had a *good job*. And a house. He owned his own house, for cripe's sake. He was *educated*. It should be *his* decision to leave *her*, or to *not* leave her, if he so chose. Either way, it should be *his* call. She had no right to cast him aside.

Walt tamped the conflicting feelings deep down inside. "When feelings begin to overwhelm you, you stuff them where they're less likely to leave you lost, lonely, or vulnerable," he rationalized. "Quit thinking about the past," he chastised himself. "Be a man." He needed to move once again towards something *else*. *Anything* else, different from the life that he was currently leading. He needed to focus on the marathon. The marathon was *real*, the marathon was *tangible*, it *meant* something. Walt turned and continued walking up river.

The buildings of Sparrow Lotus LLC were not quite in sight, but he knew that they lie not far beyond the tree line on the far side of the river. A few voices drifted his way, carrying across the river valley and sounding much closer than they actually were. He tried to make out what the voices were saying, but they were only noises floating in the wind.

He continued marching on, well past the big pond and the property lines of the yoga camp, to where the river once again funneled down to a width of no more than thirty yards across. He pushed further, and the open meadows gave way to thicker woods. There were stands of second and third-growth cedar and alder, framed by long stretches of plantation pine. The forest grew denser, and he had to fight his way through scrub brush in order to forge the trail ahead.

It was after eight when Walt finally stopped walking, some ten or twelve miles from where he'd first started. The woods were thick here, the shadows growing long. Black flies swarmed his head, and he regretted not bringing bug repellant. The hour seemed much later than it was. The trees, growing tight together, stole what little light infiltrated from the rapidly sinking sun. Walt looked at his watch and realized that he had no chance of making it back to the Samurai before the onset of darkness. He also realized, for the first time that day, that he'd forgotten to call his paddling partner this morning as he'd promised. His cell phone was back at the trail's head, sitting in the cup holder of the Samurai. He took a deep breath, adjusted his baseball cap, and turned in the direction from which he'd come. He'd just have to hurry.

DIGGING FOR CHINA
39

"Give me a break," was all he could get out. Ray had been digging this particular hole for over twenty minutes, was certain this was the spot. It was about two feet in diameter and was now almost four feet deep. Sweat matted his hair and trickled down his forehead, stinging his eyes. Ray wiped his brow with his dirty sleeve, which merely managed to create a streak of mud across his dirty visage. He had traipsed all over this stretch of the shoreline, back and forth, searching and pacing like a dog on the scent of a fresh pheasant. Everything *did* look different, but he had finally decided that this was the spot. It *had* to be. The trees were bigger than they'd been seven years ago, there were shrubs where once there were none, but this *had* to be the place. Seven years wasn't a lifetime, after all.

He paced off the yardage upstream from the dam, and yeah, he was relying on memory, memory that might be slightly impaired from seven years of hard drinking and partying, but still, if this wasn't the spot, it was damn close to being the spot. Within a few feet, anyway. He'd started to dig. He knew they couldn't be more than three feet down, the remains of that long-dead kid, and he started to dig, but didn't find a single thing. No clothes, no bones, no fishing rod or creel, no nothing. He dug a little deeper, and still nothing. So then he moved over a few feet, started carving out a new hole, kind of a "test well," as he thought of it. Again he found nothing. He'd been out here a few hours already and was now working on his twelfth hole, having created a rectangular grid composed of thigh-deep cavities, a few feet apart and encompassing a total area ten yards by twelve yards, just a stone's throw from the banks of the Sparrow River. "What the hell," he sighed again. He was tired. He was pissed off, angry at this whole stupid situation. Sand and soil covered his jeans, infiltrated every pore of his arms, his neck, his ankles. He smelled bad, even to himself, even by his standards. He was hot, frustrated, and no closer to accomplishing what he'd set out to accomplish.

He'd been sure this was the spot. And just a few minutes ago, the shovel had finally hit something solid, and he'd thought to himself "Pay dirt!" Instead, it turned out to be one more damn field stone, two and a half feet beneath the surface. It was beginning to get dark, which alone was nothing to worry Ray. He'd spent plenty of time in the woods alone after dark. But if he couldn't find the grave in the light of day, how in the hell was he going to find it in darkness? The area looked as if an alien spacecraft had landed and decided to take a set of soil core samples back to the mother planet. That, or some lunatic had brought a post hole digger out to the middle of nowhere and gone at it like a giant, drunken woodpecker. If this wasn't going to draw some unwanted attention to the shore bank, he didn't know what would. He'd have to refill all the holes, but any moron would still be able to tell that the soil had been freshly turned. And how long before someone began to wonder why? How long before someone from that camp across the river began to poke around, out for a meditative stroll, and wondered what else was out of place? He had an acre of top notch dope growing not a quarter mile away, dope that was in no way ready to be harvested for at least another month.

Ray was deeply regretting having not thought this day through, regretting not considering the potential downside to what he was doing a little more carefully, *before* he'd started digging holes. "Fuck this," he cursed as he leaned on the garden spade. He felt like crying, but knew it wouldn't do him any good. He should have brought his cousin Randy along. Randy might not be the brightest guy, but at least he'd have provided another set of hands. He rested his forehead against the wooden handle of the shovel and closed his eyes. "How could this day get any more screwed?" His answer was just around the next bend.

THE CHEETAH STRETCHES
40

"Remind me why I'm here again." Matt Amberson was not in a cheerful mood. He hadn't been for some time, when you got right down to it. The county budget was tight and getting tighter, and things seemed to have only gone downhill during his time with the sheriff's department. The Crown Vic Interceptor he was driving, for instance, had 183000 miles on it, and needed a new set of tires, amongst other things. The vehicle's starter was going, and didn't always catch on the first try. The back seat smelled as if one too many drunks had lost their lunch on the floor, and there was no way that the odor was ever going to dissipate. The suspension was getting a little soft, and she burned way too much oil. That was fine for a car you might take to the hardware store every few days, but not up to snuff if it was your rolling office for ten hour shifts, four days per week. Especially if you ever had to chase down a speeder, or hurry to the scene of a domestic violence dispute. No, the car was not in good shape, and Amberson was smart enough to recognize that it was emblematic of other things that were going to hell.

Most of his professional life was dedicated to a town full of miscreants that put twice as much effort into breaking the law as it would have taken to find real work. While he enjoyed the job, and in fact was quite good at it, he was beginning to question whether he'd found a true calling in life, or merely followed the path of least resistance. The weight of it all was beginning to crush down on Matt.

And then he'd gotten the call to drive up to Sparrow Lotus Lodge. "Suspicious activity." That could mean a lot of things, the majority of which were minor nuisances. He was near the end of his shift, and wasn't anxious to drive a half-hour plus in each direction. That didn't even include time wasted once he got there. He'd be late getting home, again. No, Matt Amberson was not at all in a cheerful mood.

"Miss?"

"Blue." The resolute woman stared back at the deputy with hard eyes. She was beautiful, in a non-traditional way, but her eyes meant business. She was not a woman to be trifled with.

"Again, ma'am, Miss Blue, Deputy Matt Amberson. To what do I owe the pleasure of this invitation to the Sparrow Lotus Ranch?" He made no effort to hide his reticence. He was standing in the main dining room of the lodge, feeling tired and covered with road dust. It had been a long day, his shift was almost over with, and he really wished he were on his way home rather than dealing with what was likely nothing more than a nuisance complaint.

"As I told your dispatcher on the telephone, *officer,*" she put a strong emphasis on the "officer," a little bit like a school teacher straightening out an impudent child, "I witnessed some *suspicious activity* while walking in the woods, and I thought you should know. If he wanted to play games, well, she'd *give him* games. "I was just trying to do the right thing." She left the ball in Amberson's court. What kind of a policeman was he? Was he going to do his job or not? A donut-eater or a real cop? She was waiting on an answer.

He appraised the situation, and decided a retreat was in order.

"I think we've started off on the wrong foot here. Could you please tell me your full name, address, what you witnessed, and I guess, a little more about this suspicious activity that you observed?" He wasn't sure why this girl had gotten her hackles up so quickly, but there was no reason to be ornery. He had a job to do, and by God he was going to do it. She was a pretty, younger woman, mid twenties, curly brown hair and eyes that could suck you right in, if you stared too long. The kind of girl to steal your heart before you even noticed it missing. He was trying to decide if he'd said something to offend her. She'd probably just picked up on his crankiness. But hell, it was almost dark outside, and he'd driven way up here to take a report on "suspicious activity" that probably wouldn't amount to a hill of beans. He'd been on enough wild goose chases to know one when he saw one. In retrospect, he should have let the call wait until the morning, or shlubbed it off on the night shift. He was here now, though, so he might as well finish what he'd started.

"My name is JoAnn Blue. I live at 308 Elm Street, Batavia, Illinois. I'm here for the week, on vacation. I've been a regular visitor to Sparrow Lotus for years, and I'm very familiar with the Sparrow Lotus property. I arrived late last evening, and will be staying until next Sunday afternoon. I was out walking the grounds about an hour ago, strolling alongside the pond. I heard what sounded like something straining or grunting on the far side of the riverbank, and went closer to investigate where the noise was coming from. I thought it might be an elk or deer, or maybe someone that was hurt. Instead, I saw a man digging a hole in the ground."

"A man digging a hole in the ground?" Amberson was trying to keep his voice level, official in tone, despite the opinions that were quickly developing in his head. He was a bit incredulous. This could prove to be the *mother* of all wild goose chases. The guys at the station would laugh their butts off when he told them about this one. At least she'd been clear and concise. Some people would have wasted another half-hour getting the story out. She'd gotten to the point in under three minutes.

"Yes, officer, a man digging a hole. He was digging on the far side of the riverbank, close to the dam but still on Sparrow Lotus property. He isn't a guest or an employee of the camp, and I can't imagine any good reason why he might be doing what he was doing. I was going to inform the manager of Sparrow Lotus, Anton Kalinik, but he doesn't seem to be around this evening. So I called the sheriff's department to report an individual engaged in what is, in my humble opinion, assuredly suspicious activity."

"Digging a hole in the ground?"

"Digging a hole," she repeated. "I believe I just said that." She returned an expectant silence to the deputy. She obviously believed that what she saw merited attention, and expected the sheriff's department to investigate. Matt could tell by looking at her body language that JoAnn Blue was the kind of woman who rarely took "no" for an answer. And she wasn't the kind of woman a man, even a happily married man like Matt Amberson, would wish to disappoint, even if it were within his power. Nope, she was the kind of girl you'd do anything to make happy, just so long as it didn't adversely impact your own marriage or career. She'd never *have* to take "no" for an answer. Any man would be a fool to utter that word in her ear.

"A hole in the ground," he muttered, realizing when he was licked. JoAnn Blue didn't bother to respond, just stared back at him with her deep brown eyes. Powerful. The woman was just *powerful*, Matt decided. Her quiet resolve and inner confidence radiated from her core. It didn't help that she was so damn cute.

"I guess I'd better look into the matter. Can you point me in the right direction?" Amberson finally acquiesced. The pair slipped out the side door of the vast room and started walking across the meadow.

THE GAMES PEOPLE PLAY
41

"Hey, asshole, what are you doing?" Walt yelled at the top of his lungs. He was still about eighty yards away, having just rounded one more bend in the river. He was almost to the dam, at least as best he could tell, and was shocked to find the same dirtbag that had sucker-punched him back at the Deer Track Inn, that worthless drug dealer Ray, digging a hole in the middle of the woods. This was too good to be true. "Justice will be mine!" Walt yelled, because he'd heard it in a movie somewhere or other and it sounded good. He was now seventy yards away and quickly closing the gap between himself and the other man.

Ray looked up, a combination of sweat and dirt glistening on his forehead, slowly seeping into his eyes. He rubbed his left eye to clear the accumulating gunk away, which only made things worse. The course grains of sand that stuck to the back of his hand scratched and irritated his eye even more, burrowing into his tear duct. "Shit. What now?" he thought. He couldn't see very well, he was tired and well past the point of frustration. He finally used his shirttail to dig out the worst of the sand in his eye, and looked up to see Walt striding quickly towards him at sixty yards. This day was going downhill quicker than he ever could have guessed.

"Yeah, I'm talking to you, dirt bag!" Walt screamed again. He didn't wait for a reply. He was close enough that he no longer had to yell, but Walt knew that screaming intimidated people. It threw them off their game, if nothing else, it made the person doing the screaming seem larger than life. "Remember me?" He was now fifty yards out and ready to fight. He remembered having been threatened with the gun by the river, getting coldcocked at the Deer Track Inn by the dirt-covered weasel. But he had yet another reason he disliked the man, he just couldn't remember why, in the heat of the moment. What was it about Ray that irritated him so? A suspicion, or something more? Things were moving too fast. His legs pumped like pistons through the sawgrass.

It took him a moment to gather his thoughts, but Ray *did* remember this man. Right here, as twilight was falling, was the source of most of his problems incarnate. It was like a gift from the heavens, or maybe some kind of a practical joke from above. Here Ray was, at his most discouraged, certain that everything he had worked for was about to be snatched from his grasp, the sun setting and his hopes flickering, and fast approaching was the very same man that had ignited this whole series of events. Had the government man not been walking out here in the first place, Ray might not have been quite as obsessed with excavating the grave. God, Ray wanted to kill him. And what better opportunity? Thirty yards and closing, Walt was bearing down with fists clenched. "I remember you," Ray finally shouted back. He hadn't moved a step. His hands gently held the handle of the spade, gunfighter's hands. Not gripping tightly, but ready to spring into action in an instant, when called upon.

"Well you better remember me. If you don't you will. I'm the guy that's going to kick your ass from here to Sunday."

"Good to know," Ray responded. "Sunday's coming fast." He still hadn't flinched, but he was ready, tightly wound and ready to spring into action. One hand twitched on the wooden shaft.

"Then you'd better say your prayers." Walt was only steps away. With all the grief that had built up inside him, a volcano of rage that was about to erupt. Losing Dora, working alongside Tom Dewers and those other smug pricks at the office who humiliated him on a daily basis, being ridiculed over the discovery of a body in the river, getting beaten up in front of Pam, and being dumped by Pam for no apparent reason, all were pieces of a bigger picture. The world had been shitting on Walt Pitowski, and it was time for Walt Pitowski to give as good as he got. Ray the drug dealer, well Walt couldn't think of a better recipient for what he was going to deliver. Three more steps and the shit was really going to rain down.

It was but one more step before he was down on the ground, writhing in pain. It was amazing how quickly you could go from predator to prey, Walt thought. Then the pain shot clear through his right leg, up into his hip, skewering his entire right side. "You're going to die, bastard!" Walt screamed, blood pulsing in his temples. He tried to roll to his left, get up from the ground, but couldn't move his leg. It was as if he were being held in place by a #16 steel bear trap. The more he pulled and twisted, the more the pain in his leg worsened. Why couldn't he stand up? It had happened so fast.

He didn't have long to worry about it, however. The head of the shovel swiftly bore down into the back of his left shoulder, as Walt helplessly tried to wrest himself away.

THINGS YOU FIND IN THE FOREST
42

"So, you've been coming here for a while, you say?"

"Since I was eighteen, anyhow. A friend of mine from college, Amy, brought me up here for a long weekend when we were freshmen, and it was love at first sight."

"You and Amy?" she couldn't help but notice the touch of disappointment in his voice. He quickly realized how his words had come across. What was it to him, any ways? He was a happily married man. To each their own. Matt knew he needed to sound less judgmental, but didn't know exactly how to apologize. "I'm sorry, it's none of my business."

"No! Me and Sparrow Lotus, me and yoga, me and nature! It opened my mind up to so many things, a small town girl from northern Illinois. Amy and I are friends. I do still like men, Officer Amberson." She smiled in his direction, a gift better than any act of forgiveness.

"Truly I'm sorry, I didn't mean to imply anything one way or the other." He was blushing and staring at his shiny black boots.

"Nothing to be sorry about. I just don't want you to get the wrong impression."

The pair were still trudging across the meadow, the grasshoppers parting like the Red Sea before them. They were following the pond's edge in a more or less westerly direction, downstream towards the dam. They walked in silence like this for a while.

"If you don't mind my asking, what did Sparrow Lotus open your mind *to,* exactly?"

"It's hard to boil it down into sound bites. I don't want to preach and I don't want to sound trite. Where did you grow up, Officer Amberson?"

"Matt would be fine, by the way. You're not a suspect or anything. I grew up in a small town in southwestern Michigan."

"So maybe you *would* understand. You grow up in a small town like that, you know how it is. The people there, not that there's anything *wrong* with it, but they tend to be, you know, *like* you. They're predominately white. They're Lutheran, or Episcopalian, or Methodist, or some other branch of Christianity. Maybe you meet a few Catholic kids growing up, but you don't see them on Sunday morning, and anyhow, well, those are probably the most visible minorities you'll ever encounter before going away to college, *if* you manage to go away to college. If your parents have money, well maybe you drive into Chicago for the occasional weekend and run into honest to gosh black folks while you're still young, or you eat out at an Indian restaurant or something once or twice a year. But you probably don't actually *know* a lot of people with varying perspectives on life, because most small towns are fairly homogenous."

"And Sparrow Lotus opened your mind to African Americans serving Indian cuisine in their dining room?"

"Very funny. No, Sparrow Lotus opened my mind to the idea that there are people in this world, all sharing this one planet, who are at once very unlike me, and who at the same time are *exactly* like me. People come from all over the globe to visit this camp. All nationalities, all religions. Sparrow Lotus is about meditation and yoga, yes, but it's much more than that. Not everyone that comes here has the same faith, or practices the same methods of contemplation. They don't even come here for the same reasons. Most visitors are here to learn about yoga, sure, some beginners, some experienced. But that's just a small part of it. I've met atheists who come here just to enjoy the north woods, and to feed off the positive energy from those of us that *do* believe in something bigger than ourselves. It's about *possibilities,* and it's about the fact we all have more in common than that which divides us, if we'd just pause to appreciate that fact. It's about finding that which makes us *human,* that which links us together."

"Plus it's a very pretty place. It beats staring at miles of cornfield in Batavia Illinois," he smiled.

"That it does, Officer Amberson, that it does."

They continued walking, stride for stride, in comfortable silence. After the rough start, there was an underlying sense that they might be kindred spirits. They kept their heads bowed, shielding their eyes from the setting sun, which was just now dropping below the horizon. Matt was beginning to understand how someone could fall in love with this place, strolling and chatting with a woman like JoAnn Blue. It was probably not a great thing for a married cop investigating "suspicious activity' to admit, but in an alternate universe, wherein he was about fifteen years younger and still single, he could readily see himself with this particular young lady. The pair were only about three-hundred feet from the dam when they heard the scream, followed by the swearing, followed by a more chilling silence.

THE PATH OF THE RIGHTEOUS MAN
43

"Why does this idiot from the Geological Service keep turning up everywhere I go?" Lord, as if things weren't difficult enough, Ray having to dig up half the frickin' county trying to rectify old mistakes. Now this bozo comes stumbling down the riverbank, sounding as if someone had pissed in his breakfast cereal. "Well screw him," Ray thought. "I've had enough of his bullshit." He watched Walt approaching, an angry man cursing and running down the shoreline, babbling about all the things he was going to do to Ray. "Just great," he thought. If this isn't the cherry on top of the sundae. "Let him come." He kept his hands on the shovel handle, ready to swing when the opportunity arrived. Ray wasn't a man who by nature actively sought conflict, but one thing he'd learned was, the first strike in any fight was often the only strike in any fight.

It was a bit of a shock to Ray, what happened next. Here he was, ready to brawl, the other man bearing down on him fast and furious, just a yard or three away. Then, quicker than the blink of an eye, Walt was down on the ground screaming, his right leg stuck almost to the hip in one of the holes Ray had just dug. And Ray hadn't needed to do a thing, didn't even move a muscle. It didn't get any easier than this. Maybe God wasn't out to get him, after all.

The man was down on the ground, rolling around howling, for all of about two seconds. Ray was ready to run, bail out of here, let the chips fall where they may. But the stupid bastard wouldn't stop screaming, and he'd latched on to Ray's pant leg and wouldn't let go. Ray shook his leg, but still Walt held fast. Ray took a kick at the man's face, as he lay prone on the ground, and Walt still wouldn't release him. One quick whack with the shovel cured that problem.

He wasn't meaning to kill the guy. He just wanted the man to release his leg, let Ray get the hell out of here. The tip of the spade connected with the back of a shoulder blade, and that, combined with whatever Walt had done to his own leg while stepping into the hole, was enough to render Walt temporarily unconscious. Ray pitched his shovel in the water and started running up the shoreline. He didn't think that his assailant was dead, but even if he was, well that's what you got when you ran around attacking innocent dope farmers.

Ray took one quick look over his shoulder as he ran, which turned out to be just enough time to bring about a new calamity. Ray's leg, like a heat seeking missile, managed to locate a hole of its own, another three-footer . He went down face first into the soil, bounced back up, and tried again to run. He'd only caught the lip of the hole, didn't really put his leg all the way down to the bottom, but damned if it wasn't enough to cause a high ankle sprain. It hurt. It hurt a lot. He could still run, sort of. He tried to take off again, and managed a fast hop, complicated by a faltering limp to his left side. "You've got to be kidding me," he cussed. Ray took another look back, and now Walt, having rejoined the conscious, was managing to lift his own leg injured out of the hole. He wasn't yet to his feet, but it was obvious Walt was going to try and give chase.

"Wait up, asshole," Walt yelled as he wobbled to his feet.

"Bite me," Ray retorted, hopping away on his one good foot, his other leg jolting his mind with pain on every bounce.

"I said wait up!"

"You wish."

Walt's leg was worse than his own, Ray thought. Walt was hopping along behind him, but unable to put any weight at all on his right ankle. It was probably broken. When Walt did try to use the right leg, he went immediately down to the ground, grudgingly pulling himself back upright after each stumble. Every time he went down, it took a little longer for Walt to get back up. At least Ray's bad ankle could make occasional contact with the ground without giving way completely.

"You're insane. Quit chasing me, dumbass!" Ray wasn't moving *all* that fast, limping and hopping up the ragged shoreline, but he was putting distance between himself and Walt. "Why doesn't this guy just go down and stay down?" Ray mumbled. He ventured another glance over his shoulder: Walt had fallen yet another time, and was a good forty yards back, but was once more rising on his one good leg. “Stay down, stupid!” Ray yelled again.

“I owe you!” Walt bellowed. Face first into the sawgrass again, back upright, then teetering on his left leg and madly hopping along. “I’m serious. I’m going to kick your ass.”

“With *that* foot?”

Ray paused to catch his breath. The other man closed the gap between them to thirty-five yards. This was getting insane, a bad comedy if ever there were one. Ray’s own foot was killing him, and he wished he had something a whole lot stronger than the homegrown weed in his pocket to help ease the pain. It wasn’t of any use anyhow. He didn’t have time to stop and light up. Why couldn’t he have brought a few Oxycodone capsules with him? Anything would be better than nothing. It was obvious Walt wasn’t going to catch him, but it didn’t seem as if he was going to quit trying, either. How long was this going to drag on? When would the guy ever give up?

Ray hopped over to the river’s edge and gazed down at the pond’s darkened surface. It was deeper here than in the lower parts of the river, thick with vegetation, but not completely weed-choked like some other places he’d seen. The bottom of the pond was dark silt, unlike the gravel and sand stream bed that existed below the dam. The current here was hardly noticeable, the water slack. “Swimmable,” he thought. Ray was a decent swimmer. In the next instant he was in the water, stroking his way upstream. The pond felt cold, and for that he was grateful. It numbed the pain in his ankle, and he was able to concentrate on just one thing: escape. He needed to get as much distance between himself and the man chasing him as possible.

“What in God’s name do you think you’re doing?” Walt shrieked. He couldn’t believe his eyes. Ray had just jumped into the pond, and was attempting to escape by swimming upstream. Walt wasn’t giving up that easily. He too, hopped over to the shoreline, deliberately faltering, face-forward, into the muddy water. It was painful at first, the shock of the cold water in addition to all the other trauma his body had endured. But the cold also had a calming effect, and he quickly realized that the pond gave his body a freedom and buoyancy that nullified the pain in his leg. The cold water was also helping clot the blood seeping from his injured shoulder.

Up until now Walt had been operating on blind rage. The original adrenalin rush, that burst of strength he'd found after getting knocked out with the shovel and then quickly coming to, had begun to wane. Until this moment, Walt didn't truly believe that he could catch Ray, not with a hobbled ankle and a cut, bleeding shoulder. He'd continued to chase the man out of obstinance, more than anything else. Walt Pitowski didn't know how to quit. He might be defeated, but he never quit. And he wasn't about to let this joker best him again, not without putting up a fight. Once Ray jumped in the water, well that changed everything. With only one leg functioning, Walt was still a better swimmer than most. The race was on.

A HAT TRICK
44

"Walt Pitowski." That's about all Matt Amberson could say. Because here he'd been enjoying a peaceful walk through the tall grasses and wildflowers of the Wolverine River Valley, on his way to locate the "suspicious activity" of "a man digging a hole." Probably somebody putting in a geo cache or some other nonsense. Matt was enjoying the company of an attractive and articulate young lady, not the usual complainant in any police situation. And Amberson was in no hurry to get to the spot where the "suspicious activity" was first spotted. This was the most relaxing call he'd had in a long time, and he was in no hurry for the sensation to end.

And all of that was being interrupted by Walt Pitowski and some other guy screaming at each other on the far side of the river. He recognized the voices, without even seeing the pair. What the hell were those two clowns doing? When he'd first heard the scream, followed by the cursing, Matt Amberson had snapped back to attention. So much for enjoying the company of a pleasant young woman. He was once more a policeman, no longer a guy out for a leisurely stroll. He still had a ways to walk before he'd be parallel to the two men, arguing with one another on the opposite shore. He'd have to go even further to get to the dam, cross over the river, then double back to where the two were going at it.

"Wait here, ma'am," he cautioned in his official voice.

"I'm not waiting here alone." It was clear that JoAnn Blue was not going to stand in an empty clearing by her lonesome.

"Alright then. I'd advise you to return back to the camp compound. I'll investigate what's going on over there, and return to the camp as soon as I'm finished." He doubted she'd oblige, but it was worth asking.

"Alright then," she agreed reluctantly. She wasn't happy about it. Her natural instincts were to stay with Amberson, a confident police officer who seemed to know what he was doing. But then, what could she really do to help? She did an about face and began hesitantly walking back toward camp. "Be careful, please."

"Yes, ma'am," tipping his hat.

Matt undid the snap on his holster and considered whether he'd have any actual need to draw his sidearm. There wasn't much call for unholstering your weapon in Rasmus, except to finish off the occasional deer, critically wounded by a car accident. He couldn't remember the last time he'd pulled it for anything other than a wounded animal. But Matt Amberson wouldn't hesitate to use his gun, should the situation deem necessary. It was always better to be safe than sorry. Out here in the woods, with no backup, you never knew what you might run into. Poachers, drug dealers, there were more than a few reasons you might want to be ready. It didn't happen often, but he'd heard stories, and had no intention of being caught off guard. He rested his hand on his weapon in hand and cautiously worked his way down the path towards the dam.

And he'd almost made it to the dam when, on the far side of the water, he spotted that local troublemaker that he recognized as Ray, limping up the shoreline in the opposite direction. Not far behind him was Walt Pitowski, swearing up a storm, haphazardly chasing after the first man. The funny thing was, Walt was limping too. He seemed to have an open wound high on his back, and blood had soaked through his shirt. It was a nasty looking sight. Amberson couldn't quite figure how you'd go about getting an injury like that, even in a fight. Both men were oblivious to the sheriff's deputy on the far side of the pond, and neither looked as if they could pass a sobriety test. They were engaged in a slow-motion chase if ever there were one.

"Walt Pitowski," Matt lamented. What was the man up to now? And what was it he'd said to Walt back at the Red Eye Saloon, not all that long ago? Oh, yeah, now he remembered. Something about if there was a pile of crap in the forest, Walt would find a way to step in it. Maybe that's why the two men were limping. Maybe they'd both stepped in shit. Deep shit. This was something far more complex than one man digging a hole in the forest. Whatever these two men were fighting about, it appeared to be personal, and appeared as if it had turned violent.

"Pitowski, stop!" he ordered. "You, Ray, whatever the hell your name is, stop!" Neither Walt nor the other man so much as glanced in Amberson's direction. The two had to have heard him, the way sound traveled out here. Why wouldn't they at least acknowledge his order? It *was* a police order, damn it. They were probably too involved in whatever argument they were having to even notice him. Well this sucked. He'd have to get down to the dam, cross to the other side of the pond, and find out what was going on.

By the time he reached the dam and crossed to the far bank, Ray had leapt into the pond, a good hundred yards back in the direction from which Matt had just come. Not so much a leap. Slithered into the pond, more like. "What is wrong with these people?" Amberson wondered, not for the first time. Why would Ray decide now was the time to go swimming? Why did the simplest things always have to turn out to be so difficult?

Matt slipped his gun safely back in his holster. These two men chasing each other might be reckless jerks, but neither appeared to be armed. Introducing a gun into the situation could only make matters worse. He checked to make sure his holster was secured, then started marching up the bank in pursuit. The men were a good hundred and twenty yards ahead of him. It was only a second or two more before he observed Walt Pitowski staggering into the pond.

"Pitowski, stop!" Amberson ordered again. Again, it fell upon deaf ears. "Police!" as if that was going to make any difference. He was going to have to run the two men down, find out what in the world was going on. He wasn't looking forward to chasing them through the woods, not at this time of the evening. The sky was rapidly growing dark. There were no lights in the valley, nothing but a few stars emerging in the evening sky. Amberson considered phoning in for backup, but knew he'd never get a cell signal out here, not in the river valley. Nope, this was all on him.

He started running up the shoreline in pursuit of the pair, and only made a few strides before Matt Amberson, too, had twisted his leg in the minefield of holes. He hit the third crater at a full sprint, and went down to the ground as if he'd been shot. A spire of pain pierced his side. He rolled over on the ground, one leg dangling in the shallow pit, and tried to compose himself. He didn't see any broken skin, no protruding bones, but his knee was a mess. It hurt to touch, and was swelling quickly. He was guessing it was nothing more than a serious sprain. He really hoped he hadn't torn an ACL or something that would require time off work. Either way, he wasn't going to be doing any running anytime soon. “How could this get any better?” he lamented.

Matt rubbed his knee gently. It was already beginning to swell. He hoped it wouldn’t swell any more before he made it back to the cruiser. When he finally let his eyes search upstream, the other men were swimming off into the distance. He glanced back down into the hole for but a second. There was something in the bottom, a scrap of brown fabric, mostly covered in sand. He reached down to the bottom, lying on his stomach and flopping the damaged leg on the ground behind him. It took a little digging and prodding, but eventually the fabric came free of the earth. “A fishing vest?” he wondered, as he dragged the garment from its resting place.

MARCO POLO
45

"Give up, bastard!"

"Get off of my back, lunatic!"

"Go to hell."

"I'm already there."

Walt had, as he'd expected, caught up with the other swimmer in just a matter of minutes. All of that cardio training was finally paying off. An occasional swimmer and full time drug dealer couldn't match the tempo of a man who'd been training for a marathon. Walt had successfully managed to block out his leg pain while navigating his way across the crisp surface of the pond. He'd closed the gap bit by bit, until he was only a stroke or two behind the other man, swimming in the darkness. Now he was draped across Ray's back, trying to punch the other man in the face, all the while wrestling in about eight feet of water. Very few of his blows were landing. It was an unnatural motion, trying to hit a guy in the face when you're behind him. And Ray couldn't get turned around or do much to fight back, other than to swing the occasional elbow into Walt's ribs. Ray landed one lucky foot to the groin, but Walt didn't receive the full force of it. The water was draining the force from the men's blows. Walt clung tight with one arm wrapped around the other man's neck. They went at it like this for a few minutes, and both Walt and Ray were tiring rapidly.

"Let go, you idiot."

"Why, so you can sucker punch me like you did back at the bar?"

"Let go!"

"I'll let go when I can bury your ass in that hole you were digging!"

Walt was still livid, still had plenty of fight left in him, but his body was telling him he needed to rest. Ray was lagging. He flailed in the water, weighed down by fatigue and the much bigger man clinging to his backside. Walt threw a few more punches, managing to land a few glancing blows to the side of Ray's head. Most failed to have any effect. The punches were getting fewer and further between.

Eventually the smaller man managed to break free, dog paddle over to shallower water, and drag himself up on shore. He retched up a mouthful of algae-laden pond water, just as Walt dragged his own battered body up beside him. The two men lay momentary, side-by-side in the mud, gasping for oxygen.

Ray finally managed to get to his hands and knees, forehead pressed to the ground, still belching up river water. He felt as if he'd inhaled an entire ecosystem. All he really wanted was to be left alone, left to puke in solitude. If he could get out of here, if he could just get out of these stupid woods and this stupid county, forget the dope and the body in the ground and everything that came with it, well maybe he'd move down to Saginaw, start over. He could move in with cousin Randy, find a girlfriend, maybe even find a job. If he could just get out of here. "What is wrong with you?" he eventually croaked.

Walt lay prostrate on his back, trying to grasp some air of his own. "That's a damn good question," he finally responded. What *was* wrong with him, Walt wondered? Here it was, less than a week before the marathon. He should be training, or at the very least resting up for the big week ahead. Instead he lay here in near-total darkness, soaking wet and with an injured leg, gasping for breath at the side of the Sparrow River. His shoulder hurt. The bleeding had stopped, but was he even going to be *able* to paddle in the big race next Saturday? He didn't know how much damage had been inflicted by the shovel. Had it cut through the muscle? Would it heal in time? Would it get infected?

And this guy next to him? Why did this guy keep reappearing, like some harbinger of doom, other than to ruin Walt's life? Had God made Walt some sort of 'asshole magnet?' He seemed to attract enough of them. Everywhere he turned, it seemed, there was yet another asshole. Downstaters and snowmobilers, old people who shouldn't be driving, and rude store clerks. Fat cranky ladies and younger women who thought they were too good for him, and fly fisherman who acted as though they owned the rivers. People he worked with. Jehovah's Witnesses that interrupted his nap while trying to save his soul, and telemarketers trying to get him to buy life insurance. This guy, this *Ray*, who he couldn't shake to save his life. A world full of jerks, and he was their true north. They flocked to him. He should get business cards printed. Walt Pitowski, Asshole Magnet.

Walt rose gingerly, attempting to bear some weight on his bad ankle. The leg gave way immediately, and he found himself once more flat on his face, in the soft black silt of the river shallow's bottom. He rolled over painfully to his back and again rested for a moment. The oozing black mud actually felt good against the open wound on his back. He thought about staying here, about just staying down and not getting up, letting life continue on for everybody else but Walt Pitowski. He could just lay here with the soothing mud against his back, lay until the morning light. He could lay here until he got fired from his job, until Ray was gone, until the marathon was over, until the winds covered him over with sand. It would all be so *easy*.

But he knew he couldn't do that, either. Because the one thing he knew for sure, the one invariable truth that had defined his life thus far, was that Walt Pitowski doesn't quit. It was not in his nature. He *had* to get back up. He didn't know *why*, he only knew that he must.

By the time he'd again scurried to his knees, Walt was barely able to see Ray, now limping erratically across the meadow. Ray was weaving his way in the general direction of Sparrow Lotus Camp. Ray must have stopped puking and slipped off in the brief moment that Walt was pitying himself. Walt was no longer sure that he could catch the man, but he'd be damned if he wasn't going to try.

"Hey loser, wait up!" Walt bellowed.

SOMEONE'S IN THE KITCHEN WITH ANTON
46

All Anton wanted was a bite to eat. He had driven to East Lansing early that morning, starting well before the sun had even come up, to meet with a potential investor. He hadn't wanted to make that long haul, but this particular potential investor was friends with two members on the Club's Board of Directors. They'd both called Anton personally to request the meeting. It was not the kind of request one could easily decline, not if he wanted to keep his job. And Anton liked his job, so he drove to East Lansing.

On his way down state, Anton had taken the direct route on the four lane divided highway of US127. There weren't a lot of cars driving south on a Saturday morning. Most people, if they were out and about, were heading north, and the road was relatively free of congestion. He'd gotten to the city early, in fact, allowing him time to take a leisurely stroll around the campus of Michigan State University. He'd checked out the Beal Botanical Gardens, managing to tour some of the facilities at the school of veterinary medicine, and even stopped by the Dairy Store for freshly made ice cream. The ice cream was actually a no-no for a guy who proclaimed himself a vegetarian, but Anton figured the gods would forgive him for taking small pleasures every once in a while.

His luncheon meeting went well, and by one p.m. Anton was sitting in the driver's seat of his 1979 Toyota Landcruiser, working his way back to Sparrow Lotus Camp. He loved the old Toyota, a throwback to the days when SUVs were called "trucks," and trucks like this were built for their serious off-road capabilities, not for their ability to seat seven kids on the way to soccer practice. He settled behind the wheel of the old FJ40, cruising along in the slow lane at sixty miles-per-hour without a care in the world, the AM radio spewing local news, weather and traffic reports. That's when his day began to unravel.

Anton made the mistake of thinking he should swing through Saginaw and pick up a small package from a friend. This really should have caused him no more than a twenty minute delay, half an hour at the most. What Anton hadn't considered was major construction on I-75, combined with significantly heavier traffic on the major expressway. The big road was a congested mess of orange barrels and road building equipment. What should have been at most a four hour drive had turned into a six hour return to camp, and Anton was just now rolling in to Sparrow Lotus, tired and hungry. It was dark out, and all he really wanted, at this late hour, was a bite to eat, a beer, and a soft place to land.

He was standing in the big walk-in cooler in the kitchen, rummaging through large plastic containers full of leftovers. Something in here should look like dinner. So far nothing had seemed remotely interesting, and Anton was beginning to think that it would be easier to throw together a quick garden salad and skip the leftovers. He was startled to hear a voice outside the cooler door. Someone else prowling the kitchen for food after hours?

"Hello, somebody in there?" the voice cried out, echoing across the tile floors and the high ceilings of the lodge's vast cooking space. Whoever it was, they were walking in his direction.

"Yeah, it's me, Anton," he answered back. "Who's out there?" he asked, as he stepped back into the warmth of the greater kitchen. As soon as he closed the stainless steel cooler door behind him and turned his head, he had an answer. He paused to buy himself time, organize his thoughts, then smiled condescendingly. "Ray man, I've told you, you can't come in here. You're persona non grata inside the camp buildings, you know that. What in the world happened to you?" He had been so concerned with formulating his own thoughts, it had taken him a moment to realize the shape Ray was in. The man was covered with dirt and sand, his clothing was wet, and he had an assortment of scrapes and bruises on his arms, neck, and face. He looked as if he'd been drawn and quartered. Ray was not a pretty sight, and Anton was hoping for, at most, a brief explanation of how he'd gotten that way. He was hungry and tired, after all.

"You don't want to know, and I don't have time to explain right now."

"Well then what are you doing in the kitchen? I mean, come on man, you know the deal. You and I are cool, but it's not good for business, you being in here. The clientele has expectations. You look like shit, by the way."

"I've got a problem, and I could use a hand." He answered curtly. He seemed anxious, fidgety.

"We've all got problems, man. I've been driving since six this morning, and I'm hungry. And now you're standing in the kitchen, where you're not supposed to be. Now *that's* a problem."

"No, I have a *real* problem, and I could *really* use a hand." Ray was wondering if all the dope he'd sold Anton over the years had begun to kill his brain cells, or if he just didn't *get it*. Couldn't he hear the urgency in Ray's voice? "Look at me, man. I'm soaking wet and I'm filthy. I need some clean clothes, to start. And then I need some transportation."

"Well yeah, I can lend you something to wear. I'm not sure how well it'll fit, my pants are gonna be way too long for you. Maybe we can find something in the lost and found, I've got a big box of stuff back in my office. You know, things people forgot in their rooms. But it's really not cool, you being in here and all. It could cause a problem with some of the guests, if you know what I mean."

The tone in Ray's voice grew decidedly more serious, picking up an edge that hadn't been there until now. He'd tried to show patience, but knew he was rapidly running out of time. "Fuck your 'clientele,' Anton. They don't seem to have a problem with smoking the dope I sell them, now do they? I need a hand. I'm in trouble, asshole. Find me something to wear and something to drink. I've got some nut chasing me through the woods, trying to kill me, and Matt Amberson wandering around out there somewhere behind him. Let me say it again: clothes, drink, car keys. I don't give a rat's ass what vehicle, just so long as it's one that runs. I need to get out of here, sooner rather than later."

"Whoa, Whoa, settle down! What's the sheriff's department doing hanging around my camp?"

"Didn't you here the part about some nut trying to kill me? I don't know what Amberson's up to, and I don't intend to stick around long enough to find out. Maybe he's after that guy that was chasing me. All I know is, I need to leave. I need to leave *now*."

"Chill, man. Alright. Let's head over to my office and see what we've got by way of clothing. I've got a bottle of Maker's Mark tucked away in my desk drawer," he added, almost as an afterthought. There was no way Anton was giving Ray the keys to his Landcruiser, but there was no sense bringing that up now, not with Ray in such an agitated state. Maybe once he got a few drinks in him, Ray would settle down, realize he was being unreasonable. If worse came to worse, Anton would let him borrow the old pickup the camp used for grounds maintenance. He sure as hell wasn't going to let Ray know that his own keys were dangling from the ignition of the Toyota.

Anton was only *slightly* concerned about "some nut" trying to kill Ray. Ray certainly *looked* like someone *might* have tried killing him, but more than likely Ray was on a bad trip of some kind. He'd probably popped some pills, fell in the river, and rolled around in the mud while trying to get himself out. It was dark out. He'd probably imagined someone chasing him. More worrisome was the idea of the sheriff's department poking their noses around Sparrow Lotus. Not that anyone staying at Sparrow Lotus was up to anything illegal, other than the occasional recreational drug use, but many of the guests were suspicious of law enforcement. Having cops wandering around would not be good for business, not at all. Anton and Ray quickly slipped out the kitchen's back door, making their way to the main office.

Anton glanced to his left, checking to see that no one else was out and about. Camp seemed quieter than usual, given that they were at full occupancy for the week. The majority of guests must have gone into town after dinner, or turned in early for the night. A lucky break at that. There was no sense drawing attention to themselves, and he really didn't want to be seen associating with Ray more than was absolutely necessary.

Anton looked to his right. What he saw almost made his eyes pop out of his skull. Charging across the clearing like a wounded bull was Walt Pitowski. "Some nut, trying to kill me" suddenly had a name. Pitowski's right leg dragged behind him, a worthless club that slowed, but could not stop his progress. He was a long ways off in the distance, yet still coming this way. Jesus, what now?

Further in the background, beneath the dim glow of the stars, Anton could make out two additional figures, traveling side by side. The first figure had a slim, short profile, possibly a child, or maybe a small woman. Leaning against the first figure was a second, taller silhouette. His gait, much like

Pitowski's, was unnatural, as if he'd tied a wooden board to one of his lower limbs. This second figure was clinging onto the first figure for support. They, too, were slowly headed in this direction. Anton peered behind him, and just now noticed that Ray, too, was limping. Three figures, each with a hobbled leg. None of it made any sense.

"Let's get over to the office, Ray. You're not the only one needs a drink."

CATCH AS CATCH CAN
47

"Son of a bitch," Walt sighed. He'd seen them, seen them both sneaking out the back door of the great dining hall. Anton and Ray, Ray and Anton. He hoped if he just kept at it, maintained his dogged pursuit, he'd catch that prick Ray and settle things once and for all. What he didn't expect, didn't see coming at all, was that Ray had gone to that flake, Anton, for help. It figured. Anton had probably been buying drugs from Ray all along, and now Ray was turning to Anton for help. "Well fuck'em," Walt cursed.

And at this point, quite suddenly and unexpectedly, a little switch clicked in the back of Walt's head. He now recognized the second voice from the bridge, the second voice he'd heard when he'd been on his "romantic" picnic with Pam. The first voice, Anton's, he'd identified right off. The second voice, that which had at the time seemed somehow familiar, well that was the voice of Ray. It was that bastard Ray, the man who had held a gun on Walt when he'd been peacefully walking the river, who'd sucker punched him at the Deer Track Inn, and who'd been making clandestine, middle-of-the-night deliveries on foot, just outside the Sparrow Lotus dining hall. Ray was the other man on the foot bridge, collecting "five grand" in "blood money."

Now it all made sense. Ray was not just Anton's drug dealer. Anton must have murdered that man, nearly a decade ago, dumped the body near the Sparrow River, and now Ray was blackmailing him in connection with it! Why hadn't Walt realized this earlier? He could kick himself for having taken this long. He'd known something was up, suspecting the hippie that ran the camp of something illegal, but until now had been unable to piece it all together. It was there to see, plain as day, all laid out before him.

Walt picked up his pace in the direction of camp. His injured leg hurt, but it no longer mattered to him. Justice was what mattered, Pitowski-style justice. This was *his river,* after all, *his county*, and crap like this didn't belong here. He'd had his fill of Ray and Anton and their "alternate lifestyles." What belonged here were people like himself, honest men trying to live an honest life, without distractions and without tourists, religious freaks, or dope peddlers polluting everything that they touched. Walt's anger spiked, and with it, his adrenaline peaked. In the distance he could just make out the two men, scuttling through the door to the main office. "Like cockroaches," Walt thought. "And I'm just the man to crush them."

When he eventually reached the building, he thrust his right shoulder, his *good* shoulder, against the thick door of the main office. The slab refused to budge. It was solid wood, undoubtedly oak, ash, or some other hardwood, and the surrounding frame was just as solid. Pain surged through Walt's tender left shoulder, and he could feel the earlier wound, tender and raw, temporarily caked over with mud and clotted blood, begin to weep anew. He stepped back, wobbling a little on the bad ankle beneath him, and once more launched his body at the hefty edifice. Walt heard a slight cracking noise, thought for a moment that he might have succeeded in busting open the latch, and then quickly recognized that the slight cracking sound had come from his own body. He stepped back once more, rubbing the "good" right shoulder that now hurt as much as his damaged left shoulder, and prayed he hadn't broken his collarbone.

So much for heroics. Walt eased his body down and sat on the stoop in frustration. This was not going the way he'd hoped, when he'd first come charging across the clearing. "What now? What next?" he wondered. He was close, so very close to getting vengeance, and yet still so far away. Anton and Ray were safely inside the building. The door wasn't going to budge. The two conspirators could stay holed up in there till eternity, and there wasn't a damn thing Walt could do about it. This was not what he'd expected, not at all. "Shit," was all he could say. Disappointment descended across him like a thick curtain. Hope was momentarily lost. And then, a faint rumbling. He could hear a motor turning over but failing to start, somewhere behind the building.

The truck's starter tried and tried, but the engine refused to catch.

"Piece of shit," Ray cursed. Anton had initially refused to give him the vehicle's keys, whining about "liability" and "procedure," but had finally coughed them up once Ray threatened to beat his scrawny butt. Ray quickly grabbed the keys and ran out the back door of the office, if you could call it running, all the while that simpering Anton hiding behind his desk, throwing back shots of whiskey as if Prohibition started tomorrow. Now Ray was sitting behind the wheel, and the stupid truck refused to start. This was the fourth time he'd turned the engine over without any results. He could tell the battery was losing juice with each and every attempt. One more try, he figured. Otherwise he'd have to find a different means of escape.

He pumped the accelerator three times, cranking the key yet again. It groaned, it turned, but in the end gave him nothing. "Idiot," he thought, "I probably flooded it." He tried anew, desperation flooding into the back of his mind. Nothing. He tried again. This time, after ten long seconds, the motor sputtered its way back to life. Black smoke belched from the exhaust, the truck backfiring twice, then settled into an irregular idle. Ray sighed with relief, grateful that the truck was running at all. He slid the shifter into gear and eased the big Dodge from behind the main office, around the corner of the building and into the Sparrow Lotus driveway. A few hundred yards and he'd be on Wolverine Valley Road.

The worst of it was behind him, Ray was sure. He'd get to that road, and keep right on driving. Saginaw wasn't far enough, the more he thought about things. No, he wasn't stopping until he got a lot further down the trail than Saginaw. He'd never been outside of Michigan, not once in his whole life. It was about time. Always wondered what it would be like to live near the ocean, with all that sun, warmth, and water. California was too far, and this old truck would never make it that far. Maybe the gulf coast would be a good place to start again. He'd drive until he hit Florida, Alabama, Mississippi, anywhere other than this god-forsaken peninsula of jack pines and snowbanks. He'd start a fresh life, disappear into an entirely new environment, and do it all over, do it *right* this time.

"Almost home," he whispered. He urged the old truck forward. "Come on, girl. You can make it."

It was a good feeling, making a clean break. In an odd way, Ray was relieved that things had finally come to a head. All this crap that was going on around him, it was giving him one last chance to reinvent himself. All he needed to do was get out of here, put some miles behind him and Sparrow Lotus Lodge, the town of Rasmus, the whole lot of it.

"This must be what it feels like to be born again," Ray told himself. He finally understood what all the bible thumpers had been talking about. All of the bad things that had followed him throughout his life were slowly seeping away. He felt, for the first time since he was a kid, *peaceful* inside. *Serene*, almost. Because the decision was made, the die had been cast. He stole one last peek in the Dodge's rear view mirror, just in time to glimpse Walt Pitowski, sliding into the driver's seat of a Toyota Landcruiser.

THE RACE IS ON
48

Walt had him in his sights, the old pickup truck lumbering up the driveway to the main road. The twin red taillights rose and fell with each bump in the path. Ray had a healthy head start on him, but Walt knew that wasn't going to be enough. On the highway, yeah, maybe the battered truck could lose him in heavy traffic or something, especially at night. It might even be able to outrun him. For all Walt knew, that old Dodge might have a big block V-8 engine. The FJ40 Landcruiser was in far better shape than that pickup, sure, but it was also four-wheel-drive, which added a lot of weight to the vehicle. And it had a transmission geared for torque and power, not for speed. If he got to the highway, Ray was probably gone. All the more reason for Walt to catch him before he ever got the chance. He'd run the man down on a slow curve before he let him get away.

Walt was surprised when the old truck got to the road and turned to the east. He'd been certain Ray would swing west, drive through the town of Sturgeon before hopping on the expressway. North or southbound, Walt wasn't sure which, but he had been sure the other man would try and lose him with speed on the highway. Instead Ray swung right, following Wolverine Valley Road deeper into the forest. A bad decision if ever there were one, Walt thought. The FJ had a decisive advantage over the rear wheel drive truck, once they reached the point where the pavement ended. There must be some reason Ray had turned right. The weathered road got worse the further it went, all twists and turns, poor grading and soft shoulders. The county road commission didn't have the budget to maintain much in this corner of the world. Ray must have a hideout, a secret pullout in mind, a plan up ahead.

Walt gunned the engine, hit a large rut in the driveway, and slammed the top of his skull against the FJ's headliner. He came down hard, landing back in the driver's seat. The impact sent bold waves of pain through both of his shoulders. Shit, he'd have to be more careful. He'd been more than lucky to find the keys sitting in this thing, like a gift-wrapped present. There was no sense wrecking it. For a second he wondered if he could get in trouble, if taking the Landcruiser constituted car theft of some kind. But then, Walt reasoned, he was only borrowing the vehicle, and the keys were in fact, just sitting there in the ignition. That was pretty much the same as having permission, right? He'd put the vehicle back when he was done doing what he had to do. In the meantime, he had bigger fish to fry.

He reached the end of the path, punched the pedal to the floor, and spun a cloud of sand and gravel behind him as the FJ's tires bit and grabbed the pavement of Wolverine Valley Road. Walt caught a fleeting glimpse of two red lenses, glowing softly in the night ahead. They were visible for but a second, veering left before disappearing into a curtain of darkness. Walt knew that not a mile past that turn, the road returned to dirt. He knew this area by heart, could drive it in his sleep. Walt double checked that the Toyota was indeed in four-wheel-drive high, quickly shifting through second, then third gear, grinding his way into fourth with the cumbersome manual transmission.

The FJ quickly reached the point where the concrete road surface reverted back to sand and gravel. Warrior Way slid by on the right, the last semblance of a true side road for over ten miles. Still Walt couldn't make out the taillights ahead. How far in front of him was the truck now? A mile? A half mile? Wolverine Valley Road weaved its way through the forest, in rhythm with the cuts and meanders of the river. Walt drove as hard as he possibly could, the old Landcruiser holding firm to the uneven surface beneath its wheels.

Once more he got a quick look at the Dodge's taillights, only to lose sight as the truck skidded around the next bend. Walt was gaining ground. The sneak peeks were becoming more and more frequent, their duration lasting longer and longer. He couldn't be more than a half mile behind the truck now, two vehicles hurtling deeper into the heart of the wilderness.

What did he envision awaiting him once he eventually caught up with Ray? What did he expect to do when the two men were face to face? It didn't really matter. He'd extract some form of retribution, some sort of recompense. As of now, the pursuit consumed him.

After a series of short curves and bends, followed by a brief straightaway, the road broke hard, ninety degrees to the right, and for one queasy moment Walt almost lost it. He eased his foot off the accelerator, since slamming on the brakes would only make the slide worse. He downshifted from fourth gear to third, hearing the engine scream as the transmission did the dirty work of slowing momentum. The vehicle yawed hard left, briefly threatening to roll over, the back end kicking loose and fishtailing wildly over the washboard surface. Walt tapped the gas, again picking up speed, and gently coaxed the Toyota back under control. The road straightened itself out once again. Two red bulbs glowed not a quarter mile in the distance ahead, and then, just as suddenly, the twin dots evaporated.

Walt let off the gas. He no longer needed to hurry, knowing what lie ahead.

THE BRIDGE THAT WASN'T
49

He was awake most of the night Sunday, after Amberson finally caught up with him, first at the scene of the accident, then back at the courthouse giving his statement. "Accident," that's how they were describing it, at least for now. The sheriff's department and the t.v. station out of Cadillac, both were calling it "an unfortunate single-vehicle accident."

"The truck reached the Sparrow River sometime shortly after ten p.m. Sunday night, according to official reports. The older model Dodge pickup truck was traveling at a speed of approximately sixty-five to seventy miles per hour, in an easterly direction on Wolverine Valley Road, a road which runs smack dab through the heart of the Huron National Forest. The accident occurred at the Sparrow River Bridge, or, more precisely, where the Sparrow River Bridge *would have been* if it were not for the bridge's earlier removal and ongoing reconstruction. Traveling at sixty-five to seventy miles per hour, the vehicle ignored signage and a barricade indicating that the bridge was out. The truck then hit a ten foot vertical drop from the road bed to the stream bed. The driver, an as yet unnamed thirty-two year-old local man, was taken to Northern Michigan Hospital by ambulance in critical condition. There is no indication that alcohol was a factor in this accident."

That was what they were reporting on the morning news, as Walt struggled through his front door Monday early. He'd been first on the scene, witnessed for himself the carnage at the bottom of the Sparrow River. He'd actually thought Ray was dead, didn't even bother to investigate, until Amberson showed up only a few minutes later. The deputy didn't say a word to Walt, not at first. Just looked him up and down, gazed down at the truck in the water, skewered by a concrete stanchion, and slowly walked back to his police cruiser. He'd reached in the open driver's side window and called dispatch on the radio. He then quietly walked back to the precipice, lowered himself from the pavement to the loose scree below, and waded out to the Dodge. Ray was breathing, but barely. A bloody mess, too. It took the ambulance nearly an hour to reach them, traveling all the way from Gaylord. Walt spent most of the time standing with his hands in his pockets, waiting.

"If you want to take that Landcruiser back to the camp, I'll follow you." That was all Amberson said to Walt, once the ambulance was away and other deputies were busily securing the scene. By that time the Television 13 news crew was setting up, with some perky, twenty-something blond girl, fresh out of journalism school, doing the "live from the scene" broadcast.

And then, still in silence, the two had driven back to the county courthouse, Walt sitting alongside the officer in the front seat of the police cruiser. Back at the courthouse, Amberson brought two cups of coffee, not bothering to ask Walt whether he wanted one or not. The deputy took a sip from his own cup, sitting down on the far side of the grey steel table from Walt, and sighed. He eased the second cup across the table's gouged surface. Walt grasped the cup and drank greedily. Amberson waited, letting Walt suck down the hot liquid.

"Want to tell me what happened out there?" No Miranda rights, no warnings, just a simple question.

"Not particularly," Walt answered quietly, licking a trace of coffee foam from his upper lip. His eyes cast downward, a dog who knows when he's done wrong. He wasn't sure he had the energy left to explain what happened "out there."

Amberson sighed again, leaning back to consider how he'd gotten here, in a dingy office taking a statement from Walt Pitowski at one in the morning. It was a far cry from what he'd envisioned as a younger man. What had he envisioned, after all? Any dreams he'd had were so far in his past, he could no longer remember them. He stared at the fluorescent light fixture in the drop ceiling above, wondered how long before someone would clean the dead flies trapped beneath its acrylic cover. He already knew that answer. Not until a bulb burned out. Well, he'd better get on with it.

"Could you try?" It wasn't your standard interrogation technique, but Matt was too tired for playing games.

Walt lifted his attention from the coffee cup, looking Amberson directly in the eyes. God, he was tired. Amberson looked even more exhausted. And that's when Walt made a choice, decided it was time to let it all go. At least for this one moment, he'd had enough. Enough anger, enough pain, enough of being a right-fighting vigilante. He started slowly, started from the beginning. He spoke with calm deliberation, retelling the story with great clarity and detail. He described his fight at the Deer Track Inn, his surreptitious trips to the forest, the picnic with Pam and two men talking on the bridge. He told the deputy everything he knew.

By four-thirty Monday morning, he was free to go. Walt limped straight out the door of the county courthouse and down the street six blocks, to the Rasmus Hospital emergency room. There he promptly received eighteen stitches for his shoulder, a prescription for antibiotics, and a tetanus shot. An x-ray showed he had a severe ankle sprain, not a break. The ankle was wrapped in multiple layers of tape, and he was advised to rest, ice, and elevate the leg as best he could. Walt then walked back to the courthouse, where one of the other deputies had been kind enough to park the Samurai, freshly retrieved from where Walt had parked it in the forest. And now, Monday early, he was finally making his way back home.

He entered through the sliding glass door, looking around for Doofus, before remembering that his dog was down at the neighbor's house. "Hallelujah for neighbors," he shouted to no one in particular. He walked over to the Zenith, turning on the local news, lay his body down on the couch, and promptly fell asleep.

THE AFTERGLOW
50

Walt was enjoying the dream. He was sound asleep, knowing on some subconscious level that it was merely a dream, but nonetheless relishing the temporary warmth and comfort of his alternate reality. He drifted freely across the ocean flats in a small wooden boat, a sturdy, deep-hulled craft with decades of layered paint peeling from its sides. The sun radiated down upon his head, enough rays to heat his body without leaving him hot or sweaty. He sprawled lazily in the generous bow, a fishing line dangling casually over its teak gunnels. The sky was the color of lapis lazuli, the crystal clear water lapping gently at the weathered sides of the boat. There were no other boats around other than one ocean-going freighter inching slowly along the distant horizon. He watched as it made its snail-like progress along the outermost edge of the vast sea. All was well with the world. And despite the absence of any fish on his hook, Walt was content.

He'd been enjoying his nirvana, this freedom from the endless cycles of ramifications and consequences that accompany daily life, when a persistent, clanging sound increasingly permeated his peace. He looked around for another boat, a buoy with attached bell, a castaway signaling for rescue in the water, all to no avail. The noise only grew louder. Eventually he succumbed to the inevitable, releasing his grasp on the dream and allowing himself to awaken.

The phone was ringing in the kitchen. Walt opened his eyes groggily. The late afternoon sun beat down through dirt streaked windows. He didn't bother to get up, was in no hurry to talk to anyone. Eventually the ringing stopped, and he eased himself up to a sitting position.

Monday. He'd have to call Jim Rivard, touch base on when the two were going to paddle again. Jim was going to be thoroughly pissed that Walt hadn't checked in with him all weekend. He'd be even angrier once he found out that Walt was nursing a bad ankle and a banged up shoulder, and with the race just five days away. There wasn't much Walt could do about it now. Jim would just have to deal with it, or not deal with it, whatever he chose.

He eased his way over to the kitchen and opened the cupboard. There were enough coffee beans remaining for one last pot. He ground the beans in the electric grinder before dumping them into the wire basket of the drip coffeemaker. He filled the reservoir in the rear of the unit with cold tap water, setting the machine to "bold brew." Walt's body didn't feel as stiff as he'd thought it might. Tired, yes, but he felt relatively well, considering all he'd been through. His shoulder hurt, but it was something he could live with. The ankle was tender, but would probably start to feel better within a few days. Maybe if he laid back down on the couch, he could return to that same dream, the one where he was floating around near the Bahamas. It rarely worked that way, he knew. You can never will your way back into a dream. Walt eased his body back onto the sofa.

The telephone began ringing again. Walt sat on the sofa and counted the number of rings, not bothering to get up and answer. One, two,.....eighteen. Eventually the caller gave up. Walt focused his attention back on the t.v. in front of him.

The local news was just winding down. The weather forecast indicated rain for the next three days, a godsend for the canoe marathon. The river was running unusually low, and any precipitation at all would be a gift. Otherwise he'd be shoveling gravel out of the stream bed with a bent shaft paddle for the first hour of the race. Walt switched over to the classic movie station. "Marty," an Oscar winner from 1955 was playing. He'd never seen it before. He'd picked it up partway through the film. Ernest Borgnine was starring, *"Ernie frickin' Borgnine from McHale's Navy starring in a movie?"* as a homely Italian butcher who's practically resigned himself to a life without love. Then he meets a girl, a schoolteacher. She's nothing special, but then neither is he. Marty's professing his love, in his own dopey way, to his equally homely girlfriend, if it's even *possible* to be equally homely as *Ernie frickin' Borgnine*.

"See, dogs like us, we ain't such dogs as we think we are," Marty tells Clara.

"Well this is a load of crap," Walt chimed in, turning off the television and stumbling to the kitchen. "Like that loser could ever get a girlfriend."

He poured himself a cup of coffee just as the phone rang anew. "What do you want?" He barked. He'd picked up merely to silence the ringing.

“Pitowski, this is Matt Amberson. I’ve been trying to get ahold of you.”

“Well, you got me.” Walt wasn’t feeling conversational. He leaned his body against the countertop, taking weight off his swollen ankle while he sipped his hot beverage. He’d have preferred not to be speaking with anyone.

“I thought you’d like to know what we’ve learned since you left the station this morning.” This was followed by an awkward silence, as Walt debated in his head whether he wanted to hear anything more. “Walt, you still there?”

“Yeah, I’m thinking.” Might was well listen.

“Well first off, your buddy Ray, he’s gonna live. Not well, mind you, at least not for a while. He’s got a lot of surgery ahead of him. Broke both legs, one wrist, a couple of ribs, and his face is a mess. Some internal stuff, too. He’s gonna need plastic surgery to put it all back together, once they deal with the major injuries. And then at least six months worth of physical rehab. But he’s awake, talking.”

“It couldn’t happen to a nicer guy. So once he’s out of the hospital, he’s going to jail for life, right? I mean, you’ve got him on Accessory to Murder, Blackmail and everything, right?”

“Not exactly.” Another awkward silence.

“What do you mean, ‘not exactly,’ Matt?” Walt didn’t like the way this was going.

“Not exactly. As in, there isn’t a murder, at least not one that we can prove, and there isn’t any blackmail. We can go after him on assault and battery, reckless driving and a handful of other traffic offenses, but I’m not sure anyone’s gonna have the stomach for that, when all’s said and done. It might look like we’re being punitive with a man who’s already down and out.”

“What do you mean ‘there isn’t a murder’? What about the body in the Sparrow?”

“I actually found the rest of that body, in one of the holes Ray was digging. I guess I owe you thanks for helping bring that to light. Ray says the guy slipped and fell while fishing the river seven or eight years ago, hit his head on a rock. Ray buried the kid because he didn't want people finding his dope plot. He panicked. Forensics won't be back for a while, but Ray seemed believable, almost as if he was glad to get it off his chest."

"Slipped and fell, you buy that shit? What about the blackmail money, the 'proof,' that he gave to Anton, back on the bridge? What about the head in the bag, delivered in the dead of night?"

"There was no head in the bag, Walt. The kid's head was in that hole I found, alongside the rest of his bones, a fly vest, and the kid's identification. Young guy, registered nurse, went missing while on vacation. Didn't really leave an itinerary, so we weren't looking for him in these parts. For what it's worth, yeah, 'slipped and fell,' I buy that shit. The coroner's report will tell us the truth, one way or the other."

"Well if it wasn't a head, what was in the bag, Matt? What was worth five grand to Anton, on the middle of that bridge in the forest?"

"Funny thing, we talked to Anton. Now there's a guy with all the resolve of a scared rabbit. He claims it was a bag full of morel mushrooms. He also claims you misheard, it wasn't five grand, it was five *hundred* dollars that he paid. Morels can go for thirty bucks a pound, so technically, it's possible. I'm guessing this 'bag' may have contained mushrooms, but they probably weren't morels. Maybe it was just good old home grown. Either way, we've got no evidence, ergo we've got no case."

"And you're going to let it go at that?"

"I didn't say we're letting it go. Like I said, Anton's a scared rabbit. I'm betting he changes his story a few times before we're through with him, but in the end, the sheriff's department has better things to do than chase small time dopers. We'll probably get him on a misdemeanor something or other. On a happier note, he refused to file a complaint for the theft of his Toyota Landcruiser, so you get a free pass."

"Like that was gonna happen. And Ray gets charged with nothing?"

"Maybe that other stuff: assault, reckless driving, gross stupidity. But no, probably not."

"So the bad guy just walks?"

"I wouldn't say *walks,* at least not for a while. 'Limps,' maybe. I don't think life's going to be all that easy for Ray, at least in the near term. Don't take it personally. The community is, however, putting together a fund to help him with medical expenses. There's a lot of sympathy out there for him."

"You're shitting me."

"No kidding, Pitowski. Local man injured in single car accident, serious trauma, mounting medical bills. Check out the news tonight. It plays well with the public. The town has pledged over twenty grand so far to help him out."

"That's not fair!"

"Walt, I hate to be the one to break this to you, but sometimes, life ain't fair."

Walt hung up the phone, went back into the living room, switching on the news channel. The perky blond reporter, cripes, she couldn't be more than twenty if she was a day, was back on screen.

"Coming up at six p.m., a local sheriff's deputy helps solve a seven-year-old mystery involving the disappearance of a downstate man. Catch our exclusive interview with deputy Matt Amberson of Rasmus, a local hero who's dogged professionalism and experience *single-handedly* broke this cold case. That story and others, at six."

Well, Amberson got one thing right. Life ain't fair.

THE MARATHON MAN
51

It was a carnival, that's the only word Walt could find to describe it. The whole town was abuzz. Thursday and Friday there'd been sprints for position, short, timed races to determine where each team would start in the marathon. Jim and Walt had done well, better than they'd expected, really. They were slated to start from the fifty-third position, which didn't sound like much, but with ninety-two teams entering the race, it gave them a head start on nearly half the pack.

Paddling the sprints had been the first real test of his shoulder, and while it still hurt, Walt was confident he could work through the pain. His injured ankle was tender, and that might present a problem. The race had a LeMans-style start, every team lifting their boat to their shoulders and carrying it, at a full run, for three and a half blocks before ever touching the water. Walt could walk without pain, running was another matter. The bum ankle was likely to cause them to drop back a few spots early. But Walt was sure he would overcome that hurdle, just like he'd overcome other hurdles in life.

Canoes were officially inspected and weighed at three on Saturday afternoon. There were no surprises. Walt and Jim had all the necessary safety equipment, were well within regulations. Walt duct-taped a few packets of Power Goop to the inside of his craft, emergency snacks for when his strength inevitably waned. He made sure that the extra paddles were secured, that everything was tied down and ready to go for the race.

The feed team was set. Elvin and his wife, along with one other couple, would wade into the river and provide food to Walt and Jim at predetermined locations. The first feed was scheduled for two hours into the race. Every paddler had his own particular tastes: Walt was partial to cold redskin potatoes, salted and buttered. He could pop them into his mouth without breaking stroke, along with mixed, dried fruit. Rivard was fond of cold pasta salad. Elvin assured them that the food was set, packaged, ready to go.

Staying hydrated throughout the race is critical. Elvin had preloaded plastic bottles with homemade energy drink, drilling holes through their lids, and fed surgical tubing through the openings. Again, hands-free replenishment was the order of the day. Walt and Jim would require a fresh bottle of that salty liquid every two hours, whether they were thirsty or not. The feed team would drop food and drink in the laps of the paddlers as the boat raced past, scoop up whatever flotsam the two men ejected from the canoe, then scurry back to the car, hurrying down the road to the next feeding station. It would be a long, wet night for Elvin and the others, but at least they could rest between feedings.

Paddler introductions were scheduled for eight that evening. The race started at nine. Walt had four hours to kill before he had to be anywhere. He knew he should go home and catch a quick nap, but was far too juiced to rest. The weather was perfect, sun shining and temperatures hovering around seventy. Not a cloud in the sky. A perfect day.

Walt moseyed over to the main avenue, watching thousands of spectators as they meandered through town. Both curbs along the main drag were lined with vehicles for the vintage car and truck show. The street had been barricaded so that pedestrians could stroll with impunity. Across the business loop, people jostled through a makeshift midway packed with food concessions. Kettle corn, freshly squeezed lemonade, and hot dogs were the big sellers of the day. There was a dime toss, raising funds for one of the local civic organizations, and a 50/50 raffle supporting the marathon committee. A line snaked its way around a portable rock climbing wall. The nonprofit River Restoration Society was busily handing out informational flyers and free lapel-pin flags. They were all here to witness the beginning, to absorb the atmosphere and become part of the throng, to see the making of Walt Pitowski and men just like him. His heart filled with pride. He was a spandex clad peacock strutting down the sidewalk.

Walt worked his way over to the river's edge, the wooden boardwalk where later that day, he and Jim would launch the Wenonah on their seventeen-to-eighteen hour odyssey. All sorts of people were milling about, lawyers and dentists, gas station attendants and party store owners, kids home from college and kids who would never finish high school. All of them chattering, catching up after yet another year had slipped from their grasps. Everyone was from Rasmus this weekend, those folks who were visiting for the first time, even some who'd vowed never again to set foot in "that shit hole town." It was a day for renewal, a temporal rebirth of optimism in an otherwise afflicted part of the world.

He marveled at the grass-sloped bank overlooking the river, carefully quilted with blankets of every possible color and pattern. Spectators had anxiously stretched out their markers, some as early as Friday night, reserving their seats at the starting line. The most exciting two minutes in sports, someone had once said. Walt considered it a miracle that one could lay claim to a prime parcel of turf with a single piece of frayed fabric. Tens of thousands of visitors, here to see those very same two minutes of pandemonium when a herd of canoes, paddles, and bulging muscles came rumbling down the hill. And somehow these visitors respected each blanket on the lawn like a flag of sovereignty, without complaint. Try that in a big city arena and see what it bought you.

At the very top of the river bank, on the small ribbon of sidewalk delineating the grassy knoll from the roadway behind it, people gathered in small groups, gossiping, drinking, eating greasy food from paper trays. Enjoying. In one of those groups Walt could just make out Pam, chatting with a tall, mustachioed man wearing a cowboy hat. Walt didn't recognize the man, but then that didn't really matter. Walt's eyes were on Pam. She had a red, disposable cup in her left hand, the same kind of cup they were dispensing in the beer tent, two blocks over. She wore a light sun dress, feminine but not flashy, a white leather purse slung casually from her shoulder. She was smiling up at the fake cowboy as they spoke. She looked happy, relaxed, free.

And for one fleeting moment Walt felt a pang of jealousy, a trace of loss. When would *he* get to be the handsome cowboy, the man with the girl in the pretty dress hanging on his every word? The cowboy leaned in close, whispering something in Pam's right ear, and a devilish smile creased her lips. Walt turned away, suddenly embarrassed by his singular moment of voyeurism. He'd been watching something that no longer had anything to do with him, mourning the loss of an opportunity that no longer existed. Maybe he and Pam had never existed at all, one more illusion in a summer full of illusions.

He departed along the side street, turning his back to the river, veered left at the next corner and slowly climbed to the top of a gentle incline. The Rasmus State Bank was across the way, catty-corner from where Walt now stood. A large white tent had been erected on one quadrant of the bank's lawn, filled with volunteers hawking commemorative t-shirts and other marathon memorabilia. This was where he'd first observed Ray, that night not so many months ago, as he'd exited the foyer and led Walt back to the Deer Track. A sense of disquiet again gripped Walt's heart. How different his summer might have been had he let his anger go, not followed that truck and gone straight home instead.

What had he really gained, after all? The fight in the bar, which really wasn't much of a fight? Nights spent in a meadow, watching and stalking? An injured shoulder and a sprained ankle, he'd certainly gained that. And all for what? So that Ray could impale himself on a bridge piling, so that smug asshole Anton could walk around free? It had all started with a single bone in the river, a conviction that someone, somewhere, should be accountable for the loss of a human life. The death of that fisherman, it turned out, was nothing more than an unfortunate accident. All of Walt's efforts, all of his certitude, wasted on a series of self-propagating misunderstandings and mistakes. There were no inviolable truths waiting to be discovered, no justice to be found. Just an unfortunate kid who died on a fishing trip and a small timer drug peddler who didn't want to get apprehended. And in the end, what little glory survived to be parsed out, bestowed upon a lucky Matt Amberson. Life *wasn't* fair, not in the least.

Walt surveyed the scene before him. To his left, and not fifteen feet away, in the small crowd of people surrounding a gold '63 Impala, stood Deputy Matt Amberson with his wife. They were both smiling, holding ice cream cones purchased from one of the many food vendors. Talking leisurely with the Impala's owner. Happy bastards. They looked happy, anyway. The last people on earth Walt wanted to speak with. He turned to his right, began walking away from it all. He passed a small office building, shuttered for the weekend. He passed the one-reel theater, its vintage marquee speckled with burned out bulbs too costly to repair. He passed the imposing facade of the Episcopal church on the next block, staffed for the day with parishioners offering free shade and bottled water to the weary.

It was on the subsequent block, the block that reminded Walt of Neopolitan ice cream, with its three Victorian homes painted, in order, chocolate, vanilla, and strawberry, that a small voice called out.

"Wait up!"

It was the voice of a child. Walt hesitated, turning to look. A boy, six or seven years old, running on the sidewalk towards him. The kid and his parents must have just exited the big church, the child turning the wrong way when he reached the curb. The kid stopped a few paces shy of Walt, his parents waiting for the child to recognize his mistake, run back and rejoin his family. Sandy hair, badly in need of a haircut. Jeans fraying at the knees, and a chocolate stain on the front his bright yellow shirt. Holding a balloon in one hand and a plastic bottle of spring water in the other. His face practically bursting with the exuberance of youth, the boundless joy of not knowing any better.

"Hey mister, are you a paddler?" the child pleaded as he caught his breath.

"Why yes, son, yes I am."

"Wow! Did you hear that, dad? A *real paddler!!*"

EPILOGUE

No one would mistake the Grand Limoneaux for the Sparrow River. Well, maybe in her upper stretches, just east of Rasmus, you will find some similarities. And if you were paddling in darkness, like ninety-some teams of competitive racers were on this Saturday night in late July, the mistake might be understandable. About the same width, about the same depth, similar speed. The similarities end quickly, however.

"Grand Limoneaux," a french name, meaning "Big Silty." An apt description. She wasn't all silt, just "with" silt. And "with" gravel, and with stumps and tiny islets, too. In the lower reaches she was more sand than silt, but the name Limoneaux stuck. The river runs due east, more or less, and for the first few hours of this great race men are praying that they don't hit a boulder or stump, some unseen menace hiding in its shadows. Perils lurking, harbingers of doom, with their ability to pierce craft and put you out of contention before you've scarcely begun.

The river is a series of twists and turns, all the while maintaining its easterly bent. The water here is turbulent, roiled and angry from canoes bumping and jostling one another. The boats leave a visible wake on the water's surface, as if propelled by small, hidden motors. And while it's critical to keep pace with the leaders, it is also very difficult to pass other vessels, in these crowded early moments. The first timed cutoff is at Rusty Bridge, the first of many key points for the marathon. The inexperienced will have quickly learned whether or not they are in over their heads, and a few paddlers will have withdrawn or been disqualified from the race, having failed to reach this first checkpoint in the allotted time.

Further downstream, near Kirtland's Bridge, the river widens and deepens. Here is where power reigns supreme, where positions are gained and lost. Pace and endurance become critical, and the leaders begin to separate themselves from the trailing hordes behind. The gap between elite and good canoes widens, the race gradually crumbling into small packs of wolves, running together in the night. Eventually the weak are culled out, dropped quickly from their grouping. They either paddle along in solitude, keeping rhythm in their heads, or falter to the next, slower group behind.

EPILOGUE

Mioe Pond, a slow moving impoundment created by the Mioe Hydroelectric Dam, eventually sneaks up and envelops the paddlers. The sky is liquid darkness, fog dancing across the water. The river here has no discernible flow. Some get lost in the slack water and inky conditions. The air is ten or twenty degrees cooler than when they'd first begun. The first paddlers reach the dam shortly after two a.m. Temporary floodlights atop the dam blind these athletes after hours spent with only a small bow light leading the way. The scores of feeders, spectators and security personnel inundate their senses. Paddlers crawl up on the concrete bulkhead with wobbly legs, having just spent five or six hours wedged in a tiny boat, hefting canoes to their shoulders. How are you doing? What do you need? Their support teams pumping them for information. Shouting and voices and cheering. It is a hundred yards to the stairs, and then a hundred and twenty steps down to the water. Sometimes they slip and fall, losing precious time on dry land to others that *aren*'t experiencing back spasms, leg cramps, dehydration. At four a.m. the Mioe Dam checkpoint officially closes, by which time another dozen teams have dropped from the race.

Then there is only water, fast water, slow water, more stagnant lake and Stygian darkness. Eventually Negwegon Dam beckons out to the lead paddlers, an imposing concrete bulwark, dawn rising on the horizon behind it. Another portage, another opportunity to fall, to drop the boat, to hurt a foot or a knee running. More flat water, more fast water, four more dams in rapid succession, and finally, one hundred and twenty miles after first charging through the streets of Rasmus, the marathoners, those that have not succumbed to any of the aforementioned hazards, reach the little town of Hohner, and the mouth of the Big Silty.

They have completed their final portage, are past the last of the six big hydroelectric dams. Sweats and chills, muscle cramping and spasms, elation and despair, all left in the shadows of that final dam. It is the homestretch now, this final lazy drift into Hohner and the finish line. Two thirty in the afternoon on Sunday. The lead teams have passed through hours before, still paddling hard, fighting neck and neck with one another through the final reaches.

Jim and Walt are both three minutes behind and three minutes ahead of their nearest competitors. It is disorienting, to be paddling on with only the occasional cheer from the banks to prompt them. No other canoes in sight, no gauge as to whether they are any more or less beaten by the river than other teams. Eighty, sixty strokes per minute have faded to ten, fifteen at best. Both men are dehydrated, their bodies long ago having lost the ability to sweat. Pain, debilitating, cry-out-for-mercy pain, no longer possible either. They are filled with aching numbness, both in body and in mind, paddling their way through this stupefying broth of an alien world.

Their canoe will pass beneath two bridges before reaching the finish line. The first bridge is in their sights as they round one last bend in the stream, and people are lined three deep against the guardrail above, urging them onward. Folks cheer for every team as if it were their own, though people indeed have their friends and favorites. Walt is suddenly transported back to his dream, that one many lifetimes ago, when, after much drama in the Sparrow Lotus Lodge dining hall, Walt became a fish, hurtling through the deep. He is that fish again, swimming with the current, shadow and light distorting everything above him. But that was the Sparrow River, not the Big Silty, this is not the same river as the one in the dream. Walt cannot comprehend how he has switched rivers, finding himself in this new world.

People stand on the overpass, yelling passionately, but Walt cannot fathom their words. It is all noise, Walt's brain too tired to process sound into meaning. For one moment he thinks he sees the girl, the pretty one from the camp, JoAnn something. She's standing in the second row of spectators on the pavement above, unintelligible sound emanating from her lips. Then that bridge, too, is in the past, and he is no longer a fish.

Two hundred yards at most, one more roadway overhead, and the finish line beyond. Walt realizes that he has stopped paddling, the canoe's forward progress attributable only to Rivard's irregular stabs at the water and the flow of the current itself. Walt attacks the river with renewed vengeance, such that he can muster, the end clearly in sight. They pass beneath this final bridge, cross the makeshift finish line, and their names and unofficial finish time are announced to a polite burst of hoots and applause. Forty-sixth place. Seventeen hours, thirty-six minutes, fifty-eight seconds. Jim and Walt drag their paddles briefly against the flow, stopping the Wenonah in place, then jettison their battered bodies into the crisp water.

He dog paddles in place, the cold clear water shocking both his mind and his body back to life. He knows he smells rank, despite being submerged to his neck, hopes some of that stink will wash away by the time he reaches dry land. In a temporary first aid tent ashore, volunteers tend to miscellaneous aches and ailments of some previous arrivals. Rivard is already on shore, being escorted to that haven by Elvin and his wife. A quick burst of people cheering, another canoe in the distance, grinding out one last stretch of water before that team, too, will have completed the marathon. Walt swims across the dark channel, reaches shallow water, and cautiously pulls himself upright on the big rocks near shore. He stands on wobbly legs, river swirling mid-calf. The sun has hidden itself once more behind the suspended cloud cover, a slight chill in the air. In this singular moment, water dripping from his battered body, Walt finally feels complete. He has been baptized.

THE END

About the Author

Kevin J Garrity was born in 1964 and raised in the city of Detroit, the eighth of nine children. Throughout his high school and college years, he performed as a musician of some local renown. After studies at Wayne State University he moved to Traverse City, Seattle, back to Detroit, Chicago, and then Grayling. Kevin currently resides in southeastern Michigan with his wife Deanna and two sons. He is an avid hunter and fisherman. This first novel, *Sparrow River*, reflects his great love of the outdoors and all things wild.

Made in the USA
Charleston, SC
26 June 2012